Once Upon An Enchanted Castle

An Enchanted Realms Novel

MICHELLE MILES

Book Cover by Erin Dameron-Hill

First edition May 30, 2025

ISBN: 9798989854264 (eBook)
ISBN: 9798989854271 (paperback)

Published by Dusty Tome Books, LLC

Port
Leclare
CASSONÉ
Rothshi
ROTH
B
Driftbell

Thornhurst
Castle

PROLOGUE

Early Spring, Present Day

When Hilde got word her favorite niece had fallen and broken her arm, she dropped everything and headed to Drumchapel Village, where her sister still lived. Granted, it took some effort to return to the human realm, but she was determined to make sure her little Marigold was all right.

Linnea, her sister, had sounded so distraught on the phone.

The past three years proved difficult for her and her niece. Hilde visited as much as possible, but she had to return to the other realm to rejuvenate herself. She found renewed vitality and energy in the other realm.

Her sister seemed unaffected by being in the human realm.

Marigold, however, was showing signs of illness. Doctors were puzzled by her recurring breathing problems, leading to multiple hospital visits. Of course, they were a mystery. Hilde, unlike her sister, understood her condition. They remained clueless.

Linnea intended to keep the secret. She refused to allow Hilde to tell Marigold the truth. At some point, the girl *had* to know. Now that she was in those tween years, she noticed she wasn't like the other girls her age. She was more of an old soul with a vibrant personality, stunning looks, and far more intelligence than her peers.

That was because of her bloodline.

Hilde pushed all those thoughts away as she hurried up the sidewalk. The house on Crown Lane hadn't changed a bit. At least on the outside of the house. After her brother-in-law unexpectantly passed, Linnea started redecorating. New flooring. New paint throughout. Kitchen renovation. Bathroom renovations.

She rang the bell and waited. Moments later, Linnea opened the door and ushered her in.

"You don't have to ring the bell. You're family," she said.

Hilde kissed her on the cheek in greeting. "It feels odd to barge in."

"Don't be silly," she said.

"Auntie!" Marigold's joyful voice greeted her. She hurried through the living room, her arm in a sling.

"Marigold!" her mother said, chastising.

But the girl ignored her and flung her body toward her. Hilde caught her in a big hug, squeezing her tight, but being careful of her injured arm and thankful the girl was all right. When she pulled back, she held her at arm's length, looking her over.

"Now, how did you do this?" Hilde asked, nodding to her arm in the sling.

"I fell at school. I'm all right."

"She's not all right. It's broken. The doctor wants her to see an orthopedic surgeon in the morning," Linnea said.

Hilde took her by the hand and led her back into the living room. Gone was the well-worn furniture replaced by newer, more functional pieces. Two three-seat cushion sofas were on either side of a square oak coffee table.

"That sounds serious," Hilde said.

Together, they sat on one of the sofas. Marigold snuggled up next to her, holding her injured arm against her chest.

"How about some tea or coffee?" Linnea asked.

"Tea, please."

Nodding, Linnea headed off to the kitchen to prepare it.

The house was old. Instead of the open concept that was popular in floor plans in the newer homes, this home still had the rooms sectioned off. Linnea disappeared into the kitchen to prepare the tea, which gave Hilde time to question her niece about the fall.

"How did you fall?" she asked.

With her sunny blonde head down, she said, "I don't want to talk about it."

"Why not?"

"Because I *don't*," she said, sounding angry.

Hilde thought she understood. She glanced over her shoulder to make sure her sister was still in the kitchen, then lowered her voice.

"Were you pushed?" she asked.

Marigold lifted her head, her blue eyes big and round. "How did you know?"

"Tell me what happened," she said, instead of answering her question.

The girl settled down next to her again, plucking a stray string off the edge of her shirt. "The other girls are mean to me."

That sent a pang right to heart. How could they be mean to her sweet Marigold? She wanted to have a few strong words with these girls, whoever they were.

"They pick on me and call me names. Why would they do that? I've done nothing to them," she said and glowered.

"They're jealous of you, my sweet girl."

"But why?" She looked up at her again. Tears stood in her eyes. It was hard to see her hurting.

"Because you are..." She paused, trying to choose her words. Hilde wanted to do everything in her power to make Marigold understand those girls didn't matter. They never would.

"I'm ugly, aren't I?"

"Heavens, no!" she said on a shocked breath. "Marigold, you are *far* from ugly. You're smart and pretty and special. You have a kind soul. I wish you knew how special you were. That's probably why they treat you that way." It was the closest she came to telling her the truth.

She frowned. "I don't feel special."

Linnea returned carrying two steaming mugs. She handed one to Hilde, who took it, grateful for the warm brew. As she sat across from them, her cell phone rang. She answered it and a moment later, her face fell. News she didn't want.

"There's no one else?" Pause and then she said, "All right. I'll be there as soon as I can."

When she hung up, she looked at the two of them.

"What is it?" Hilde asked.

"It was work. They need me to come in. Someone called in sick."

"You go. I can stay here until you get back," Hilde said.

"You don't mind?" She glanced at Marigold, who said nothing.

"Not at all. We'll be fine. Won't we?"

Marigold nodded, a smile on her youthful face. "Auntie will take good care of me."

She rose and headed for the front door, where she grabbed her coat and purse from the coat rack. "I'll be back as soon as I can. There are some leftovers in the fridge if you get hungry."

The front door opened and closed, and then she was gone.

"Do you want to tell me more about these mean girls?" Hilde asked.

She shook her head. "No. I don't want to talk about them." She scooted away from her, turning toward her. The light had returned to her face. "I want you to tell me a story."

"A story?" Hilde grinned. "Haven't you had enough stories?"

"I *never* have enough stories. Tell me one, *please*. It will make me feel ever so much better." She blinked her wide blue eyes at her, batting her lashes.

Hilde chuckled. The girl always knew how to get her way. How could she refuse?

"All right. Let me think." She tapped her chin with a forefinger as though deep in concentration. "Ah. I have just the one."

"What's it about?" Excitement lit the girl's eyes, a marked improvement over her earlier mood.

"Why, it's about a beautiful young woman who can read magical languages. One day, she finds herself in an enchanted castle with a mysterious half man, half beast."

The girl gasped. "Half beast? How?"

"He was cursed."

Her mouth formed a wide O. "Cursed?"

"Yes. Once upon a time, there was a girl named Bella..."

Chapter 1

Colorful light from the stained-glass window splashed across the book's yellowed pages, giving them a multi-hued illumination. The only sound was that of Bella's quill as she dipped the tip in the inkwell and then scratched out her translations on the parchment. Silence and the musty smell of old books were her constant companions this late afternoon.

She was lost in the ancient manuscript with an extraordinary alphabet of roses and thorns that no one else was able to translate or read. She, however, had a gift for it. Her whole life, she could examine foreign writings and understand the concealed words within their secret scripts.

Father called it her magical gift.

She turned the page of the book, her gaze skimming across it. Her mind translated the climax of the story she'd been writing. It was the tale of a wicked enchantress and the prince who caused her heartbreak. She cursed him to exist in isolation within his castle's dark and lonely confines. His eyes would never again behold the sun, for its light would be his ruin.

Bella sat a moment, staring at the words and thinking about the tale. It was heartbreaking. Surely, it was fiction and not a tale of truth. She could not imagine being alone for all of her remaining days, locked away in a castle without the sunshine to warm her cheeks.

A faint tap at the library door interrupted her thoughts. She looked up as the door swung open and the butler stepped inside the library, his hand on the knob.

"Hello, Archie," she greeted.

He winced only a little at the nickname she'd given him. "Miss Rinaldi, his lordship asked if you would like afternoon tea."

She and Archie—Archibald was his proper name—were on a first name basis since coming to Lord Vincent's extravagant manor in the seaside town during the past few weeks. Port Leclare was home to some of the richest, fattest nobles in the northern realm of Cassoné. And some of those rich nobles liked to collect ancient works that required translation.

That's where she managed to help them—for a price, of course. She made a handsome sum for each book she translated and had garnered quite the reputation in the sleepy seaside village. Her father was a merchant and was often away on business, which left her to her own devices most of the time. She started translating for fun and then realized the nobles were happy to pay her for the services.

Sometimes it took her days to translate. Sometimes weeks. And always she spent the time in their extraordinary personal libraries in their mansions where she was pampered by their staff and treated as though she, herself, were royalty.

"I would love afternoon tea," she said.

"Very good, my lady." He nodded and closed the door.

She settled into the plush, oversized chair. Her fingers were ink stained. She didn't mind. Her penmanship, she had been told, was some of the best ever seen. The Port Leclare General Library often requested she scribe for them when she had a free moment, but that was volunteer work. She much preferred her work as a paid scribe and translator.

It must be after midday since it was time for afternoon tea. Father would arrive in port later that evening, returning from a long voyage across the sea to another continent, Cappadocia, where he planned to sell his wares and buy textiles to bring back to their small sliver of land. Though her father, Enzo, was not a noble, he was treated as such. His shop on the wharf was among the most popular selling the latest fabrics to the local dressmaker for their fine gowns. Everyone in town knew the Rinaldi's which made it quite easy for Bella to find work as a translator in the port.

The door creaked open again, and the soft scent of Earl Grey drifted into the room as Archie wheeled in the tea cart. The porcelain cups clinked and rattled with each tiny bump, a delicate, familiar sound that made her smile. Her eyes immediately locked onto her favorite finger sandwiches—fresh cucumber slices glistening on buttery bread—and next to them, the tiny lemon cakes, their golden tops shimmering under a light dusting of powdered sugar, sending the tangy sweetness wafting toward her.

Lord Vincent Blackwell entered next.

He was slender and tall, his dark hair streaked with white at the temples, giving him an air of wisdom and experience. He wore a fine three-piece suit, the kind that spoke of class and sophistication, and his black shoes gleamed as if polished for this moment. Time etched lines into his face, proving a long and full life. She couldn't help but feel the weight of all he had seen and done in a life of luxury. His wife passed away several years ago from consumption. They never had children.

"That will be all, Archibald. Thank you."

Archie bowed low and then left the room, closing the door behind him. Lord Vincent poured two cups of tea.

"How is the manuscript coming along?" he asked. He dropped in a lump of sugar in each cup.

Bella suspected his visit was to check on her progress and she was right. "I should be finished soon. Only a few more pages or so left to transcribe."

He handed her one of the cups. "Will you sit with me?" He gestured to the sitting area on the other side of the room.

"Of course."

She took the cup from him and rose from the desk, leaving her papers and the book behind. Lord Vincent's private library ranked among the best she'd seen in her line of work. Bookshelves lined the walls, soaring to the twenty-foot ceiling. One end of the room had a desk. That's where she liked to work. Next to it, the colorful window that let in shafts of colored light. That was her favorite.

On the other end of the room, the wall of windows overlooked the south lawn that was always immaculate. The sitting area had two sofas facing each other. To the right and left of the sofas were two oversized wing-backed chairs. In the middle, a large table hosting a small candelabra. She imagined it lit in the late evening, giving off a warm, inviting glow to the sitting area.

He took one of the sofas. She sat across from him. For a moment, she thought he seemed disappointed she did not sit next to him.

"Tell me about the rose and thorn language you've been translating." He sipped his tea.

"It's a fascinating story about a powerful sorceress who fell in love with a prince who broke her heart."

He lifted a dark brow at that. "Fascinating. The gentleman I purchased the book from didn't know what it was about."

"It's a sad story, really," she said. "With a terrible ending."

"How does it end?" he asked.

"A curse dooms the prince to a solitary life, locked away in his castle." She sipped her tea.

That seemed to have struck a nerve with him. He placed the cup and saucer on the table in front of him and leaned forward, his elbows on his knees.

"That sounds horrid," he said.

"It's terribly sad," she agreed with a nod.

"Miss Isabella..." The way her name rolled off his tongue sent warning bells clanging in her mind. He clasped his hands together and gave her a weak smile. "I cannot tell you how I've enjoyed having you here these last few weeks."

Her fingers tightened on the cup handle. "Have you? I've been here in the library the whole time. We've hardly seen each other."

A small smile slipped across his face. "Yes, I know. And a pity that. Perhaps you would like to dine with me?"

Her heart rammed hard against her chest. Dine with him? Lord Vincent? She knew where this was going, and she had to stop it before it got out of hand. He was much too old for her.

"I do thank you for the invitation, my lord, but I'm afraid I cannot. My father is due to return this evening. I need to be home to greet him." She placed the cup on the table in front of her and rose.

"Oh, perhaps another time then," he suggested.

She cut a glance at the desk with her scattered papers and the still open book. "Perhaps. I'll return tomorrow and finish the translation."

"Of course." He got to his feet.

She headed for the door, and he followed, reaching past her to open it for her. As she passed by him, he placed a hand on her arm.

"A moment, please," he said, his voice low.

Stopping abruptly, her heart pounded in her chest. She hated having to wave off the men who wanted to court her. She was not interested in courting anyone, for none of the men in the port city were of an interest to her.

"Yes?" she asked, looking up at him.

"I do not know how to say this, Miss Isabella, but...I find you to be in my thoughts more and more and—"

"I do thank you for that, my lord, but I must tell you straightaway I cannot reciprocate any feelings you might have for me."

He blinked, surprise evident on his face. She rushed on.

"I have learned that it's best to say my feelings up front, so that there is no misunderstanding later. While I do appreciate your kind thoughts and your offer of dinner, I must make it clear I'm here for work and work only, my lord. I do hope you understand that."

He swallowed hard then, his throat working. "I do, of course, my lady. Thank you for your candor."

She dipped a quick curtsy. "Good night, my lord."

She hurried from the library. At the front door, Archibald waited. When he saw her coming, he opened it.

"Leaving, miss?"

"Yes."

Archie, of course, sensed her departure and was ready for her. Her wrap was in his hand. He handed it to her, along with her gloves. She pulled on the gloves first, then took the wrap—a silk shawl with fringe—and draped it about her shoulders.

"Good night, Archie." She dipped a curtsy.

"Good night, miss. Do travel home safe." He gave a nod of his head as he held the door open for her.

With that, she hurried out into the late afternoon and headed for home.

CHAPTER 2

Bella walked away from Lord Vincent's house at a brisk pace. The evening air had turned cool, and she tasted the salty breeze from the port. The house she left was on a hill. In the distance, she saw the ships coming into the port for the evening. Her father would be on one of those ships.

He was gone this time for nearly a month. She hoped he returned with wonderful treasures. Sometimes, he brought her gifts from across the sea. Books, candles he thought she might like, hats, scarves, and other things. But mostly she liked when he brought her books. He visited all the port cities and had access to all the places of the world she didn't.

And yet she didn't mind he traveled without her. When she was small, just after her mother passed, she traveled with him on his voyages. The high seas were exhilarating and full of wonder. But mostly she preferred to spend her days at home at their manor, Belcourt. When she was older, she remained behind with her governess and the other servants. Now that she was of age, she was able to run Belcourt while he was away on business.

She supposed they were wealthier than most. They had several servants in their manor house who kept her company when her father was away. The butler, Gerald, was a stoic man who tried to hide his emotions. Bella understood he was a man of little words who preferred his solace with books. She, of course, understood his love of books, for she was the same. He was a private man, never sharing any personal details of his life outside of their home. Bella respected that, too, and never asked prying questions.

The cook, Edith Graves, was a merry woman who had a big laugh and loved to talk about her family. She was widowed, but her children were grown and had children of their own. She had a ruddy complexion and wide blue eyes, and hair the color of a farthing. She was the youngest of six children who had a penchant for baking. Bella found her lemon cakes and other sweet treats irresistible. But she was also a terrific cook.

Her own maid, Emmaline, was attentive and sweet. She was young. Working at the manor house was her first real job. Her parents wanted a better life for her and had sent her on several interviews. Bella quite liked her the moment they met and hired her on the spot. That was three years ago. Beyond that, Bella had to admit she didn't know much about the girl other than she was looking forward to spending her days off at home with her mother and younger sister.

Belcourt Manor sat the bottom of the hill close to the port. A most ostentatious name for their home, truly. Bella thought it silly to name it, but her father liked naming things. Even his fleet of ships had names. His favorite ship in his fleet was named the Emerald Voyager. Another he named Azure Starlight. And yet another Golden Tempest. He liked names for his ships that had a color in them. All of them did.

She smiled, thinking of that as she watched the ships sail into port with their sails flapping against the wind. She spotted the Emerald Voyager right away with its deep green sails. Her father would be home in time for dinner.

Thinking about that made her step a little quicker, a little lighter, as she hurried down the hill to their home. She pushed open the white gate and walked down the stone walkway to the front door, where she stomped up the steps to the porch. Moments later, she entered the foyer, pulling off her gloves. Gerald came bustling toward the door.

"Ah, miss, welcome home. I trust your day was productive?" he asked.

She handed him her shawl. "Yes, quite, thank you, Gerald. I saw Mr. Rinaldi's ship coming into port on my way home. He'll be here in time for dinner. Will you let Mrs. Graves know?"

"Of course, my lady." He took her shawl and gave a low bow.

"Thank you, Gerald."

She headed for the grand staircase to change her dress and prepare for dinner. Emmaline met her on the stairs.

"Oh, miss, you're here early. I didn't expect you so soon." She paused in the middle of the staircase and waited for Bella to catch up to her.

"My father will arrive shortly. I want to dress for dinner and be ready for his return," she said.

"Very good, miss. Would you like a bath as well?"

"Perhaps after we dine," she said.

Emmaline nodded as they made their way up the stairs and down the hallway to Bella's room.

Her room was on the east end of the manor and overlooked the port, with double doors leading out to a balcony. It was one of the things she loved about her room. At any time during the day or night, she could step out onto her balcony and inhale the salty air, watch the ships coming into or out of port, and hear the seagulls squawk as they hunted for food.

The four-poster bed was in the center. Across from that was the wardrobe where she had all her gowns and shoes. She was lucky enough to have an en suite bathroom complete with running water. Not many houses in the port city had running water, but her father was well off enough to make sure they had it.

"Did you enjoy your visit to Lord Vincent's, miss?"

Bella expelled a sigh as she toed off her slippers. "I have to say I do enjoy his library, but something happened today."

Emmaline's eyes widened. "What happened?"

"He wanted me to dine with him."

The girl looked confused. "You didn't wish to stay?"

"I knew Father was coming into port today and I didn't want to miss seeing him," she said. "Aside from that, no, I didn't. He's much too old for me."

Emmaline began unbuttoning the back of her gown. "I suppose. He's a widower, isn't he?"

"Yes. He's never remarried."

She helped her remove the dress, then stepped to the wardrobe to find something suitable for dinner. She chose a long gown in dark blue silk with a dropped waist, full skirt, and long lace sleeves. She held it up for Bella to approve.

When she gave her a nod, she helped her into the gown, then she sat at the dressing table while Emmaline brushed out her long, brown hair to rid it of the tangles from the day. She pulled back the sides and secured it with a sliver hair clip at the back of her head.

"I see you were hard at work writing today," the girl remarked.

"Oh?"

She grinned at her in the mirror over the top of her head. "Your hands, my lady."

Bella looked down and noticed ink still on her fingers. "I'm afraid there's not much to be done about that, but I can try to scrub them clean."

She spent a good amount of time with a bar of soap and warm water. She got most of the ink off her fingers, but they were still stained. She finally gave up after nearly half an hour of scrubbing.

As she exited her room, she heard the front door and knew her father had returned. She picked up her skirts and hurried down the stairs as he called out hello. Gerald was there in an instant, taking his hat and coat as they exchanged pleasantries.

"Father!"

Bella flew down the stairs and launched herself at him. He hugged her tight.

"There's my girl." He pulled back and held her at arm's length. "Have you stayed busy while I was gone?"

She nodded. "Yes. I've done several translations while you were at sea."

He hooked his arm in hers. "You have? You must tell me everything about it." He paused and turned back to the butler. "Gerald, they'll be bringing my trunks up from the ship. Will you have them delivered to my room?"

"They have already arrived, my lord," he said, his face devoid of emotion.

"Wonderful!" Then he patted her hand. "I'll go change for dinner and then join you in the dining room. I have a gift for you."

"A gift? What is it?" Excitement lit within her.

"You'll have to wait and see." He grinned as he released her and headed for the stairs.

Bella could not wait to see what he brought her.

The dining room was one of her favorite rooms. The room was large, with a long mahogany table in the center and enough chairs for twenty. A plush rug in an intricate design was under the table. The soaring ceiling and dark damask wallpaper above the wainscoting added to the dramatic effect of the room. A sideboard was to one side. The table was set with their finest china.

Though they had enough space for twenty, she and her father rarely entertained. It wasn't that they didn't have friends or acquaintances in the city—they knew everyone in town. It was because they preferred not to have ostentatious parties. There was the occasion when her father would have several of the higher-class folks join them for dinner, but it was a rarity.

Bella sat back in her chair, her hands resting in her lap, after demolishing the delicious meal Mrs. Graves prepared for them. She was happily drowsy, with a full stomach and a glass of wine. All throughout the meal, she waited for her father to present her with his promised gift. Finally, she was unable to wait any longer.

"You said you had a gift for me, Father."

He laughed. "I knew you wouldn't forget. I wondered how long it would take for you to ask."

He rose and left the dining room, then returned moments later with a large parcel in his hands wrapped in brown paper. He handed it to her.

"I thought you might like this."

She ripped open the paper and then halted, peering down at a leather-bound book embossed with a circle of interwoven thorns forming a perfect ring. In the center of the thorns was a fragmented rose, as if caught mid-transformation from bud to bloom. There was a gold embossed border around the edges, and the title was in a language she had never seen before.

"What is it?" she asked, shoving aside the paper. She pushed away her empty plate and placed the book on the table in front of her, opening the cover. It cracked with age.

"A book, of course." There was humor in his voice.

"But what kind of book?"

She flipped the pages yellowed with age and written in a careful, perfect hand with more of the same language inside. It was not written in traditional lines, but in spirals or what appeared to be blooming clusters. Whenever she came across a book with a unique language, she was almost immediately able to translate it. But not this one. It did not speak to her like the others.

"What language is this?"

"I thought you might like a challenge, my dear. The bookseller I bought it from had never seen this language, nor did he know where it came from."

The book fascinated her. Her eyes skipped down the pages, trying to pick out a word or two she was able to understand. So far, nothing. Her language skills were definitely put to the test.

"I love it," she breathed, though she wasn't sure why she loved a book she was unable to read. "But I have no idea what it says."

He chuckled. "You will in time, my dear. I have no doubt about that. Now, tell me what you've been working on."

She closed the book and sat back in her chair, placing her hands in her lap. She told him about the rose and thorn language she was translating for Lord Vincent and the terribly sad story of the prince who was cursed to live alone locked away in his castle for eternity.

"I have a few more pages to translate, but I'm not sure I want to return to Lord Vincent's."

Her father arched a brow as he reached for his crystal wine glass. "And why is that?"

"Well..." She paused, unsure how to tell him the man invited her to dinner. "He asked me to dine with him this evening. Of course, I declined, because I knew you were returning today."

He blinked surprise, and then the corner of his mouth lifted in a faint smile. "And you don't want to return because you don't want to turn him down again."

She flushed as she looked at her father from across the table. She reached for her glass and took a sip of the too-sweet wine. "I do like him just...not the same way he likes me."

Her father chuckled. "I'm not surprised he asked you. It was only a matter of time."

Bella tipped her head to the side. "What does that mean?"

"He asked permission to court you," he said, as though it were common knowledge.

The blood drained from her head in a whoosh. "Oh. What did you say?"

"I told him you were headstrong with a mind of your own and if you wished to be courted, you would certainly let him know."

She stared at him as the shock rolled through her. Her father often surprised her. Now, especially. Though he didn't want her left alone in the world when he was gone, he also would never make her marry for the sake of marrying. She, of course, knew that but hearing him reinforce that made her happy.

"Thank you, Father."

"I know you want to marry for love," he said. "I do hope some security will come along with that."

Meaning, he wanted her to marry well. She understood that, too.

"But I'm sure whoever you choose will make you happy." He downed the rest of his wine and pushed back his chair. "I think I shall retire for the night."

She got to her feet and picked up the book he gifted her. "I think I'll read for a while in the study, if that's all right with you."

"Don't stay up too late." He kissed her cheek and then headed out of the dining room.

Clutching the book to her chest, she left the dining room behind and headed to the study where her inks and parchments were in the hopes she could begin translating this odd book.

Chapter 3

The grandfather clock in the hallway chimed the midnight hour. Bella crumpled another piece of paper and tossed it in the wastebasket, the frustration edging through her. Her fingers were stained with ink even more than they were earlier that day. She'd wasted several sheets of parchment in her attempts to translate the book. The candles had nearly burned down to a nub as she sat at the desk in the gloom trying to translate the language on the pages before her.

She so far had no luck.

Stretching her arms over her head, she yawned and then rose from the chair and walked toward the wall of windows on the west side of the study. The other walls of the room hosted floor-to-ceiling bookshelves. She and her father were both book lovers and enjoyed getting lost within the pages of a good story.

At the window, she parted the gossamer curtain and peered out at the night. Since the study was on the second floor, the view was across the rooftops down toward the harbor. The harbor lights twinkled across the smooth water. There was not a soul in sight. It was quiet at this time of night as the shops were closed and the sailors who lived in port had returned to their homes. Others were snoozing on the decks of the ships under the stars.

How lovely to sleep under the stars in the cool night air.

As she stood at the window, thinking about the language in the book she was unable to translate, movement in the shadows caught her eye. At first she thought it was nothing more than a vagrant staggering through the streets near the port, but then she realized it was someone moving from shadow to shadow. No, not someone. Some*thing*.

How odd.

From her distance, she was unable to make out what or who it was moving through the streets. She pressed her face against the cool glass as if that would help her see it clearer. When she breathed out, she fogged the glass in front of her face. Stepping back, she used the sleeve of her gown to wipe it away.

When she peered back into the street, the shadow figure was gone.

Turning from the window, she decided it was nothing more than her imagination. She walked back to the desk and closed the book. As she scooped it up, she blew out the candles and, with a yawn, headed to bed.

Her footsteps were light as she headed down the hallway to her room. Emmaline had left her nightgown at the foot of the bed. The blankets were turned back. A long candle flickered in its candleholder on the bedside table.

Bella placed the hefty tome on the bedside table by the candle. She wished Emmaline was there to help her out of her dress. Likely the girl was sleeping. She didn't want to wake her, but she was too tired to wiggle out of her gown herself. With a yawn, she kicked off her shoes and slipped into the bed still fully dressed. She blew out the candle and then curled around the pillow. Before long, she was fast asleep.

The acrid smell woke her. The back of her throat burned. In her sleep haze, she was unable to decide what that was.

A pounding on her bedroom door jarred her. She sat up straight, her heart ramming hard in her chest as she realized smoke seeped under the door.

"Bella, wake up!"

It was her father's frantic voice. Before she was able to respond, the door flew open.

"We have to go at once." He waved for her to hurry out of the room.

She heard shouts somewhere in the house. "What is it? What's happening?"

"The house is on fire. Hurry. We haven't much time."

He waved to her again, this time stepping into the room and holding out his hand. He held a handkerchief in his other hand pressed against his mouth and nose.

Bella sprang from the bed, thankful she was still dressed, and her shoes were nearby. She started for the door, then halted and turned back wondering what, if anything, she should grab. There simply wasn't enough time to save all her things.

"Bella," he urged, his voice near frantic.

Then she saw the mysterious book on the bedside table. On impulse, she snatched it, cradling it against her chest and dashed from the room after her father. The hallway quickly filled with smoke. She covered her mouth and nose with her sleeve as she made her way to the staircase. The foyer was full of smoke, but the front door was open making a square of light through the haze.

She headed for it and stumbled outside into the yard. Outside, Emmaline and the butler stood in the street looking up at the house. She stumbled along next to her father as they joined them, then turned to see the flames beginning to engulf their home. They were all out of the house safely and that was all that mattered. Still, it was difficult to stop the feeling of horrific loss from pounding through her.

It was a horrible thing to watch their lives burn to the ground. There wasn't much anyone could do to stop it. The volunteer firefighters came, certainly, but buckets of water tossed onto the raging inferno was not enough to extinguish it.

When the fire was finally out, the constable arrived to question them all. Her father had retired for the evening. Gerald secured the house before turning in and Emmaline was abed by the time Bella left the library. She thought of the eerie shadowy figure she saw creeping through the port, but she said nothing to the constable about it.

"A terrible loss," the man said. "You have my sympathies. If you can think of nothing more, I'll write this up as an accident."

"Nothing more," her father said with a glance at her.

She shook her head. The constable and the firefighters left them as the house smoldered, gray smoke curling upward. There was nothing left but a burned-out shell with blackened walls. She stared at it with an overwhelming sense of sadness and despair. They got out alive, but at the cost of losing everything.

Bella stood in the yard next to her father clutching the strange book to her chest. If she'd had more time, she would have grabbed more things from her room. But she didn't have more time and now everything was lost. Their vast library of books. Her mother's china. Her father's antiques he had collected from all over the world. All gone.

And here she stood still in her evening gown while her father wore his night clothes. He appeared to have haphazardly pulled on his overcoat. While he buttoned it, the buttons were off, making it look uneven. The collar stuck up and his hair was disheveled.

"What are we going to do now?" she asked, her voice rough and raw from the smoke.

"We're going to Hawthorne Hall," he announced, sounding sure and strong.

Bella snapped her head in his direction. "Hawthorne Hall?"

Hawthorne Hall was in the southern provincial town where her father owned a small, but modest manor house on the outskirts. They spent quite a bit of time there when she was younger. Her mother loved it there, but Bella not so much. They hadn't been back since her mother died when she was a child.

"Gerald, you, Mrs. Graves and Emmaline will come with us, of course," he said, as though she hadn't spoken.

"As you wish, my lord," Gerald said with a nod.

"Pack what you can in the wagon, though I daresay there isn't much left."

There was a bitterness in his tone as he peered at what was left of their manor house. A bitterness she, too, felt.

"Emmaline was looking forward to her days off to spend with her mother and sister," Bella said. "We should at least ask her if she wants to come."

She wasn't sure why she thought of that now. She craned her neck to look for her. She and Edith were huddled together on the edge of the lawn. The girl's face was tear streaked. The old woman had an arm around her shoulders and spoke to her, as if trying to comfort her.

"Of course, dearest. I need to make some arrangements for us. I think we should spend the night in town, then we can take the train in the morning."

She gaped at him. He was not thinking clearly. "Father," she said, her tone soft and patient. "Hawthorne Hall has been closed up for years. Do you think this is a good idea? Besides, I don't have any clothes and neither do you."

"Pardon me, my lord," Gerald said, moving a little closer. "If I may, your daughter makes a good point."

Her father's gaze bounced from hers to Gerald's. "She does?"

"Yes, sir. Allow me and the others to go on ahead to make the house ready for you both. That way, we can make sure the larder is stocked for your arrival. In the meantime, perhaps it would be prudent for you and Miss Rinaldi to stay in town a day or two to purchase a new wardrobe?"

Relief settled through her at Gerald's suggestion. Truthfully, it was the most she'd ever heard the old butler speak. She flashed him a grateful smile.

"And Emmaline," she added, hastily. "I need her with me."

Consideration flickered over her father's face before he finally nodded.

"Ah, yes, quite right, Gerald. I'm not thinking clearly." He put a hand to his forehead and rubbed. "Bella and I will do just that. We'll meet you there in a day or so."

"Very good, sir."

"I'm going to ask Emmaline."

Before her father answered, she bounded off toward the two women. They were both dressed in their nightclothes, a dressing gown hastily thrown on and slippers on their feet. They both looked exhausted and terrified but, thankfully, uninjured.

The moment the young girl saw her heading her direction, she whisked away the tears and straightened, as if she wasn't allowed to grieve losing the manor.

"Are you two all right?" Bella asked, her gaze flickering between the two of them.

"We're fine, miss. Thank ye for asking," Edith said.

"I'm relieved to hear it," Bella said, still clutching the book to her chest.

"What's going to happen to us, miss?" Emmaline asked.

"We're going to stay at the inn in the port for a few days. Then, after that, my father intends to move us to our country home in Driftbell, Hawthorne Hall." She reached out a hand to her maid, placing it on her arm. "Emmaline, it would mean a lot to me if you came with me and then travelled on to Hawthorne Hall with us."

Emmaline's face paled as indecision flashed through her eyes.

"You don't have to, of course, but I find I cannot dress without you." She gave her a weak, hopeful smile. "Of course, you can always return to visit your mother and sister. Anytime you wish. It's only a short train ride."

"Do you mean that, miss?" Emmaline asked, her eyes shining and bright.

"Of course, I do. You're such a help to me. I couldn't bear being in the country without you." She turned to Edith. "Or your fine lemon cakes, Mrs. Graves. That is, if you'll agree to come with us as well. Gerald is going to go ahead to make the house ready for our arrival."

"Oh, miss, ye do go on about those." She chuckled. "If ye don't mind me returning to visit the grandchildren…"

"You can visit them anytime you like." She released Emmaline and reached a hand to the older woman. She took it, squeezed her hand and gave her a bright smile.

"All right, then. I accept," Mrs. Graves said.

"And so do I," Emmaline said.

Bella blew out a breath. "I'm so glad. The country would be dreadful without you both."

"Bella, come along," her father called.

Still clutching the book, she gave Mrs. Graves a wave. Emmaline fell in step besides her, and they joined her father. The three of them walked down the street toward the port, leaving behind the charred remains of their life.

CHAPTER 4

Her father secured them two rooms at the local inn in the port. The sleepy-eyed innkeeper, though, looked them over with a curious eye. She in her formal dinner gown, her father in his nightclothes with his dressing gown hastily thrown over and no hat, and her maid in her nightdress and slippers. The girl remained behind Bella with her eyes downcast.

It was a relief to be in their room, though it was small. One narrow bed on either side of the room and a small wardrobe between the two. At least the view from the one window was of the port. Moonlight glistened on the water beyond the ships.

Emmaline unbuttoned the back of her gown and hung it in the wardrobe while she kicked off her slippers and slid under the blankets. Emmaline climbed into her own bed across from her, but Bella sensed apprehension rolling off her.

"Everything will be all right," Bella said, trying to reassure her. "You'll see."

"It's just that...I've never been out of the city, miss. In the morning, I'd like to send a message to my mum and sister."

"I'll help you with that."

Fatigue pounded through her as she laid on the soft mattress, trying not to fret over the loss of their home and things. The book she brought with her rested next to the unlit candle on the low table between the two beds.

"What is Hawthorne Hall like?" Emmaline asked.

Bella yawned. "I've not been back for many years, but I remember it as a quiet, serene place where my father and mother liked to spend summers. There's a pond behind the manor house with a short pier. My mother loved roses and had quite a large rose garden that smelled sweet with all the colorful blooms."

"Sounds wonderful." Her voice was thick with sleep. "I look forward to seeing it."

She yawned, curled around the pillow, and moments later was fast asleep. But sleep eluded Bella as she laid on the bed, peering up at the window with the gossamer curtain filtering out the moonlight. She thought of the strange shadow she saw in the port before she retired to her room.

She wasn't sure what made her do it—some deep impulse she was unable to deny—but she shoved off the blanket and stood between the beds, peering through the curtain. Several ships bobbed in silence in the harbor, their sails down and secured. She parted the curtain to peer into the night, her senses on high alert. As she did, she thought she saw the shadowy figure moving through the port. The same one she saw earlier.

A strangeness pierced her as she watched the figure move from shadow to shadow as though floating through space. She resisted the urge to throw on Emmaline's dressing gown and rush out to the port to investigate. As the thought flickered through her mind, a dark voice whispered through the room.

The hair on the back of her neck stood at attention. Her head snapped over to Emmaline, but the girl was still sleeping. She hadn't moved and her face was in repose.

She let the curtain fall back into place and backed up against the bed. When her legs hit it, she sank into it, pulling the blankets to her chin to ward off a sudden chill that flickered through her. She needed to sleep and put the strange shadow figure out of her mind. She squeezed her eyes shut and calmed her mind, regulated her breath, and finally slept.

Bright morning pierced her closed eyelids. When Bella awoke, she was momentarily disoriented as she tried to recall where she was. Then it all came crashing back to her. *The fire.*

Across from her, Emmaline's bed was empty and perfectly made into neat, straight lines. She sat up, running a hand through her tangled hair as she peered around the room. Where could Emmaline be in her nightclothes?

She pushed aside her blankets and stood, remembering the strangeness of the night before. She peered through the slit in the curtain at the port. There was the normal activity in the harbor.

A tall ship unfurled its sails, its bells clanging, in preparation for departing. Shouting orders from the ship captain was nothing more than a muffled voice as the men readied the ship. Seagulls squawked as they swooped through the air searching for a morsel of food.

Dockworkers were loading and unloading crates, barrels, and sacks using their rope pulleys and wooden ramps. Horse-drawn carts rambled down the cobblestone street, wheels clattering and drivers shouting. Fisherman and traders called out their prices of their wares as they tried to make their wages for the day. Sailors swaggered off their ships to gather in the local tavern for their morning breakfast.

As she stood there, watching and listening through the pane of glass, a pang of sorrow clutched her. She realized, with some desolation, she would miss the bustling port, as well as the wealthy nobles whose libraries she frequented. The book sitting on the table was the only one she'd translate now. Her finger ran down the aged leather-bound cover and over the thorny vines and brambles. Perhaps, at Hawthorne Hall, she would find the key to deciphering the odd language.

As she pondered this all, the door scraped open. Emmaline entered, her eyes bright and cheery and her cheeks ruddy. She carried an armload of packages and kicked the door closed with her heel. She was fully dressed in a cream high-waisted gown. The sleeves ended at her elbow and were trimmed in lace.

"Oh, my lady, good morrow!"

She hurried to her bed and dumped the packages. Curiosity sparked through Bella as she moved to stand next to her.

"What's all this?"

"I woke before dawn and, well, I hope you don't mind, but I slipped out to visit my mum and sister," she said. "I told Mum we were headed for the country. And then I picked up some of my gowns since I lost everything else in the fire." She turned to the bed and picked up one of the brown paper packages tied with string, extending it to her. "It's not much, but since you only have your dinner gown, I thought this might be more appropriate until you can purchase a new wardrobe. You're the same size as my older sister."

Bella was touched she thought of her. She slipped the package from her hands and pulled the string to untie it. Unwrapping it, she peered down at a pale blue gown embroidered with tiny white roses. It was simple yet lovely.

"Emmaline, this is very kind of you. Thank you."

"I'll help you dress. Your father is waiting for you in the tavern."

After dressing and brushing the snarls out of her hair, Emmaline twisted her hair into a low chignon and pinned it. Then she headed down to the tavern to meet her father. Sunlight filtered through the grimy windows, casting golden shafts along the scarred wooden floor. Most of the chairs were turned upside down on top of the tables, save for a few that were occupied by early morning risers—her father included. The barkeep behind the counter rinsed mugs in a wooden basin, the soft clink of glass on wood the only sound in the hush. A tired barmaid wiped down the length of the counter, her movements slow, mechanical. The faint scent of stale ale and wood smoke lingered in the air.

Her father sat at one of the old wooden tables near the fireplace, where smoldering embers popped quietly and glowed with the last breath of the night before. He wore a threadbare shirt that hung too loose on his frame and trousers a shade too short—borrowed clothes, all of them, ill-fitting and smelling faintly of smoke and someone else's home. He held the morning newspaper and peered at it intently. When he heard her enter, he lifted his gaze, smiled, and folded the paper.

"Ah, there you are, my dear. Did you sleep well?" he asked.

"Well enough, I suppose."

She didn't want to mention the apparition she saw skulking through the docks or the eerie whispering sound she heard coming from the book. She took the seat opposite him, her chair scraping along the wood floor as she pulled it out to sit. He eyed her with a curious look.

"Where did you get that dress?"

She placed her folded hands in her lap. "Emmaline brought it to me. Where do you get those clothes?"

He flushed, as he cut a wayward glance to the barkeep. "The innkeeper took pity on me. Seems news of the fire has already spread." He cleared his throat and leaned his elbow on the table. "I have business in the port, right after I visit the tailor and pick up some new clothes for myself. You and Emmaline should go on to the dressmaker. Tell them to put everything on my account. And get something for the young lady, too. I insist."

"That's very kind of you, Father. When will we be making our way to Hawthorne Hall?"

"I reckon we'll take the evening train." He reached for his pocket watch and realized it wasn't there. Frustration lined his face. "I best be off. We'll meet back at the inn this afternoon."

"All right," she said.

He rose and came to her side of the table. He kissed the top of her head. Then he was off, disappearing through the tavern door leaving her alone with the barmaid and the barkeep who both ignored her presence.

She pushed from the table. It had been a while since she had new gowns. She decided to collect Emmaline and then head to the shop for a day of shopping.

Chapter 5

Bella spent a small portion of her father's fortune in Miss Etta's Fine Attire, the ladies' clothing shop on Main Street. The finest gowns were displayed on mannequins with corseted waists. The shelves were stacked with folded gowns, skirts, and petticoats of the finest material. Drawers were full of gloves, lace collars, handkerchiefs, stockings, and shawls. Hat stands displayed wide-brimmed bonnets. Some ostentatious with brightly colored plumes and ribbons. Others unadorned. In the back room, seamstresses feverishly worked on custom orders. But Bella was there to purchase whatever was on hand in her size.

Miss Etta was more than happy to help her since her father provided the shopkeeper with bolts of fine material from his travels all over the world. She happily put the cost onto her father's account. It seemed fitting to spend the money for the gowns she and Emmaline purchased. Emmaline grinned from ear to ear, clearly enjoying herself. It made Bella smile to see her so happy.

When they stepped out into the bustling street in the early afternoon, Bella's stomach growled. She realized, then, she'd missed breakfast.

"Let's go to the wharf for something to eat," she said.

With their arms loaded with packages, they headed down the street to the docks where they would find street vendors hawking their street food including everything from grilled fish to fruit skewers.

"I've never done that." Emmaline's face beamed as she continued to grin, her eyes wide and shiny as she took in all the sights, the sounds, the smells.

"You're in for a treat. Father used to bring me here when I was younger and he had business in the port with his ships."

As they neared the docks, the fishermen shouted their catch of the day. Wooden crates were full of slippery silvery fish, the afternoon light gleaming on their damp scales. Lobsters crowded their cages. Mounds of oysters were on ice.

One side hosted the street food carts where there was a variety of treats. Fruit skewered, roasted meat on a stick, meat pies, fried potatoes, roasted nuts. The food smells intermingled with that of the salty sea air. Bella paused a moment to bask in the afternoon sunshine, closing her eyes and lifting her face to the sky to enjoy the warmth on her skin.

"My lady, you'll burn," Emmaline said on a gasp.

"The warmth feels delicious. Don't you agree?" she said without opening her eyes.

"I do agree."

The charming male voice made her eyes pop open. Standing near her, with a faint smile on his handsome face, was Lord Vincent. He was dressed in an elegant navy frock coat, finely tailored to his broad shoulders and cinched at the waist with a silver-buttoned closure. A crisp white shirt peeked out from the high collar of his dark brocade waistcoat. A silk cravat, knotted and pinned with a glittering sapphire, gave him a dash of effortless elegance. Charcoal-gray trousers were tucked into black boots polished to a high shine that gleamed despite the dust and grime of the wharf. His gloved hands held a matching cane and, tucked beneath his arm, was his top hat, allowing his brown hair to have a windswept look as though he were merely strolling the docks.

"Oh, Lord Vincent. It's nice to see you."

She hadn't expected to see him again. It left her a bit flustered. After their last encounter, she thought for sure he would never speak to her again, though she did try to be kind when she rebuffed him.

"I daresay I'm delighted to see you, Miss Rinaldi. Especially after hearing about the devastating fire that took your home. Are you well? Your father?" Concern etched his face as his gaze flickered from her to Emmaline and back again.

"Yes, we're fine. Thank you for asking. We all made it out in time." She noticed he continued to look at Emmaline, who stood a few paces behind her. "This is my lady's maid, Emmaline."

He gave a brief nod and a pleasant smile in greeting, his eyes lighting with interest. "A pleasure to make your acquaintance, miss." His gaze roved over the mountains of packages in her arms, but he said nothing. Finally, his eyes flickered back to her. "What will you and your father do now? Surely not stay at the local inn."

A flash of fear went through her that he would open his home to them. She forced a smile, voice light and causal. "Oh, no, we're heading to our country estate in Driftbell this evening."

"I see." He sounded rather disappointed hearing she was leaving the port.

Truth be told, disappointment tugged at her too—but not for the same reason. She'd miss the clamor of the docks, the clang of rigging in the wind, the gulls shrieking overhead, and the coarse shouts of fishermen haggling over the morning's catch. The port had a pulse, a life of its own she couldn't quite explain but felt deep in her bones.

He was still looking at the packages. Her arms ached from carrying them, but pride and determination kept her spine straight.

"May I help you with your packages? You both look quite overloaded."

"Oh, that's very kind of you, but we can handle it."

As the words left her mouth, one of the packages slipped—tilting, tumbling. He caught the hatbox before it hit the ground, smooth and swift. But though he gave her a polite smile, his eyes said he knew the many packages were far too much for her.

"I must insist," he said gently. "Allow me to have your packages sent ahead to your home in Driftbell. It will make your travels much easier."

Bella shifted from one foot to the other, suddenly aware of the weight she carried in her arms, which cramped. She had the sneaking suspicion he was interested in helping her so he could call on her later at Hawthorne Hall.

She cut a glance back at Emmaline. Her wide eyes took in his appearance and a flush bloomed high on her cheeks. She gazed at him with shy dreamy admiration. Lord Vincent's gaze flickered toward Emmaline and, for the briefest moment, his polished composure cracked into a smile that was meant only for her.

A grin wanted to pull up the corners of Bella's mouth, but she suppressed it.

"I do believe you're right, Lord Vincent. Thank you for the kind offer. Our home in Driftbell is Hawthorne Hall."

Lord Vincent signaled for his valet who stood a few paces behind him. He was dressed in a dark livery coat and black pants, his hands clasped behind his back and his expression unreadable. He stepped forward, offered a small bow and immediately took the packages from Bella's arms.

"Hollis, please see these packages are delivered to Miss Rinaldi at Hawthorne Hall in Driftbell."

"As you say, my lord."

Hollis handed off the packages to another manservant who materialized out of the crowd. Before long, she and Emmaline had offloaded all of them to the men. She had to admit it was a relief not to be carrying them. Lord Vincent lingered, though, even after Hollis and the other man melted away into the crowd.

"May I escort you somewhere?" he asked.

"We were headed to the food stalls," she said with a breezy air. "But..." She cut a glance to Emmaline and her rosy cheeks. "I just remembered I need to see my father. He's on his ship. Would you mind escorting Emmaline instead?"

She reached behind her, taking the girl's hand in hers and tugging her toward Lord Vincent. When his gaze landed on the girl, there was a definite spark between them. He placed his hat on his head and then held out his elbow to her. Emmaline, flustered and a tad breathless, took his arm. She gave Bella a winsome smile as the two headed away.

Bella remained a moment, watching the two of them walk toward the food stalls. He with his tall, broad shoulders in his finery, and her with her hair in a long braid down her back. They made a fine pair. A sense of smug satisfaction swept over her, pleased at her matchmaking skills, as she headed for her father's ship.

As she approached the ship, though, she heard shouting coming from the decks. And not the normal shouts of boisterous men. This had a hint of fear in it. She picked up her skirts and hurried toward the gangplank as one of the sailors appeared on deck with a shout for her father.

Several of the crew members were clustered on the dock at the foot of the gangplank, huddling together and whispering. There was a palpable tension in the sea air, and something made the hairs on the back of her neck stand at attention.

She halted a distance from the gangplank as her father, who was talking with one of the merchants, left the man and headed to the deck.

"What is it, lad?"

The young man—who could not be much older than Bella—was clearly frightened by whatever he saw in the hold. He pointed behind him and uttered nonsensical words. Her father approached him, took him by the shoulders.

"Easy, now. Tell me what this is all about," her father said.

"He's dead, sir."

A stillness settled over the ship. Bella's heart dropped to her shoes as she stood there, still as a statue, wondering who was dead. One of the crew?

Her father dropped his arms to his side. With his back to her, she was unable to see his reaction.

"You best show me, lad."

He waved in the direction of the hold, then followed the young sailor from the deck to the cargo hold. Intent on finding out what happened, Bella headed for the gangplank. But when she approached, Tobin, a longtime boatswain on her father's ship, stepped in front of her to stop her.

"Ya don't want to be goin' there, miss," he said.

"Why not, Tobin?" She put her hands on her hips, determined to step around him and find out what was going on for herself.

She'd known the man since she was a little girl. When she sailed with her father, he looked out for her, told her seafaring stories of the high seas that were surely fiction, and made sure she was treated with respect by the other deckhands.

"Still headstrong, ain't ya, miss." He gave her a wink and a wide smile, then turned serious. "Trust me when I tell ya, there's nothing but trouble there."

Something about the way he said it sent cold tingles dancing up her spine. "What do you mean?"

"He means, miss, there be whispers from below. Like chanting. It's cold as the grave down there, it is," said one of the deckhands.

"Whispers you say?" She instantly thought of the book whispering to her in the middle of the night.

"Aye, miss." He lowered his voice and leaned in close, as though sharing a secret with her. "Happened in the middle of the night. Cold wind blew below deck. Lanterns snuffed out. And that shadow thing—it was in the cargo hold."

"That's enough, Jory," Tobin said, cutting him off. He gave him a nudge away from her and stepped in front of him, as if to shield her from the deckhand.

But something about the way he said *shadow thing* sent definite cold chills through her. She shuddered and clutched her elbows. She'd seen the shadow herself creeping through the port. Not once, but twice.

"A shadow thing?" she repeated.

"And now a man's dead," Jory continued.

Tobin turned to him and grasped him by the arm. "Get back to yer post, you scallywag." He gave him a shove in the direction of the gangplank.

But Jory and the others weren't too keen on boarding the ship once again. Tobin turned back to her, plastering on a wide smile.

"Don't ye be worrying about that, miss. It's for Mr. Rinaldi to worry about."

She clutched her elbows tighter, hugging herself. "Yes, of course. You're right. Tell my father Emmaline and I will meet him at the inn."

"My pleasure, miss." He tipped his well-worn hat to her. "I'll let him know soon as I see him."

With her heart in her throat, she turned back to the wharf. A sort of numbness took residence in her as she walked across the planks, thinking of the strange whispering from the book and the odd shadowy apparition. Were they connected? She wasn't sure. All she knew for sure was she had to get back to the inn and collect her things. The book included.

CHAPTER 6

Later that day, she, Emmaline and her father boarded the train to Driftbell. Emmaline had a dreamy look about her as she, no doubt, continued to think about Lord Vincent. There would be time later to query her about how things went when they visited the food stalls together. Her curiosity was definitely piqued.

Her father shuffled through papers, a pinched expression of worry on his face. He had mentioned nothing that happened at the ship, but he was unsettled that something dreadful happened to one of the crew. She was too cowardly to ask. She clutched the book, holding it in her lap, fearful of opening the pages and perusing them once again. And so, they rode in silence.

By late evening, they arrived at the train station. Bella was relieved to see Gerald had sent along the horse and carriage with a driver and footman. Another bumpy ride later and they would arrive to the place she hadn't seen in years.

The carriage wheels crunched over gravel, the lanterns flickering as they bumped along the winding country road casting halos of light dancing across hedgerows. Road dust smudged the glass panes, but the warm glow offered a small circle of brightness in the puddle of darkness.

They slowed as the iron gates creaked open, welcoming them into the yawning abyss of night. Beyond the trees, Hawthorne Hall rose from the mist like a memory half-remembered—larger than she recalled, and lonelier, too. Moonlight caught on the old wood façade, casting long shadows across ivy-covered walls and shuttered windows that stared back like melancholy eyes.

Her father gathered his papers as the driver slowed the carriage to a halt and moments later, the door opened. Her father was out first, tucking his leather folio under his arm. When he was on the ground, he turned back and offered her his hand.

Grasping it, she stepped out of the carriage and tilted her head back, trying to reconcile the childhood image in her mind with the darkened silhouette before her. The front doors loomed tall and weathered, their iron fixtures dulled with rust. Somewhere within, the house creaked—settling or perhaps remembering her.

She swallowed hard. Next to her, Emmaline peered up at the imposing structure with wide eyes. A flagstone path led to the front of the old house. They had bought it years ago when it was shiny and new but now it appeared time and age and neglect had taken its toll. The shutters were faded, the paint peeling. The wood exterior needed new paint to brighten it from the dreary gray.

The air smelled of damp earth and wild roses, overgrown and untamed. The once-proud hedgerows had grown thick with brambles, and the old fountain at the center of the circular drive stood silent, its basin choked with leaves.

The driver detached one of the lanterns, the flicking flame dancing within the glass and led the way to the front door. As they approached, it opened casting Gerald in a slash of light as he waited for them to make their way inside. It was a comfort to see the old butler there.

"Mind your step, ladies. I daresay the place is wildly overgrown. I can see I need a groundskeeper straightaway." Her father paused in front of the butler. "Thank you, Gerald. Is the house in good order?"

But this was no mere house. This was a manor. And much larger than she remembered.

"Of course, my lord."

The butler stood aside from the heavy oak door allowing them entry. Her father entered first, moving deeper into the foyer. Bella paused inside the doorway to take in all the sights of the house.

Before her, the staircase led to the upper floors where the bedrooms were. On the left, the parlor. The right, the dining room and beyond that the kitchen. Another room behind the stairs, she recalled, was her father's office and library.

The furniture was uncovered, ready to welcome them once again to Hawthorne Hall. Through the open parlor door, she saw the loveseat the color of mint and two chairs, a low table between them. She remembered with some clarity her mother sitting on that sofa combing her hair and telling her stories of the high seas when she traveled with her father to distant lands to buy satin and lace.

"Well," her father said, his voice loud in the silence. "Good to see things are as we left it."

"Several packages arrived for the ladies, my lord," Gerald announced from his place by the front door. "I had them put in your room, miss."

Surprise flickered through her. "They did?"

"A courier delivered them late this afternoon on behalf of Lord Vincent," Gerald said.

"Very kind of him," her father said. "Once we're settled, we should invite him for dinner to thank him properly."

Behind her, Emmaline sucked in a breath. Bella nodded.

"Yes, of course, Father. Thank you, Gerald, for seeing to our things."

He gave a nod of acknowledgment.

When Bella remained rooted in place, still clutching the book, her father walked to her. His face was creased with concern.

"Go on up and rest," he said. "I want to have a look about to make sure all is well."

Gerald handed her a candle to light her way.

"All right. Goodnight, Father."

Truthfully, she was exhausted and ready to fall into a soft bed. She was glad Emmaline was with there to help her.

She started for the stairs, the wood floor creaking under her steps. Up and up and they ascended, the lone candle lighting her way casting long, ominous shadows along the wall with its damask wallpaper in muted colors her mother surely picked.

Her room was off the top of the stairs. She pushed open the door to see it was as she left it all those years ago. With her candle, she lit the others in the room, illuminating it in a warm golden glow.

The white four-poster bed still hosted the satin and lace coverlet. Perched against the pillows at the head of the bed was her well-worn, well-loved teddy bear. She forgot she left him behind hoping he would guard the place while she was gone. The bed was piled high with packages from their shopping excursion earlier that day, which now seemed to be more than a few hours ago.

Emmaline started sorting and unwrapping packages as she placed the single candelabra on the bedside table, still clutching the book in her other hand, and reached for the bear. His eyes were made with two black buttons sewn into the brown material. He was all she had left of her childhood in the country, and she was unable to resist hugging him to her chest.

Emmaline opened the wardrobe. "Miss, you have some gowns here."

"They're all from my childhood. I suppose they will need to be packed away."

The girl reached for one of the dresses, but Bella moved to stop her.

"Let's not worry about that tonight, Em. We can sort that out tomorrow. I'm tired."

"Yes, miss."

She moved the rest of her unopened packages to the nearby chair under the window while Emmaline turned back the bed. At least the room was clean and had fresh linens. She was grateful for that.

After helping her out of her gown and taking down her hair, she decided to sleep in her shift rather than unpack everything. Emmaline picked up her packages but paused at the door, a look of confusion on her face.

"Where do I sleep, my lady?"

"Oh, how thoughtless of me. I'll show you." Bella shoved back the blankets and rose.

"It's all right. You can tell me where the servants' rooms are. I can find my own way." She gave her a smile.

"On the third floor right above me."

She dipped a curtsy. "Good night."

Emmaline juggled the packages and closed the door behind her, sealing Bella inside. She slipped back under the blankets, curling around the pillow. It wasn't long before she was fast asleep.

Morning light filtered in through the lace curtains at the window. Normally, she would be awake before dawn. But this morning, after their long night, she slept in. With a yawn and a stretch, she rose, pushing back the blankets. Her stomach growled. She hoped there was breakfast. She rang for Emmaline to help her dress and as she released the bellpull, she heard the low whispering coming from behind her.

It was coming from the book.

Her heart rammed hard against her chest as she stepped to her dressing table and peered down at it. The whispering stopped. She opened the cover, the aged leather cracking. Then she flipped several pages, staring at the arcane language her translator brain refused to decipher.

A sharp, sudden chill slid down her spine. The air around her shifted—heavier, darker—as if the book exhaled something foul. Something *wrong*. It seeped from the pages, pressing against her chest like invisible hands. Her breath caught.

She slammed the book shut and stumbled back, heart pounding.

That wasn't ink and parchment.

It was alive. Watching. Waiting.

Wicked.

She didn't want to touch it again.

A sharp knock on her door startled her. Her hand flew to her throat as she emitted a strangled gasp and spun toward the door, her eyes wide and her mouth suddenly dry.

"My lady?" Emmaline's muffled voice filtered through the wood.

She blew out a sputtering breath. "Yes, come in."

Emmaline headed inside and then started opening all the packages, chatting on about the house and how she liked her third-floor bedroom. But Bella didn't hear much of it as she was too distracted by the oily feeling the book left crawling over her skin. Her hand was still at her throat as she stared at the offending tome, thinking of the dark whisper and the strange shadow she saw in the port.

What was she going to do with the book?

As she recalled, there was a bookshop in town. Perhaps she should take the book there and talk with the owner to see if he had ever seen anything like it before. In this small village, though, he may not have seen anything so unusual. Still, she wanted to give it a try.

Or, even better, offload the book if he was willing to buy it.

"Miss? Did you hear me?" Emmaline asked.

She shook herself out of her thoughts and focused on the girl in front of her. She held two gowns. One a pale yellow, the other a pale green.

"Which one?"

"Oh..." She glanced between the two of them, still preoccupied with thoughts of whispers and ghostly apparitions. "Either is fine with me. Em...would you care to go into town with me today?"

"Town?"

"Yes, I'd like to visit the bookshop."

Her youthful face broke into a wide grin. "I'd like that very much."

Then it was settled. She would take the offending book into the shop and be rid of it.

CHAPTER 7

After dressing, she put the book in a basket, covered it with a cloth, and headed down to the dining room to find her father. She wasn't going to tell him she intended to sell the book. She didn't want to hurt his feelings after he brought it to her from his travels.

But when she arrived in the dining room, he was nowhere about and had already hastily eaten his breakfast. According to Gerald, he received a message that left everyone scratching their heads and took off without his hat or his overcoat muttering something about the morning train and that he'd be back by nightfall.

Odd, that.

But then, her father was often distracted when it came to business.

So, she and Emmaline buttoned on their bonnets and headed for town. The path from Hawthorne Hall wound gently downhill, skirted the farmer's lush green fields in the late morning light. It was sprinkled with old oaks, casting a long shade across the gravel. The faint breeze carried the distant scent of chimney smoke, roasted meats, and baking bread. All signs they approached the little town of Driftbell.

"Thank you for coming with me, Em."

"Em." She grinned beneath her bonnet. "My mum and sister are the only ones who call me that."

"Oh." Bella breathed out the word. "I'm sorry. I didn't think—"

"I don't mind." She continued to grin and then hooked her arm in hers. "I hope that means we can be friends."

Bella felt the weight of the basket on her other arm and realized she was glad she had the girl with her, though she wasn't prepared to tell her anything about the whispers or the skulking shadow figure yet.

"I think it does." She returned her smile.

As they walked, the humming village rose to meet them. The shuddering sound of wheels through the gravel street, boisterous laughter, a dog barking behind a garden wall.

The rooftops of Driftbell came into view through a break in the hedgerow, and with them, the narrow spire of the old chapel and the green-painted sign of the bookshop proclaiming *The Quill and Scroll* swinging gently in the breeze.

The moment they stepped into the town, Emmaline's eyes were round and wide as she took in all the sights and sounds. The streets wound through the aged buildings with their slate roof covered in moss and their shutters painted in faded colors of blue, green, and ochre.

Horse-drawn carriages rumbled down the dusty road. The village was a bustle of activity. The smell of bread and roasted meats permeated the air. And somewhere in the distance, she heard the bellow of a deep voice hawking his wares.

A flower cart was bursting with colors—flowers in every color. A smiling young woman with eagerness burning in her eyes stood behind the white cart, hoping Bella would stop and make a purchase. Next to her, local farmers sold their fruits and vegetables, fresh eggs, and cheese. And beyond that, a weaver who made straw baskets.

A narrow stream cut through the southern edge, crossed by an old stone bridge arched just enough to let small boats pass beneath. Beyond it rose the chapel spire, a weathered bell at its peak. The source of Driftbell's name, some said, was because the bell once drifted downriver before being claimed by the town.

"I have business in the bookshop," she said. "If you want to explore—"

"Oh, can I? I mean, do you mind ever so much?" Excitement buzzed beneath her normally cool exterior.

Bella grinned. "I don't mind at all. Meet me back here."

She dipped a quick curtsy and then bounded off through the colorful crowd. Smiling over the girl's enthusiasm, Bella turned toward the door of the shop and pushed it open. The bell chimed her arrival. The moment she stepped inside, a sense of ease calmed her. The smell of dusty tomes, aged parchment, and ink comforted her. It wasn't a large shop. But even so, several patrons were already inside perusing the shelves.

Bookshelves lined the walls of the shop from floor to ceiling. A sliding ladder was in place to reach the uppermost shelves. A young boy stood on the ladder shelving books. Another bespectacled man was behind the counter at the front of the store.

A tall man stood off to one side, his head titled slightly as he ran a gloved finger along the well-worn and new spines, as though he were looking for something in particular. The morning light filtered through the shop's windows as he stood in the pool of light making several strands of his dark, unruly hair glisten.

He wasn't dressed like most men in town—no stiff collar or polished arrogance. And yet his coat was of fine material, threaded with silver and hosting gold buttons. His cravat was a bit loose, as though he'd tugged it away from his throat from frustration or annoyance or perhaps even out of habit. There was a quiet confidence about him. As if he were used to slipping through the world without drawing attention to himself and yet impossible to notice.

He cast her a glance as she entered. His pale brown eyes seemed to glow within that circle of light as their eyes met, sending a shiver through her. For a moment, they shared an unexpected connection making it impossible for her to look away.

"How can I help you, miss?" the man behind the counter said.

It broke their connection, forcing her to look away and toward the counter. She plastered on her best smile.

"I was wondering if you buy used books?"

He smiled and gave a brief nod. "If they are unique and unusual, I do."

She assumed this was the owner. She placed the basket on the counter and uncovered the book. "I have something that's unique and unusual."

He peered down through his spectacles at the book with a *hmmm*, then glanced back up at her with a gesture toward it. "May I?"

"Of course."

He plucked it out of the basket and placed it on the counter, opening the antique cover. He paused at the first page, staring down at the thorny language. He flipped through the pages, the parchment fluttering and exuding that ancient paper odor. As he did, she watched the archaic writing shuffle by, still unable to read it. He flipped past the drawings of symbols, not pausing to give them a second look. But as the pages turned, she saw the drawings appear to move.

"I've never seen the likes," he said. "Where did you get this?"

"My father brought it back from his travels. I'm not sure where he found it."

"What language is this?"

"I was hoping you could tell me." She flashed a winsome grin.

He shook his head. "I've never seen it before."

"Nor I."

She started to lose hope at the way he questioned the book and the reluctance that emanated off him. He paused on a particular page with symbols that appeared to be ancient runes. From this angle, it looked like a blooming rose across the page, entangled with the peculiar-looking rune.

His finger ran down the yellowed page. As he did so, she heard the soft whisper that seemed to come from the parchment itself.

He heard it, too. He jerked his hand back, snapping his head up and looking at her with wide, wondrous eyes. She kept her face impassive, hoping not to give anything away and pretend as though she never heard the indistinct whispering. She heard the rustle of fabric behind her and was aware one of the shop patrons stepped closer to her. Her heart quickened, but she kept her breathing even.

The shopkeeper closed the book with a snap and slid it across the counter to her. "My apologies, miss, but I'm afraid I can't buy this one."

Disappointment flooded her as she picked it up and tucked it back into her basket, covering it with the cloth. "Thank you for your time."

She turned for the door and came face to face with the tall man. He eyed her with curious interest. She sucked in a quick startled breath, then dipped a quick curtsy.

"Pardon me, sir."

Then she headed for the door and slipped out into the morning light, the warmth of the sun on her face as she considered what to do next with the haunted book. Because that's what she decided it was—haunted with a ghostly presence lingering between the pages. She didn't know how that was possible. That with the fact she was unable to translate it was all the warning signs she needed to get rid of it, and quick.

The bustle of the street was in front of her. She scanned the crowd for Emmaline, but didn't see her pale blue bonnet bobbing among the throng. She took one step toward the street when the bell chimed as someone exited the shop behind her.

"Miss?" the male voice said.

She turned to see the mystery man standing outside the shop on the sidewalk. In the morning light, she got a good look at his face. Not only was he tall, but handsome as well. He had broad shoulders. His face was sharp lines, regal, aristocratic. When he looked at her, she sensed something otherworldly and ancient about him. Underneath that, a twinge of melancholy, as though some tragedy overshadowed his soul.

"Yes?" she managed, sounding a bit more breathless than she intended.

It wasn't often she was taken aback by a man such as this, but she suspected this was no ordinary man. There was a spark between them the moment their gazes collided in the bookshop.

"That book you carry. May I see it?" Hope glimmered in his pale brown eyes.

"It was a gift from my father." She didn't know why she said it as she clutched the basket tighter on her arm, her gloved fingers cramping.

He smiled. "And yet you wished to sell it."

"Oh. Yes, well, I can't read the book." Flustered, she was unsure why she said that.

"Neither could the shopkeeper. Perhaps I buy it from you?"

Had he also heard the eerie whispering from the book? She hesitated with her uncertainty, wondering what to make of the man standing before her.

"My name is Leopold Thornhurst. I collect books and have an extensive library. I'm always on the lookout for new volumes to add to my collection. Yours seems exceptionally interesting, though it is a pity it's written in an obscure language."

That got her attention. "You have a library?"

Visions of magnificent libraries flashed through her mind. Lord Vincent's with the stained-glass windows immediately brushed her thoughts. How she once again longed to step foot into a noble's private library filled with dusty volumes that held long past secrets.

He grinned, his eyes lighting with humor. "Yes. Quite a large one."

She chewed on her lower lip as she considered this. "My name is Isabella Rinaldi. I agree it's a pity about the language. It's one I can't seem to decipher."

It was unlike her to offer this information straightaway. But there was something about this man, this Leopold Thornhurst, that intrigued her. Something that made her want to know more about him and his magnificent library.

He tipped his head to one side. "Decipher?"

It was her turn to smile. "I'm a translator of archaic languages. But this one is quite the enigma."

"A translator, you say?" Interest glittered in his pale brown eyes.

She nodded, though again, she didn't quite understand why she was telling him this. She was never this forward or chatty with a stranger. Bella slid the basket down her arm and flipped back the cloth to show him the book. The embossed circle of thorns appeared to gleam in the morning light. She hadn't noticed that before.

He stared at it for a long, quiet moment as contemplation flickered over his face.

"How much?" he asked.

She pushed the basket toward him. "It is my gift to you for your library."

His surprised gaze flickered back up to her. "Are you certain?"

"Yes, it's not dear to me. Not really."

He remained silent as a carriage rattled down the street near them leaving a cloud of dust in its wake. He took her by the elbow and gently eased her away from the street, closer to the building.

"Perhaps you keep the book," he suggested, "and I hire you to translate it for me."

She considered this, wondering if there was some way to translate the book when she'd already had a difficult time of it. The words didn't make sense to her. The longer she stared at the pages, the more elusive it became.

"Allow me to offer you my personal library as a resource, as well as room and board, if that suits you. And, of course, pay you for your services."

A tingling of excitement skipped through her. When she left port, she was certain she wouldn't have the opportunity to step foot into a nobleman's library again. And now, here was the chance to do just that as well as find the answers to the inscrutable language within the pages of the book. An extensive library, at that.

Without another thought, she heard herself say, "When can I begin?"

CHAPTER 8

L eopold left behind the town of Driftbell, hope blooming in his breast for the first time in long, quiet, lonely years. He rode hard back to his estate on the southern edge of town, shrouded in mist and oak trees that hid the Castle Thornhurst from the road and prying, inquisitive eyes. Brambles and climbing roses the color of ink clawed their way down the stone wall to the iron gate that was the barrier between the real world and his dark, desolate world.

It was difficult to get the beguiling Isabella Rinaldi out of his mind. She was dressed in the latest fashion, but her bonnet concealed most of her face in shadow. Yet when she tipped her head back to look at him, the sunlight glistened on her face, illuminating it just right. She was breathtaking with delicately carved cheekbones, a full mouth, a dainty nose, and eyes that rivaled the sea, fringed in dark lashes. Eyes that were intelligent, full of wisdom, and gleamed with curiosity.

She seemed flustered by his offer of room and board. Indeed, he felt it was the best way to keep her working as she studied the book. If she was able to translate it as he hoped, then all things would be returned to as they were before. She told him she lived at Hawthorne Hall—truthfully he thought the place abandoned—and that she would need to speak to her father first. A bit of hope died right there, but he had to believe she would find a way to help him, even if she didn't realize she was helping him.

His horse trotted up the gravel drive where he halted, dismounted, and gave the mare a pat. The signal for her to return to the stables. She trotted off as he entered the castle and was immediately greeted by his valet, Dickens.

"Welcome home, my prince." He bowed low in greeting.

"Dickens, I told you not to call me that."

It was an age-old discussion and one that continued to be ignored.

He and Dickens were the only two remaining in the castle. Where the halls were once alive with boisterous laughter, enchanting balls, and lively music, they were now dark and desolate with creeping shadows that seemed to curl along certain hallways. The curse had not spared Dickens, affecting him in inexplicable ways. Not only was his life force was tied to Leopold's, but he also gained interesting magical abilities. While he was able to remain a part of his life, the rest of his staff and court didn't fare so well—they disappeared in a flash.

"As you wish, my prince." He took his hat as Leopold handed it over giving him his best thin-lipped expression.

"You were gone quite some time. Are you sure that was wise?"

He and Dickens had been together since he was a boy. The old valet served his father and now him. Now that they were alone in this together, he wanted Dickens to call him a friend instead of prince. Old habits, and all that. He knew as well as Dickens did he'd never not call him prince.

The man eyed him with curiosity.

Leopold said, "A risk, yes, but worth it. Are you going to ask me about the girl? For surely you know about her."

There was always that knowing his valet had—part of his interesting magical abilities. The sagacious light was deep in his dark eyes. His valet's face remained impassive, as if Leopold's guess was neither right nor wrong.

"If you wish. But I know you prefer I not spoil the telling for you."

Leopold chuckled, a sound rumbling low in his chest. A sound, he realized, he hadn't emitted in ages. In fact, he couldn't recall a time when he last felt so light, so optimistic, so encouraged.

"She's a beauty, I gather," Dickens said.

He slipped off his waistcoat and handed it off. "You'll see for yourself. She'll be here tomorrow. I've hired her."

That seemed to get a reaction out of the old man. His pinched expression was clear on his aged face. One thin dark brow rose. "You hired her *and* invited her here? My prince, no one has been invited here in decades."

"Yes, I know. So, I look to you, Dickens, to make sure everything is ready for her arrival. She may be staying with us for some time."

"Staying with us?" He sounded utterly confused by the notion. "Forgive me, my prince, but are you certain you wish for this girl to be here? In this castle? Alone? With you?"

He laughed again, enjoying the way it felt to allow it to bubble up through his throat. He reached for his old friend, his valet, and clapped him on the shoulder.

"I am. You won't believe what she has."

"I'm sure I won't."

"She has a book, Dickens. A book, I believe, that can at last break the curse. I saw the pages myself. It matches this."

He dropped his arm to shove up the sleeve of his white shirt revealing the rose that was branded on the inside of his forearm. The blood red rose caught in a snarling twist of brambles and thorns. The same symbol was embossed on cover of her book.

Dickens's brows rose to his receding hairline. "Indeed."

"So, make the castle ready. For tomorrow, Miss Isabella Rinaldi arrives." He headed for the stairs, then halted, turning back. "And one more thing, Dickens. First thing in the morning, send the carriage to meet her in town."

This elicited another shocked expression from the old valet. "As you say, my prince. It will be done."

Bella and Emmaline hurried back to Hawthorne Hall. She remained quiet as she considered Leopold Thornhurst and his invitation to stay at his residence during her translation work. She had no certainty regarding her father's response to the news. She doubted it would be proper for her to depart Hawthorne or remain with the gentleman without an escort. He said he lived south on the outskirts of town, not far from Hawthorne as it turned out. She chewed on her lower lip as she considered how to break the news to her father.

She half-heartedly listened as Emmaline chattered endlessly about everything she saw in town. Her step had a definite bounce as she talked about the shops she saw, the flower cart with an array of bright-colored flowers, the baker with his scones, and how the clock tower in the old chapel chimed the hour.

"Everything all right, miss? You seem distracted."

She clutched the basket tight in her hand as she glanced up at Emmaline, wondering if she should tell her about her encounter with Leopold. She wanted to. She *needed* to tell someone.

"Was your trip to the bookshop successful?" she asked.

Bella pressed her lips together into a thin line and kept her gaze forward. "I suppose you could say that."

"Oh? Were you able to sell the book?"

"No," she said, almost too quickly. She came to a jarring halt in the middle of the road and turned to Emmaline. "Em..." she started, then shook her head and started walking again, changing her mind about telling the girl.

"Yes?" she asked, bouncing alongside her. "Did something happen at the bookshop?"

"Oh, Em, I'm not sure what to do." Again, she came to a halt, both hands clutching the handle of the basket now as she held it in front of her. "I met someone."

Her eyes lit with joy. "You did? Was he as handsome as Lord Vincent?"

He was ever so handsome, but that wasn't the point. A business transaction formed the sole connection between them. She intended to translate the book for him. What he decided to do with that translation did not concern her. She was going to use his extensive library. Excitement skipped through her at the thought of once again being in her element.

"He hired me to translate the book," she blurted.

Confusion shifted over her face as she tipped her head to one side, trying to understand. "Translate the book? Why?"

"I'm not sure. But he was quite interested in it. And there was something..." Bella paused, searching her mind to find the right words. "It appeared there was a bit of sadness about him. But when he looked at the book, his demeanor changed. I shouldn't have told him I was a translator, but it slipped out."

Emmaline considered her words as she looked at her from under the brim of her bonnet. She adjusted it a bit to see her better. "Well, are you going to translate it for him?"

"I want to."

A breath escaped her as she thought, once again, of his *extensive library*. Her imagination ran wild with what that library looked like. How many books did he have? A hundred? A thousand? More? Did he have stained glass windows like Lord Vincent? Comfortable furniture? A butler who served tea and cucumber sandwiches?

She shoved all those spiraling thoughts away. There was no guarantee she would be able to take on the position, even though she jumped at the chance when speaking to the man.

"But I must speak to my father first."

And even then, he might refuse to release her, as he had the right to do. She remained a maiden, after all, and it could cause quite the scandal. Still, relinquishing the notion of a book-filled room's appeal proved difficult.

Emmaline hooked her arm in hers. "I'm sure he'll say yes. Let's go tell him!"

Bella giggled at her enthusiasm. "Yes, let's!"

But when they arrived home, everything changed.

CHAPTER 9

Grievous news awaited when she and Emmaline arrived back at Hawthorne Hall.

Her father's fleet was *gone*.

All of it, save for the Golden Tempest, which was still at sea.

She couldn't breathe. Couldn't think. The words tumbled around in her head, meaningless at first, until they landed like the weight of cannonballs.

He sat at the end of the dining table, hunched over, head in his hands as he tried to hold himself together. His voice cracked as he spoke, rough and uneven. Every word difficult. The news unsettling and tragic.

The Emerald Voyager. *Burned.*

The Azure Starlight. *Sunk.*

Gone. Both of them. Just like that.

She didn't speak. Couldn't. Her mouth was dry, her fingers numb around the teacup she hadn't touched. This was real. Not a dream. Not some far-off tale of tragedy in a foreign port.

Most of the crew had made it off, he said. Somehow. Including Tobin—the gruff old boatswain who once taught her how to tie a sailor's knot when she was barely tall enough to reach the rail.

Her stomach twisted. This wasn't just business. This was loss. Real and raw and far too close.

"I'm ruined," her father said, his voice muffled against his hands as he raked them down his face.

His hands dropped into his lap, fingers limp, useless. He slumped back into the chair like the strength had gone out of him completely. She'd never seen him so pale. So still. His eyes were glossy, unfocused. Holding back tears he wouldn't let fall. He was thinking about the men. The ones who didn't make it. The silence was heavy and tense between them. Thick and cloying in the room.

"How did it happen?" she asked.

"Tobin said it started in the cargo hold of the Voyager and spread quickly. None of the other ships in the harbor were harmed."

Hot tears pricked the backs of her eyes as she thought of the incredible loss they'd experienced. First, their home. Now the ships. And it was hard for her not to think it had something to do with the book. She'd handed off the basket to Emmaline and asked her to take it to her room. Now, she sat next to her father at the dining table. She dropped her hands to her lap and clasped them together to keep from shaking. She hadn't even removed her gloves or her bonnet. When she arrived, Gerald immediately asked her to see about him as he was in a state of despair and disbelief.

Shadow things and whispering pages.

How were they tied to the destruction of their lives?

"You still have the Tempest," she said, trying to sound optimistic. "All is not lost."

"Yes, the Tempest." He blew out a heated breath. "I've sent word with Tobin to make sure it sails to the other continent and remain there."

The continent across the sea was where her father spent time in port visiting merchants and trading goods, buying silks and spices.

"I'm so sorry, Father. I wish there was something I could do to help."

His gaze lifted to hers and he managed a weak smile. He reached a hand to her, and she took it, letting him clasp it tight for reassurance.

"You being here is enough." He released her and sat back again, his grave expression lining his face. At that moment, he looked old, frail, and utterly desolate. "But I daresay I will have to return to port to deal with all this business."

"Then Emmaline and I will come with you."

"No." He waved off the thought. "There are reports to be filed and meetings with the port authority, not to mention the crown. I have shipments to reroute and negotiations with suppliers. All tedious dealings. You stay here with her and the others. I trust you to run the household in my absence."

Running the household in his absence was not foreign to her. She did it every time he was at sea. But somehow this time it felt different.

She remained silent as she thought of Leopold Thornhurst. Now was not the time to bring that up with her father. Now was not the time to accept the job with the nobleman, either, even though she desperately wanted to. Even though his carriage would be waiting for her in town to transport her to his home. Her place was here, with her father, to offer her support and comfort during this horrible, devastating time. Disappointment flooded her as she shoved the thoughts aside. Remaining here was the right thing to do.

"When will you leave?"

"In the morning. That will give me tonight to make arrangements and pack a bag." He leaned towards her, reaching once again for her hand. "I do hope you understand, dearest."

She gave him a reassuring smile. "Of course, I do, Father."

It was their livelihood at stake, after all, not to mention his reputation as a reliable trader. She was aware rivals might seize the opportunity to undermine him. She understood there was an enormous amount of pressure on him in the aftermath of this disaster.

"I hate to leave you, but—"

"Do not worry for us here, Father. All will be well," she said, quickly cutting him off and giving him her best supportive smile. She sounded far more confident than she felt.

He blew out a breath of relief. "My dear daughter, you are intelligent and brave like your mother, may she rest in peace. I'm so grateful to have you." He pushed from the table and rose, the chair scraping along the wood floor. "Ask Gerald to bring supper to my room, will you?"

She nodded. "Of course."

He left her alone in the dining room with her whirling thoughts. She was distraught about the ships and the crew. But she knew they had enough money in their accounts to last a few months. She would speak to the staff and make sure they were aware of their situation and ask them to be mindful of their spending. At least until things settled with her father and the business. A merchant without a fleet of ships was like a sailor without the sea—adrift, useless, and destined to drown.

A cold knot twisted in her gut at the thought.

Not just financial ruin, but his reputation, his pride, and everything he'd built.

Before long, they'd need money to survive. But perhaps there was hope yet. The only way she knew to get that money was through her translations and scribing.

She was going to see Leopold Thornhurst.

Nerves jangling like bells in her chest, Bella practically flew down the stairs. Sleep was a lost cause—if she'd managed more than an hour, it hadn't been restful. Her body ached with exhaustion, heavy and buzzing all at once, but she shoved it aside. She didn't have time to be tired.

As soon as her father left, she'd hurry into town to meet the carriage waiting for her. She would go to Mr. Thornhurst. No more waiting. The thought sent a sharp thrill straight through her. Her hands wouldn't stop fidgeting. Her feet barely touched the steps.

This was happening. *Today.*

Her father was already in the foyer when she reached the landing—coat half-buttoned, a leather folio tucked under one arm, suitcase by his feet. He slipped on his gloves with quick, practiced movements, then settled his top hat into place. He was leaving. No hesitation. No delay.

Through the front windows, she caught a glimpse of the carriage waiting at the drive, Gerald standing nearby with the driver and footman, everything in perfect order.

Her chest tightened. It was all happening so quickly. He was leaving for Port Leclare, and, after that, she would meet Mr. Thornhurst.

"Ah, Bella, thank you for coming to see me off." He extended his arms to her for a tight hug. When he pulled back, he held her at arm's length. "Are you sure you'll be all right here?"

"I'm sure. I have Gerald and Edith and Emmaline to keep me company. I'll be fine." She granted him a smile. She didn't dare tell him her plans to earn some coin while he was back in Port Leclare. "I'll miss you."

"I'll be staying at the inn," he said. "Should you need me, send word there."

She nodded. "I'll keep you posted of everything happening here at Hawthorne. I promise. And you'll let me know how things are going for you?"

He brushed her cheek with the back of his gloved hand. "Of course, I will. You're a good daughter, Bella. What would I do without you?"

And then he was off. He picked up his case and headed out the door, climbing into the carriage without another look back. She stood in the open doorway and watched as the carriage clattered down the gravel drive, leaving dust in its wake, until it disappeared around the corner and was finally out of sight.

She spun on the heel of her slipper and bounded back up the stairs to her room where she grabbed her shawl, wrapping it around her shoulders. She pulled on her favorite lace gloves and tied on a bonnet that matched her pale blue silk gown. As she was tying the bow, Emmaline entered.

"Miss?"

"I'm going out for the day, Em," she said, securing the knot under her chin. "Tell Gerald I will not be home for supper."

Emmaline stood in the doorway, blocking her exit. "Where shall I say you're going?"

"I'll be in town."

It wasn't far from the truth. She would, at least, be starting there. She snatched up the book and cradled it against her chest, turning toward the door. But Emmaline refused to move, as though she were a roadblock. Her gaze landed on the book.

"Em—"

"You're going to see that man, aren't you?" she asked.

"I—"

"Did you tell your father about him?" she demanded with a stern look in her eyes. She had never seen Emmaline so serious.

Heat washed over Bella as she stood rooted in place, clutching the book. "No."

She pursed her lips in disappointment.

"I *must* go, Emmaline," she said. "In light of recent events, our very livelihood depends upon it."

She relented then, her shoulders sagging a bit as she stepped aside. "Perhaps I should come with you."

"No," she said quickly. Far too quickly. "I must go alone."

"But my lady—"

"He won't be expecting the two of us," she said hastily. "Besides, I'll be back by nightfall. Don't lock me out."

Bella breezed past her into the hallway. Emmaline followed.

"Are you sure about this, miss? It seems rather reckless to me."

It *was* reckless, but what choice did she have? She had to do this. She had to earn the coin to keep them going until her father sorted out his merchant business. It was the only way to keep their household afloat and pay the bills that would surely come due.

She turned back to Emmaline, stepping close to her and lowering her voice. "It's the only way I can make sure we will be able to continue to eat."

The gravity of the situation hit the girl then, and her face blanched. She pressed a hand against her throat.

"Is it all that serious, miss?"

"I'm afraid it is. Please do not tell Gerald where I'm going. He'll find a way to send a message to my father, no doubt. Just tell him and Edith I have business in town, and I'll be home before nightfall."

The girl's gaze flickered from her face once again to the book clutched in her arms. "As you wish, my lady," she said, sounding formal and stiff.

Bella reached for her then, placing a hand on her upper arm and giving her a light squeeze. "I'll be fine. I promise. I can hold my own against pretentious nobles." She flashed a quick smile.

When she did, Emmaline grinned and stifled a giggle, then immediately turned serious. "Please be safe, my lady. I do not wish to see any harm come to you."

"I will," she said. "You have my word."

And then she was off down the stairs and out the door before anyone else stopped her.

CHAPTER 10

The carriage rattled down the gravel road, the distance expanding between her and the small town of Driftbell. With every turn of the wheel, her heart pounded harder, her stomach clenched tighter. She was a ball of nerves.

She had made it to town and found the carriage Mr. Thornhurst sent for her. It waited at the edge of the square, sleek and dark, its polished frame catching the morning light like black glass. On the door beneath the handle, she spotted the emblem of knotted thorns and curling vines, from which a cluster of roses bloomed, delicate yet defiant against the dark lacquer. The driver and footman were thin-lipped, quiet, and stoney-faced. The footman didn't speak except to greet her with a nod as he held open the door. She thanked him and, once she was inside and the door was closed, they were away.

Now, they headed down the road shaded by large trees and moving deeper into the country, leaving behind the vibrant, lively town. An ominous mist pressed all around the carriage as they made their way through the tall oak trees. Then they were through the iron gate that swung open with a creak as if it sensed their approach. It was as if no sun pierced through the gloom, making the hairs on the back of her neck stand at attention.

As they approached, she saw this was not a manor house as she expected.

No, this was no mere castle tucked away between the trees and hidden by shade and shadow. It loomed like a dream sculpted by twilight. It was an imposing fortress that exuded an otherworldly aura, the dark-blue façade appeared as though it was dipped in starlight and shadow. The spires and towers pierced the ever-night sky, reaching for the stars, the moon, or perhaps even a dapple of elusive sunlight.

The carriage came to an abrupt halt in the curved driveway. Bella clutched the book to her chest as the footman opened the door. With her heart in her throat, she stepped down from the carriage and gazed up at the commanding castle with gargoyles peering down with soulless, stone eyes.

What had she gotten herself into?

For a moment, she wanted to turn and run away, return to the cheerful warmth of Hawthorne Hall. But as the thought crossed her mind, the door opened and a tall, wisp of a man stood in the threshold.

Black hair was slicked back from his high forehead. Dark, baleful eyes peered at her from under two bushy eyebrows. He had a hawkish nose, thin pale lips, and high, severe cheekbones. His face was pale—as though he had been carved from marble. He wore the livery of a butler, stood straight and stiff, and peered at her with curiosity.

"Miss Rinaldi, I presume?" he asked in a pinched voice.

"Yes, I am." Her voice was strong, making her sound more confident than she felt.

He stepped aside and motioned for her to enter. With her heart pounding a wicked beat against the book she clutched to her chest, she stepped inside the cavernous grand entry hall. Her feet were silent on the black-and-white checkered tile. Dimly lit, blue-flamed candelabras hovered in the air above their heads illuminating the room in an otherworldly glow. The ribbed arched ceiling stretched high above and was painted with murals of frolicking imps among dark clouds threaded with gold and copper. In the heart of the castle, the grand staircase rose before her and then split off in each direction—one to the right, one to the left—disappearing into shadowy halls unseen from the entry.

"Wait here, if you please," the man said. His feet were silent on the tile as he disappeared down a hallway. Overhead, one of the floating candelabras followed him.

She remained where she was, standing stiff and eyeing her surroundings. Somewhere deep in the chasm of the castle, a clock chimed the hour. In the shadows, it felt as though she was being watched which did nothing to calm her already ragged nerves.

Finally, she heard footsteps approaching. The floating candelabra came back into view and suddenly, there he was. Leopold

Thornhurst, striking in his classic good looks and the pale circle of the blue-white light that followed him.

He wore a long charcoal velvet coat, the collar turned slightly up, its silver buttons dulled with age. Beneath it, a midnight waistcoat embroidered with a barely visible pattern of thorny vines shimmered only when the light caught it just so.

His shirt was crisp but collarless, open at the throat—a nobleman's elegance worn with the carelessness of someone who no longer bothered to impress. Though he carried himself with the air of a man who once ruled ballrooms, there was something in the way the shadows clung to him that whispered of solitude and sorrow. Something she had sensed when she first met him.

But now, that sorrow was pushed aside as his pale brown gaze landed on hers and his face broke into a welcoming smile.

"Miss Rinaldi." He reached for her hand, took it, and pressed a warm kiss on the back of it. Even through the lace of her glove, his breath was warm and sweet. It sent a tremble of delight through her. "I'm glad to see you again."

Her breath shuddered out of her. "I apologize for being late. I was delayed this morning." There was no need to tell him why. Her father's affairs were no one's business.

He glanced around as though looking for something. "Your bags?"

"Oh," she said on a breath. "I'm afraid I can't stay. I must return to home this evening."

A flicker of disappointment flashed through his eyes and then he concealed it. "Your father will be wanting your safe return. I'll have the carriage return you at sundown. If you'll follow me, I'll take you to the library so you can get started."

"Thank you."

He started down the hallway, those ominous floating candelabras following. She fell in step behind him, her heart still jangling in her chest. And every step she took was another step toward the unknown, toward uncertainty. She wasn't sure she should be here. She wasn't sure she should have accepted the job to translate the odd book. She wasn't even sure if she should *have* the book. It had crossed her mind to leave it and return to Hawthorne and never think about it again.

He turned down a hallway and headed for soaring double wood doors. Along the walls were oil paintings with watchful eyes that seemed to follow her every movement. She was suddenly very glad she wasn't staying in this strange place overnight.

The hallway was sparsely furnished. A low bench under an oversized painting of a dignified older man in a navy waistcoat with silver buttons and a white cravat at his throat. Next to the bench, a tall vase in moonlight with the oddest arrangement she'd ever seen—roses the color of spilled ink, their blooms full. The petals looked soft as velvet. Moving along the hallway, there was a chair here and there, as if the walk to the library was taxing and someone needed to pause and rest before finishing the trek.

She had to admit, it was quite possibly the longest hallway she had ever seen.

At the doors, he pushed them open with a creak, as though they were rusty from nonuse, and stepped inside. He paused inside the threshold and waited. She followed him through the door. When she stepped inside the library, she came to a standstill and gaped, a small gasp escaping her.

She had never seen so many books in all her life. Books that soared upward so high, there was a winding iron staircase on one end that led to the upper level. On another end, a sliding ladder that glided the length of that end of the room. There were so many books, so many shelves, she had to tilt her head back to see them all. It wasn't enough every wall was lined with books, there were free-standing shelves, too. Tucked between a couple of them was a long wood table with four chairs, an unlit candelabra in the center.

The domed ceiling was painted a pale blue with float-ing clouds appearing to move across it buffeted by an in-visible breeze. Hanging from the center, another one of the blue-flamed candelabras giving off enough light to see the shapes and colors of each and every leather-bound volume.

In front of her, across the great expanse of the room, a lancet window rose tall and elegant, the arc narrow and towering with stained glass that was like a blade of colorful light nestled into the cold stone wall. Faint sunlight struggled through the panes of colored glass, casting odd shards of crimson, violet, and emerald across the marble floor.

The design in the center was a single deep red rose, blooming, its petals unfurling in flawless detail. Thorny vines curled around it, twisting in spirals with their glass thorns etched in glistening silver. Some reached toward the edge of the window. Others curled protectively around the bloom—embracing and imprisoning it.

She had seen this image before. It was emblazoned on the cover of the book in her arms. She gaped at it a long moment, her mind trying to make sense of what her eyes saw. She blinked and looked away, deciding it was nothing more than her vivid imagination.

A comfortable seating area formed a cozy conversation area in front of the window—a loveseat and two wing-backed chairs. Between them, a low table. Underneath the furniture, a garnet plush rug that looked so thick and so inviting, she wanted to slip off her shoes and dig in her toes.

Leopold remained standing at the door, watching her as she gaped at the room, as though he were pleased with her reaction to his massive collection.

"I've never seen a library like this before," she said, finally finding her voice. "When you said you had an extensive library, I never pictured *this*."

He chuckled, a sound low and deep in his broad chest. It pulled her attention from the beauty of the window, and she turned to him. His smile held a hint of pride.

"It's my life's pursuit. Do you like it?"

"Like it?" She looked at him as though he'd grown a second head. "It's the most magnificent library I've ever seen."

And she'd seen a lot of libraries. Certainly, none this spectacular. Nor would she ever see one that compared.

"Good, then perhaps you'll find the answers you seek for the translation. Come." He motioned for her to follow as he took off across the room.

She fell in step behind him as he headed for the table between the free-standing shelves. As he approached the table, she noticed the wicks on the candelabra flickered to life, as though sensing his nearness.

His castle was certainly a wondrous place.

"You can work here." He motioned to one of the chairs.

She eyed the table, her brows knit.

"Is it not to your liking?" he asked.

Her gaze met his as she placed the book on the edge of the table. "Oh, it is, thank you. But I'll need parchment, a pen, and ink."

"Of course." He waved toward the table.

There was a stack of parchment, a quill, and inkwell. She swore those items were not there a moment ago. She tipped her head to the side, trying to recall if she simply overlooked the items. She was certain she hadn't, and they appeared. She stared at them as an unusual sensation crept over her.

"Let me show you where to find the best resources for our project," he said.

That snapped her out of her thoughts. "Our project?"

"Yes." He flashed a grin as he headed off toward the shelves.

She forced her feet to move and followed him, hurrying to catch up as he disappeared between two of the shelves. He paused in the middle between the two as he looked at the dusty volumes, contemplation on his face.

"You'll find some of these are quite old. Do take care of them."

He reached for one particular book with a dark green cover, the edges of the pages yellowed with age. He handed it to her. There was no title on the cover or the spine, but it was a hefty book. As she examined it, he pulled another off the shelf and handed it to her.

"This one will be a good one."

This one was a dark blue cover with an embossed title so faded it was unreadable. She ran her finger over the indention as if that would yield the name.

"Ah, and this one."

He slipped another book from the shelf and handed it over. She stacked it on top of the blue one. This one was a dark brown cover with words emblazoned across it—*Curses and Cures.*

"I don't think—"

"It may not help you, but there is an off chance it will." He cut her a glance. When he realized she gaped back at him struggling to carry the large books, he stepped closer to her. "Apologies. I didn't think."

He offloaded the books from her arms. When he did, their hands brushed. Though she still wore her lace gloves, a tingling sensation spiked through her. He must have sensed it, too, for he stood a moment, peering at her with those pale brown eyes that held a twinge of regret.

"This should be a good start for you."

He breezed past her to head back to the table. She hurried to follow. He placed the books on the table next to the stack of parchment, then turned back to her as she paused behind one of the chairs.

"You'll let me know if you need anything?"

"Yes." She glanced around the vast room looking for a bellpull.

He must have realized what she was looking for and pointed. "It's over there."

The gold cord hung on the far wall next to an oil painting of a horse.

"I'll leave you to it, then."

He seemed reluctant to leave. Truthfully, she was reluctant for him to leave as well. After a long moment of silence, he gave a brief bow and then headed back to the door, disappearing into the hallway and leaving her quite alone.

CHAPTER 11

"**Y**ou were right, my prince, she *is* quite the beauty."

Dickens's voice startled him as he closed the door behind him and paused in the hallway. His valet seemed to blend in with the shadows and tapestries. He pressed a hand against his rapid beating heart.

"You do enjoy skulking around the castle, don't you?" Leopold said as he started down the hallway.

"My prince, you intend to leave her in there all alone?" Dickens sounded perplexed at the idea.

"I can't very well hang about while she translates the book, now can I?" he retorted.

"But the library—"

"She will be fine in there," he interrupted.

He tried not to think about how her beautiful face looked when the parchment and inkwell appeared on the table. Her expression contorted into a mixture of surprise and confusion tinged with fear. He wanted to reassure her that everything was all right, but if he did that, he would have to explain things he was not prepared to explain.

The library was much like the rest of the castle but with its own mysteries and quirks. At times, the books whispered the words from their haunted pages. Other times, they sang melancholy melodies that echoed throughout the large room. And sometimes, without warning, they would fall from the shelves and land on the floor with such a clatter it would wake the dead.

He hoped the books behaved themselves in the presence of the young lady. Not that he could do anything about it—he simply hoped they sensed she was a guest and remain quiet.

At any rate, he suspected hovering around her while she tried to translate, and concentrate was not going to do either of them any good.

"I think I make her nervous," he added.

"Of course you make her nervous," Dickens replied. "You're a prince—"

"Not to her," he interrupted, halting midway down the corridor. He turned to his old friend. "She doesn't know who I am."

A brow lifted in question, wrinkling his pale forehead. "Forgive my impertinence, but I'm sure she can guess who you are. This isn't exactly a cottage we live in."

Leopold frowned. It hadn't occurred to him she would use her deductive reasoning to figure out he was someone of importance. Naturally, she would assume he was part of the nobility, but certainly not from an ancient royal bloodline that had ruled this part of Cassoné for centuries. His family name had fallen into disreputable ruin after the scandal that rocked them to the core. His parents were long gone, and he was cursed to live in his enchanted castle. Hope bloomed like the dusky evening rose crawling along the low stone wall that someday he would find a way to break that curse.

He had almost given up that hope until he saw Isabella carrying the book. It had renewed his faith that, in fact, the curse *could* be broken before the sands of time finally ran out.

The enchanted hourglass was almost empty. He tried not to think about that these last few months as he watched the glimmering iridescent sands flowing from the top to the bottom.

"She cannot know who I am," he said, firmly and pointedly at Dickens.

"You intend *never* to tell her?" he asked, then, clearly shocked by his determined resolve.

"Quite right." He spun on his heel and headed back down the hallway, leaving Dickens behind. Then, as an afterthought, he called over his shoulder, "And neither will you."

Dickens fell in step next to him, his long legs having no trouble keeping up with him. "Might I ask what you intend to do to conceal your situation at the full moon? Which, I might add, is tonight, my prince."

"She's not staying." As he said it, a pang of disappointment pierced him. He hadn't realized how disheartened he was to hear she intended to return to her home before nightfall. "In fact, we must have the carriage ready at dusk to take her back to the town."

"And tomorrow?"

"The same, if she agrees to return." He paused and cast a glance back at the library doors on the other end of the hallway.

Perhaps Dickens was correct in that he shouldn't leave her alone in there for too long. He was also correct in that if he intended to keep his identity a secret, he couldn't allow her to see him in his true, terrible form.

"Which is something you hope she does," Dickens said.

Leopold stood rooted in place as he considered this. Yes, of course, he hoped she returned. But a part of him realized he didn't *want* her to see what he was when the moon was full and bright in the night sky. For if she did, she wouldn't look at him the way she did outside the bookshop. As though there was an intensity in her gaze that bound them together. As though a light inside him had ignited, making him come alive with feelings he thought long dead.

Dickens cleared his throat. "My prince?"

"Dickens, perhaps you are correct in that I shouldn't leave her alone in the library for any length of time. Tea and finger sandwiches seem appropriate, don't they? And perhaps some sweet treats," Leopold said.

Dickens cast a glance down at the double doors, where his gaze was firmly fixed.

"I'll see that it's done, my prince."

He clasped his hands in front of him as he headed off to the kitchens to see to his request.

After Leopold left, Bella pulled off her lace gloves and bonnet and got to work. She sat at the table with the candelabra lighting the pages of the opened book before her. When she had trouble seeing the pages and squinted or leaned forward for a better look, the candlesticks moved closer to give her more light. Every time she glanced up at it, it appeared normal. But she was certain it moved closer when she needed it the most.

She pulled a piece of parchment from the stack and slid it to her, then reached for the quill and dipped it into the ink. Across the top, she wrote in her flowing handwriting, *the book with no name.*

She stared down at her handwriting, recalling the previous text she translated for Lord Vincent. The text she never finished. She thought about the alphabet of roses and thorns that told the tale of the sorceress whose heart was broken by a cruel, spoiled prince. A prince she cursed to live out his days in solitude in the depths of his castle. A castle that, it seemed, was not so different from the one she was currently sitting in.

Funny she remembered that story now as she sat at the table chewing on the end of the quill. Did that story have any correlation to the ancient language she was unable to read in the book with no name?

She reached for the book, then paused. Her hand hovered over the cover with the strange thorns and roses.

Roses and thorns. An alphabet of roses and thorns.

She glanced at the stained-glass window across the room. *Roses and thorns.*

Thornhurst.

Everywhere she looked, there seemed to be roses and thrones and brambles. As if the symbol meant something. It was all around her. In the stained-glass window. On the low stone wall surrounding the gate. She even spied a vase full of the inky roses in full bloom on a table on the way to the library.

There was some bit of knowledge buried in the deep recesses of her mind. Some scrap of story she could not quite recall. An old fable, perhaps? She shook off the vestiges of that haunting story and opened the book her father gave her.

The language stared back at her. Unreadable in every way.

She glanced back at the green covered tome and pulled it to her. The one with the yellowed pages. She flipped it open. The cover cracked from age. She peered down at the cover page and one word stared back at her.

Hexes.

Hexes? Curses and Cures? What, then, was the blue book he gave her? Curious, she pulled it to her and opened it.

Spells and Incantations.

She shoved back from the table, the chair scraping along the marble floor with a loud squawk. It was such a violent move she knocked it over. It made a loud rapping sound as she stumbled away from the table. Even the candelabra was startled by her sudden movement, the flames flickering and snuffing out, plunging the room in nothing but shade and shadows.

She backed away from the table of books, her hand at her throat.

Leopold gave her those books—what was he trying to make her do with them? How would they help her decipher the language of the book her father gave her?

It was all so confusing and a bit terrifying.

Perhaps coming here was a mistake. Perhaps she should go home and never return.

As the thoughts pounded through her, she heard a soft voice singing. She glanced around, but no one else was in the library. The singing grew louder, as though someone was trying to get her attention, and she realized with some horror there *was* someone in the library with her.

A ghost?

No, that was silly. Now her frightening thoughts were starting to spiral.

But the singing grew louder, the voice stronger. It sounded like it was coming from one of the shelves.

With her heart pounding a rapid beat, she took a step toward it. Deeper and deeper into the library she went until she found the source of the voice.

It was a book.

With every stanza, the cover and pages flapped in concert with the words.

"It's...singing," she said on a rough whisper.

The singing stopped. "Of course, I'm singing, dear child," the book replied in a falsetto.

She sucked in a sharp breath. "Y-you heard me."

"Yes, I heard you. I'm not deaf." This time the book sang it in a deeper voice, the cover and pages flapping with its response.

How curious.

Unable to resist, she picked up the book. It was a biography about an opera singer. She thumbed through the pages with interest then replaced it in its place on the shelf.

"Did you not find anything of interest, dear child?" it sang.

She snickered, amused by the response. "Not this time."

As she started to leave, a belch of mist emitted from one of the books on the other end. Interested, she hurried toward it. As she approached, there was the distinct sound of a train chugging along on a track. She snatched up the book and read the title—*History of the Steam Engine.* More mist—no, steam!—emitted from between the pages.

Fascinating.

Birdsong came from a book about an aviary. War cries emitted from another book that told the history of a war in a place she had never heard of. Construction sounds came from another describing how castles were built. A howl from a book about wolves got her attention long enough to page through it. And on and on she went, discovering all the peculiar and wonderful—enchanted—books in Leopold's library.

At last, she found herself standing among the furniture under the stained-glass window and gazed up at it. As she peered at the thorn-ensnared rose, she noticed movement. As though the rose wanted to bloom in full but couldn't because of the thorny vines constricting it. The silvery thorns themselves seemed to shimmer under the pale light seeping through the colored glass.

When the door to the library opened, she spun around, her heart in her throat. Then surprise took over as she watched Leopold Thornhurst push a polished tea cart into the library, the wheels squeaking as they turned. He halted when he noticed her standing across the room under the stained-glass window.

They stared at each other across the expanse of the room. Her heart beat wildly. And though she could not see his features, those pale brown eyes were quite distinct in the shadows. There was something inherently wild about them. Something that made her pause and tip her head to the side as she gazed at him and tried to work out where she'd seen eyes like that before.

"Tea, Miss Rinaldi?" he said, his voice echoing in the room.

Without waiting for her reply, he wheeled the cart toward her. When he stopped, he reached for the delicate porcelain teapot and poured the dark brew into one of the cups perched on a matching saucer. The cart also had a tray full of small sandwiches, delectable tiny cakes, biscuits, and scones.

"Did you make any progress?"

She flushed at his question. How could she tell him the truth? That she was ready to bolt from the castle and never return? Then that she was enamored with his odd collection of books.

He handed her the cup. When he did, their fingers brushed. It left a tingling sensation zipping through her. He poured himself a cup and then motioned to the seating area. He perched on the edge of one of the chairs, holding the delicate cup between his large hands.

She hadn't noticed his hands until then. Perfect, strong hands with long, fine-boned fingers. She took a sip of tea to calm her raging nerves.

"Would you like the truth?" she asked, and her voice was stronger than she expected.

He peered at her, indecision in his eyes, and then lifted one dark brow. It was hard not to notice the rakish look he gave her with his mussed hair, as though he'd been shoving his hand through it. One out-of-place strand fell over his forehead.

"I hired you, so, yes, I would like the truth. Is it a difficult text to translate?"

Bella pressed her lips together as she tried to decide how to answer. It appeared he expected her to tell him she was unable to translate the book when, honestly, she was terrified of the books he'd given her as a resource.

"I haven't tried yet." She sipped her tea to keep from telling him more.

"You haven't?" His voice was even with a hint of curiosity.

"No. Because..." She moved to sit across from him, holding the teacup in her hand as she gazed at him. "Why did you give me those books?"

He looked perplexed. "I'm sorry?"

"Curses and Cures. Spells and Incantation. Hexes," she said. Even saying the words aloud sent a shiver through her.

His face blanched, but only for a moment. His fingers tightened on the cup as he stiffened, his back ramrod straight.

"Apologies, Lord Thornhurst—"

"I am no lord," he interrupted. He shot to his feet and dropped the cup back onto the tray.

She snapped her mouth shut, peering at his rigid back. If he was not a lord, then...what was he?

"Your grace?" she tried.

He said nothing as he remained standing there, his stiff back to her. She wasn't sure if that was the right title of address, either, since he didn't respond.

She cleared her throat and tried again. "I fail to understand how those books could help me translate mine."

His shoulders drooped a little—an imperceptible movement that she might have missed if she hadn't been looking at him. Finally, he turned enough to give her his profile.

"I haven't been completely honest with you, Miss Rinaldi."

It was her turn to stiffen. She held the teacup tight in her hand. Her fingers cramped. "You haven't?"

He picked up one of the small cakes and placed it on a saucer. She watched intently, expecting him to eat it, but he didn't. Instead, he brought it over to her and extended it. She took the saucer and balanced it on her knee as he moved back to the cart.

"It will be difficult for you to hear this."

He leaned against the cart, his hands gripping the edge and his knuckles leeching of color, as if what he was about to say was something horrible. She braced herself.

"I am cursed."

He said it so softly, she wasn't sure she heard him correctly. Her brows drew together as she kept her gaze on his strained shoulders and the clenched muscles in his back.

"Cursed?" she repeated. A quiver of fear slipped through her.

She wondered what sort of curse but since he didn't offer more information, it seemed rude to press for more details. Was he cursed to live in this strange, enchanted castle for the rest of his days until it was broken? And how would it be broken?

So many questions floated through her mind.

"Yes." He spun to face her, his face creased with worry. "If you wish to leave and never return, I understand. If you wish to terminate our agreement, I understand that, too. But…"

His gaze dropped as he moved a little closer. For a moment, she thought he might pause in front of her and drop to a knee, but instead he perched on the opposite chair, clasping his shaking hands in his lap. He was nervous. He was afraid of her reaction, of how she might see him now.

Finally, he lifted his gaze and met hers. She saw deep in them, the desperate hope glittering there.

"But?" she asked, sounding more breathless than she wanted.

"Seeing that book of yours…with the rose and thorns on the cover…I've never seen anything like it before in all my travels and all my searching. My last hope was the bookshop in town. And that's when I met you."

His face flushed, as though it made him uncomfortable to tell her this.

Though he didn't say it, she suspected he thought their meeting was kismet. And though she never truly believed in destiny or fate or luck—she believed one made one's own destiny—she was compassionate enough to understand why he felt this way. Perhaps it was a last hope or desperation that drove him to follow her out of the bookshop.

He continued, "I believe that book is the key to breaking the curse. I apologize for not explaining that to you before. That's why I gave you those other books. I thought, perhaps, they would aid you in your translation. But perhaps I was wrong."

Silence stretched between them as she considered his words. She was in no position to turn down a paying job such as this. She thought of her father returning to Port Leclare to sort out the messy affairs of this merchant business. She thought of the potentially empty larder back at Hawthorne Hall if they ran out of money trying to pay for his business expenses. She thought of how Edith, Gerald, and Emmaline depended on her to make sure the household ran smoothly, and all were taken care of.

And that was what made her decision easier.

"Mr. Thornhurst—"

"Leopold, please. Call me Leopold."

She flushed, the heat pounded through to her cheeks and settled there. She glanced down at the tepid tea and the buttery cake resting on the saucer to hide her blush. In her line of work, she'd been around noble men, but she'd never called them by their given name. Not once. When she reigned in her emotions, she lifted her gaze back to his.

"I will stay and attempt to translate the book."

When she said it, his face broke into a wide smile. He flopped back in the chair, relief creasing his features as he blew out a breath.

"Thank you, Miss Rinaldi."

"Bella," she corrected.

Surprise flickered over his face. She flushed again.

"My friends call me Bella," she said.

He got to his feet then and walked over to her, dropping to one knee. He held out a hand, waiting for her to accept. Her heart rammed a wild and erratic beat against her chest as she reached for him, placing her hand in his. His warm fingers closed around hers as he tugged her hand closer and pressed a breath of a kiss on the back of her hand.

"I'm honored to call you friend."

The breath of his words fanned across the back of her hand, making the hairs stand on end and gooseflesh rise. She pulled her hand back as demurely as possible and then held the teacup between both of them. She sipped the now-cold tea.

He got to his feet, then, and backed away a few steps. "I should let you return to work. The carriage will be ready and waiting for you at dusk."

"Thank you," she said with a nod.

And then he was gone, leaving her alone once again in the enchanted and mystical library.

CHAPTER 12

When she had her fill of food and tea, she returned to the table, glancing up at the snuffed-out candelabra. The wicks were cold and dark.

"Light, please?" she asked, her voice timid and quiet.

The wicks flared to life with their blue-white flames, not exactly pushing back the shadows but clinging to them.

She did find it odd that Leopold hadn't noticed the snuffed-out candles, but then, he seemed distracted by the tea cart and the fact she was hovering near the seating area of the library. The book her father gave her was off to one side. She pulled it toward her and examined the cover. A twinge of familiarity skipped through her as she stared down at it.

Turning, she gazed over her shoulder at the stained-glass window. The rose on the window was almost exactly like the one on the cover of the book.

An eeriness spilled through her as she gaped at the window and then turned back to the book. She traced the outline of the rose with the tip of her finger. What was the connection to the two of them? *Were* they connected?

Her father stated he bought it from a bookseller, but beyond that he gave her no more information. He traveled a lot, stopping in various ports across the continent and the adjacent one. Perhaps he didn't even recall where he bought it, but it was worth asking him.

When she opened the book to a random page in the center, it cracked with age. She pushed it under the puddle of light to get a better look at the oddly flowing script that curved down the page. The script that seemed to be intertwined with the runes and symbols that meant...what? She hadn't a clue.

As she moved the book under the silvery light of the candles, her breath suddenly caught in her throat. The ink shimmered with a low, pulsing sheen, like moonlight across dark waters. Almost as if the letters themselves were alive and breathing. The writing curled across the page in long flowing loops and sharp barbs. Sliding across the page as though it were a living thing. As though it were a flower about to bloom. But as the petals tried to unfurl, the thorny barbs snarled them, keeping it from opening. Keeping them from flourishing.

Even as she stared at it long and hard, her talent for translating the words failed her.

Then she noticed something astonishing. One of the swirling loops that seemed to travel across the page wound around one of the runes and in the center of that rune was a letter. Curved at the top. Curved at the bottom.

The letter S?

With excitement burning through her, she reached for a parchment and the quill and ink. She hastily scribbled that first letter in her flowing handwriting.

What was S? A name? Or merely a word?

She placed her finger on the book under the mystical S. The page was warm against the tip. She followed the scrolling loop to the next rune. Before her eyes, the next letter formed as her heart pounded hard and fast.

H

She quickly wrote that down next to the S.

Her finger moved down the page. When the tip paused at the rune, another letter appeared. And so on and so on. Until she had scribbled down an entire word. She sat back in the chair and stared down at the word she'd written.

Shadows

"What shadows?"

As she said it aloud, the book seemed to whisper the word back to her.

Gooseflesh erupted along her arms and crept up to the base of her neck. A hot tingling sensation was there, piercing through her. It was as though the book heard her and replied.

She continued moving her finger down the page and writing the letters she saw. Sitting back a second time, her eyes glanced over the two words she'd written.

Shadows stir.

She pressed her lips together. Though she wanted to say the words aloud, she was worried what might reply when she did.

What did *shadows stir* mean? Was this the beginning of a long, spine-chilling tale? Or was there something else buried within the brambles and thorns of the book's language? She contemplated this when the library doors opened, catching her attention.

Leopold stood in the shaft of light from the hallway. His elongated shadow splashed across the marble floor. He seemed to pause there for a long moment, but she was unable to see his features as he was nothing more than a silhouette. She blinked, trying to focus, and realized she was squinting at the pages of the book for so long in the dimness, her eyes were gritty and tired.

"Bella?" he queried.

The doors banged closed behind him. As he moved toward her, his face came into focus. Worry and concern creased his handsome features. He paused near the table, his gaze flickering from her to the open book in front of her, to the parchment on which she scribbled words.

"It's incredible." She breathed the words in a roughened whisper, as though she did not want to disturb the book or garner its attention.

"You found something?"

His worry was replaced by hope as he moved closer. He leaned on the table next to her, his body heat radiating toward her. When he did, she caught his scent. He smelled like winter and wildfire—wood smoke and something sharper beneath it, like frost and sorrow. It caught her off guard, that scent. It was him. Of course, it was.

She glanced up at him, but his pale brown gaze was focused on her hastily scrawled handwriting.

"You were able to translate this?" he asked.

"Only the two words."

"*Shadows stir*," he read.

And when he did, the book whispered back something that neither of them understood. The faint whisper was still there, curling from the pages like breath brushing the edges of her mind. She shivered. As soon as the ghostly whisper emitted from the book, he jumped back, his eyes wide.

"I think the book understands," she said. "It did the same thing when I read it aloud."

"It...understands?"

She nodded. "And when you say the words from the book...well, it seems as though it responds. But I don't understand what it's saying."

He stared at the open book as though it were a foreign object he'd never seen before. As though it were something wicked. Something dangerous. Something *threatening*. Uncertainty was in his eyes as he continued to peer at it, not moving, not speaking. His mouth formed a thin line.

Finally, he shook himself from his trance and straightened, moving away from her. The moment he did, he took his warmth with him. A weak smile creased his lips.

"You made good progress today."

"I did. I think I can get a little more done—"

"It's nearly dusk," he said, interrupting her.

"Oh."

She breathed the word as disappointment flickered through her. She wasn't ready to stop translating. She folded the parchment with her scribbled handwriting in half and placed it in the center of the pages as a marker, then flipped the book closed.

"The carriage is waiting for you outside," he said.

"Thank you." She scooped the book off the table and cradled it against her chest. "Given that it's nearly dark, I wonder if your carriage could take me as far as the gates of Hawthorne?"

He gave her a long, quiet look as though contemplating whether to agree. He nodded. "Yes, of course. You wouldn't want to be walking home alone in the dark."

She blew out a breath she hadn't realized she was holding. "Yes, thank you."

Leopold made a motion to the door. "May I escort you to the carriage?"

Her gaze lingered on his handsome face. "I'd like that."

She pulled on her lace gloves, then her bonnet, tying it under her chin. As she headed for the door, he fell in step beside her. They walked in silence from the library down the long hallway with the oil paintings with their watchful eyes following them. From there, he led her to the front door of the castle where Dickens stiffly waited with his head held high.

"Will you be returning tomorrow?" Leopold asked, eyeing the book she still cradled against her chest.

"I hope to," she said. "But things are...unsettled and I may need to remain at Hawthorne."

"Unsettled? Is everything all right?"

She flashed a smile, realizing she might have said too much. "Yes, of course, it's just that my father was called back to Port Leclare on business and he looks to me to run the household while he's away."

"Ah," he said. "I didn't realize your father was in Port Leclare."

"He's a merchant," she heard herself say. And before she could stop the words from flowing, she said, "A few of his ships were destroyed."

Concern creased his face. "I'm sorry to hear that."

She wanted to smack her forehead for revealing that information to this almost stranger. She didn't know much about Leopold. She certainly should not be telling him their private family business.

"I should be going, your grace." She dipped a curtsy and turned toward the door.

As she did, Dickens pulled it open. She headed into the balmy night air and climbed in the carriage, relieved to be putting distance between the dashing Leopold Thornhurst, his ghostly castle, and his stern-faced butler.

Leopold watched her bolt through the door as if her dress was on fire and climb into the waiting carriage. The footman closed the door with a snap behind her. He stepped across the threshold of the door and made a motion to the driver to catch the man's attention.

"Take her to Hawthorne Hall. Make sure she arrives safely."

"As you say, prince." He gave a nod as he took up the reins.

He winced at the title but was hopeful Bella didn't hear. The driver turned the carriage and away they went, clattering down the gravel drive toward the road that led them off the castle grounds.

Dickens was at his side then. His stoic façade firmly in place on his face.

"Why did she call you *your grace*?" he asked.

Leopold pressed his lips together, trying to decide how to answer. She called him that because of his own stubbornness that refused to tell her the truth about him. That he was a prince. That the blood running through his veins was from an ancient royal line that was all but extinct. All except him.

"I told her I was no lord." He hadn't meant to say it in a haughty, insulted tone.

Dickens sniffed derision. "An insult, of course. Much beneath your stature. But, again, why *your grace*?"

"She assumes I'm a duke. I allowed her to think so."

Truthfully, he didn't want to be a duke or a prince or a king or any title. He wanted to be a man. A man who was looked at by a woman like her. But she only looked at him like that because she didn't know what he truly was. If she knew the truth about him, she would find him repugnant and she would never return with her book.

He *needed* her to return with her book. He needed her to translate the rest of the words. To see if there was a way to break the curse within those yellowed, aged pages. But what surprised him the most was he needed to see her sitting in his library every day, scratching away with the quill looking lovely and distracted.

"Rather than tell her the truth, I see. Do you think she'll return, my prince?"

He shook his head. "I don't know. Find out about her father's merchant business, Dickens. I want to know everything. Who he is. What he sells. How many ships were destroyed. Everything. She mentioned Port Leclare. Start there."

"As you say, my prince."

"And I want to know before morning," Leopold added.

"Of course, you do." There was the lilt of annoyance in his voice as he stepped inside the castle.

He suspected there was more to the story than what Bella told him. He intended to find out.

He cast a glance up at the sky. Night was falling. The sky was turning a deep indigo. Soon, the full moon would rise. A sharp edginess stabbed through him.

"Come, my prince. 'Tis almost moonrise," Dickens called.

He was right. He stepped through the threshold, pulling the door closed behind him. He hoped this night would be a calm one. But judging by the way he felt deep inside, he suspected it would not go that way.

CHAPTER 13

The carriage took Bella all the way to the gates of Hawthorne Hall, as requested. She was relieved she didn't have to walk home alone in the dark. Emmaline waited for her in the foyer as she slipped in through the front door. The girl appeared to be pacing the length of the front hall, her hands clasped tightly in front of her. The moment she saw her relief flooded her youthful face.

"Oh, I'm so glad you made it back, miss."

Weariness settled through her. She handed off the book to Emmaline, then untied her bonnet and removed it.

"Gerald asked about you," she said.

"What did you tell him?"

"What you told me. That you were in town. But I don't think he believed me," she said, worry creasing her face.

"I'll deal with him. Did I miss dinner?"

"Edith is ready to serve in the dining room, miss."

She was glad to hear there was a hot meal waiting for her. She handed off her bonnet and gloves to Emmaline. "There isn't time for me to dress for dinner. Will you take those items to my room?"

She dipped a curtsy and headed upstairs while Bella made her way to the dining room. The table was set for one—her. As she sat, pulling up her chair, she realized how much she missed her father. A bowl of steaming split pea soup was before her. Gerald entered the room, looking pristine in his black suit with white gloves.

"Welcome home, miss. I trust your visit in town was successful?" He lifted a brow in curious interest.

"Yes, thank you." She took up her spoon, ready to eat, but found her appetite had waned.

Her father wasn't there to chatter away about his business or what happened in port or his next trip and what he might find. Though Gerald was there, the silence was isolating and deafening.

"Any word from my father?" she asked.

"None yet, miss."

It was all the conversation they had while she finished her meal. It gave her time to reflect on all the happenings of the day and, most importantly, Leopold Thornhurst.

He was an enigma. Handsome, yes. But she sensed he held closely guarded secrets. Secrets he wasn't ready to part with—if ever. What was it about him she found hard to resist? Was it his eyes? Pale brown eyes that seemed to see right through to her soul when he looked at her.

Or was it something else? The fact he lived in an enchanted castle crossed her mind. How did he navigate that strange shadowy world every day? For it seemed as though the sun never touched the ground or the spires or towers of the sprawling estate. As though it were permanently cloaked within the gloom.

The floating candelabras with their blue-white flames seemed to have an otherworldly glow. The magical library with its singing and chattering books. The magnificent rose and thorn themed stained-glass window that dominated the center of the room.

When she finished her meal, she headed up to her room, her steps suddenly light with excitement as the thought of the book waiting for her. Emmaline had left it on her dressing table. And though she was weary from the emotions of the day, she found she was unable to resist picking up the book and heading back downstairs to her own library. She still had some energy left to continue her translation. Perhaps when she next visited Leopold, she'd have more to tell him.

Their library was a modest room. Small and compact with shelves on every wall. A fireplace dominated the far wall, its hearth cold and silent. On the mantle, a set of copper candlesticks. She searched for a match and, finding one, struck it to light them. They emitted their familiar warm yellow glow. Not the cold blueish glow of Leopold's.

An oversized leather chair was near the fire with a knitted blanket cast across the back of it. She grabbed the blanket and wrapped it around her shoulders to ward off the chill of the room. She was too tired to find Gerald and ask him to build a fire, nor did she want to do it herself. Instead, she lit more candles around the room, casting it in a pale light. It gave her enough light to see her work. A narrow writing desk was under the one window which hosted antique lace curtains, the only barrier between night pressing against the pane of glass and the room.

She placed the book on the table, sat in the chair and got to work.

Hours later, her eyes gritty, she had a long phrase she translated from the book. She sat back in the chair, her fingers stained with ink as she peered down at the words wondering what they meant.

Shadows stir. The sands of time slip away. Silence forever in the gloaming.

What did it all mean?

As she pondered this, a distant howl shattered the silence. Hot pinpricks danced down the back of her neck as her head snapped up and she stared at the darkened window.

It was unlike any howl she'd heard. Not a wolf. But something...*more.*

The howl pierced the air again. This time, it sounded closer.

She rose, leaning across the desk to push aside the lace curtain, which was silly because there was nothing to see. Moonlight cast down through the trees in slashes of blue-white, shining across the back of the manor house and alighting on the overgrown garden. Her father was right in that they needed a groundskeeper, but how could they possibly afford it now that his business was in such shambles? Finding coin for that would be a challenge. It made her sad to think of the out-of-control bushes that had taken over the yard.

The howl came again. A mournful sound, as though the creature—a wolf?—lost something dear. Or it was a cry of loneliness in the darkness. Either way, the sound was dreadful and haunting and chilling.

As it pieced the night air once again, she decided it was a wolf. But this time it sounded as though it were closer to the front of the manor. As though it was right outside the gates at the end of their gravel drive. With her heart pounding, she stepped into the hall and stared toward the front door. A coldness settled inside her as she stood there, still as a statue, wondering what was out there.

Gerald heard it, too, for he bounded down the stairs in his nightclothes, his dressing gown flapping behind him. He headed toward the front door as the wail sounded again. As he stomped toward the door, agitation in every step, she hurried to catch up to him. She lunged at him as he reached for the knob and stopped him.

"No, don't." Her voice was a fierce whisper.

He startled as she grabbed him. His head snapped to her in surprise, his eyes dark orbs. His face momentarily drained of color, clearly stunned to see her standing there with him. Question creased his face followed by a myriad of other emotions. He wasn't sure whether to chastise her for still being up or that she had the gall to stop him from opening the front door.

"But miss—"

"Do not open the door," she said in a terse, determined tone. "It's too dangerous."

She couldn't explain why she called it dangerous, but a powerful intuition warned not to open the door. So, she held on tight to Gerald's arm and then gave him a gentle nudge to push him back.

The wailing continued from the lone wolf which was now joined with a chorus. There must be three or four now. She clung to Gerald as he wrapped an arm around her shoulders for comfort. She shuddered against him with cold fear. It was the closest to the old butler she'd ever been. He smelled like peppermint and old shoe leather.

She wasn't sure why he thought opening the door was the best idea, but perhaps he thought it nothing more than a feral dog. When silence descended and the yowling stopped, she relaxed her tense muscles and stepped away from him.

But he remained where he was, still peering at the door and then glancing her way. "I did not realize you were still up at this time of night, miss."

"I couldn't sleep." She bit her thumbnail, distracted. "Why were you going outside, Gerald?"

"I thought to scare off whatever was making that bloody noise," he grumbled.

He ran a hand through his hair, making it stick up on the ends. She noticed then the dark circles under his tired eyes. He fought off a yawn.

"Whatever it was, I don't think it was friendly. Get some rest, Gerald. I need to tidy up the library before I retire."

"Yes, miss."

He shuffled up the stairs, taking the steps slowly as he ascended. She waited until he was upstairs before she dashed to the library and snuffed out candles around the room. When she got to the small writing desk, she was about to snuff out the last candle when something caught her eye. She halted as she looked down at the open page. In the pool of faint, flickering candlelight, she noticed something had changed.

The page she'd been translating was different. Altered. The runes were the same shapes, only they were in a different place on the page. As if they had rearranged themselves into a better order. Moved down further. New runes appeared above it. Runes she had not yet translated.

But the strangest thing of all was what appeared in the center of the page—it had not been there before. In fact, she was certain it was not there before.

A rose wrapped in thorns. And it was leaking red ink.

CHAPTER 14

After the curious happenings with the book, Bella slammed it closed and headed to bed. She left it on the writing desk in the library and refused to look at it.

She also refused to go into town and meet Leopold's carriage. She did not want to face another day in his eerie library trying to translate the supernatural language in that infernal book. And so, she put on her hat and gardening apron and decided to tackle the wildly overgrown gardens behind the manor house.

It was the perfect day for it. A brilliant blue sky was overhead. A warm spring breeze fluttered, lifting tendrils of hair at the nape of her neck. She stood at the end of the footpath, her hands on her hips, as she stared at the brambles, the overgrown hedges, the rosebushes out of control and yet bursting with color.

She decided to start with cutting back the rosebushes. In the abandoned garden shed, she found cobwebs, creepy-crawlies, and ignored gardener tools that had seen better days. It would have to do. She picked up the largest pair of pruners she'd ever seen, hefting them over her shoulder, and headed out to work.

The sun was warm on her back as she labored. Her arm muscles were throbbing, but she refused to stop. It gave her time to think about everything that had happened, about the book with no name, the destruction of the fleet and the house in the port, and meeting Leopold.

Her thoughts were stubbornly stuck on Leopold. He was handsome, indeed, but something simmered under the surface she was unable to discern. Some sense of despair or longing.

"Hello!"

The man's voice stopped her, her heart leaping to her throat. She turned to see Lord Vincent standing at the end of the footpath, eyeing her handy work with a curious gleam in his eyes. As she looked back at him, she realized there was a pile of thorny branches between the two of them.

"Lord Vincent," she said on a gasp. She dropped the pruners. "What are you doing here?"

"I wanted to call and see how you were doing. Though I daresay you appear to be doing quite well?" He eyed the cuttings warily.

She glanced down at her hands, which were now red with forming blisters. She picked her way her through to the other side.

"We haven't a gardener, you see. So, I thought it would be good to do a bit of work to keep myself occupied." She paused in front of him and looked back. She cut so much back, she was able to see the edges of the footpath. There was now a mess to clean.

"I was sorry to hear about your father's ships," he said. "I do hope you don't find my arrival too impertinent."

Recalling her manners, she plastered on a bright smile. "Not at all. Shall I ring for tea? We may be in the country, but we haven't lost all sense of propriety."

She made a motion toward the house and started to walk, acutely aware of the sweat dampening the back of her gown. Tendrils of hair stuck to the back of her neck.

"I should also say, Lord Vincent, I appreciate you coming to check on us." She suspected he was there for Emmaline, not her, though she was unsure how to ask him about that without sounding bold. "It was quite a shock when we received the news about the ships. My father left for Port Leclare straightaway."

"I don't doubt that. The destruction was quite devastating."

She halted and looked at up at him, the brim of her bonnet shading her face from the morning sun. He was a head taller than her. His top hat, though, did not offer much relief from the bright sunshine.

"You saw it?"

"It was hard not to." Sorrow and compassion crossed is face. "You could see the black smoke for miles."

She looked away, her gut knotting into a tight fist. She pressed her sweaty palm against her abdomen. The thought of the ships destroyed like that make her sick. Not only for the loss of life, but for the loss of everything her father worked for and built.

"There is one more thing…" He paused as though it was difficult for him to say.

She glanced back up at him, the light behind his head blotting out his features making it difficult to read his expression. "What is it?"

"It may be difficult for you to hear," he said. "Leclare Port Authority has opened a formal inquiry into the loss of the ships. They believe there may have been some sort of contraband on board."

The world tipped on its axis. Blood drained from her head in a sudden whoosh. Black spots danced in her vision as she pitched forward, swaying on her feet. She hated he was the one to tell her the news. Lord Vincent wrapped his hand around her elbow. She let him steer her toward the back of the house, her feet moving of their own volition.

Of course, he'd know. He had contacts everywhere. Whispers carried on dockside winds before anything ever reached official channels. And now, the gossip would spread about her father.

"I am sorry," he said, his voice low.

She didn't answer. The weight of humiliation and fury pressed down on her. When they reached the back of the house, she pulled her elbow free, picked up her skirt and hurried up the steps. She needed space. She needed to *think*. And she didn't need him to see her unravel at the seams.

But he continued to follow and moments later they were in the parlor. The door clicked shut behind them, closing them inside the deathly silence. She sank into the soft, worn cushions of the sofa, her head in her hand. Numb. She was *numb* as she tried not to think about how their lives were turned upside down. Trying not to place blame on the magical, cursed book on the writing table in the library.

But it *was* there. Waiting for her to return to it.

"Bella," he began.

He stood in the center of the parlor, his hat in his hands.

"Is there more news you wish to share with me, Lord Vincent?" Finally, she looked up, meeting his gaze, her stomach twisting and her breath shallow. Frankly, she wasn't sure she wanted anymore news.

The look on his face said there *was* something more, but he pressed his lips together into a thin line that said he didn't want to tell her. His face went impassive as he moved to sit in the chair opposite her.

"Allow me to send my gardener."

She was shaking her head before he finished. "I cannot allow you to do that, for then I would be in your debt."

"It would be my pleasure to help you—"

She shot to her feet. "Please, my lord, I cannot accept your help. For I would want to pay for his services and surely you understand that under the circumstances, that simply is not possible." Realizing her sharp words bordered on rude, she plastered on a bright smile and clasped her shaking hands together in front of her. "I do thank you profusely for the offer, though. It's most kind and gracious of you. I'll fetch Emmaline. I know she'll want to see you before you leave."

"Emmaline?"

She dipped a curtsy. "Thank you again for coming, Lord Vincent."

Before he responded, she was out the parlor door and into the breezy hallway, shutting it behind her. She closed her eyes, a breath shuddering out of her. What was she going to do now? If the port authorities were involved and investigating, she worried that something dreadful had happened to her father.

"Bella?" Emmaline's soft voice floated to her.

Her eyes flew open to see the girl standing near the foot of the stairs, question in her eyes. Bella rushed over to her.

"Oh, Em, Lord Vincent is in the parlor. Perhaps you'd be kind enough to see to him? I'm feeling rather faint." She pressed her cold shaking hand to her forehead. "Please give him my apologies."

"Of course, miss."

Before Emmaline said another word, Bella rushed up the stairs to her room. She flung herself on her bed, burying her face in her pillow, and allowed the tears of worry and fear to slip from the corners of her eyes.

CHAPTER 15

Leopold paced the length of his private sitting room for the third time, his hands behind his back as he waited for Dickens to return. He counted the steps on the same worn path of the carpet where the light didn't quite reach. The blue-tinted sunlight bleeding through the tall lancet windows made everything feel colder than it was.

Books lay in loose stacks on the shelves and floor, exactly where he'd left them. He hadn't touched any of them in days. Couldn't focus long enough to read or research. Not since the day Bella walked into his life with that cursed volume.

The hearth stood cold. The firewood untouched. He could light it with a word, but the silence felt cleaner somehow. Less like pretending to be civilized. He was far from civilized, though he put up a good façade.

Dickens was gone most of the day, giving him hope that when he returned, he would have more information for him about Isabella Rinaldi and her father's merchant business. Now, the day waned, and twilight was upon them once again.

Disappointment flooded him when the carriage returned late that morning without her. It was a sure sign she refused to return. He hadn't expected the ache deep in his chest when she didn't. He suspected it was because of his eccentric library. Or perhaps his brazen confession he was cursed. Her face paled when he told her. He shouldn't have told her.

It was even more disturbing when he woke up in the middle of the foyer at sunrise face down on the floor. The cold tile seeped into his aching bones. All he wore were his trousers with ripped hems. His shirt was gone. His shoes were nowhere to be found. The rose branded on the inside of his forearm pulsed with an agonizing throb. And he knew, the moment his eyes opened, what had happened the night before.

He halted his pacing to rake his hand through his hair, making it stand on end. Frustration edged through him. He and Dickens had taken every precaution necessary to keep him contained and still it was not enough. He'd broken through the manacles that had chained him to the dungeon wall. That meant he likely burst through the cell door, too. He hadn't gone to see about the destruction because he didn't want to face the reality. The shame of it all.

The curse was getting stronger. His ability to remain confined to the castle during a full moon was becoming more difficult. Perhaps it was for the best the lady did not return, for he would never forgive himself if anything happened to her when he was in his ghastly form.

His gaze flickered to the desk.

The hourglass waited there, a foreboding presence that overshadowed his life's existence. Its iron frame curled with delicate vines, tiny rosebuds etched into every twist, like it had been grown rather than forged from magic. The sand shimmered in shades with no name. Not gold, not silver, but something older, like starlight and blood.

The sands were still slipping through it. Slowly trickling from top to bottom. Soon, the remaining shimmering sands would all but fall through the narrow neck, forever sealing his fate.

At last, there was a knock on the chamber door. His gaze flew to it as Dickens opened it and stepped inside, the shadows following on his heels. He pushed a tea cart inside the room. His face looked grim, which told Leopold the news he had was not going to be good news.

"What did you find?" he asked, an urgency pounding through him.

"My prince, perhaps you'll wish to sit." He motioned to a nearby chair with a calm wave of his hand. Then reached for the teapot and poured a steaming cup.

"I don't want to sit, and I don't want bloody tea. Tell me, Dickens. What news?"

Dickens replaced the teapot with reserved calm, then grasped the cup in his hand. He stepped toward him and extended the tea, even though he insisted he didn't want it. He took the cup, holding it between his hands and allowing the porcelain to warm his fingers. He had not realized how chilled to the bone he was until that moment.

His old valet returned to the cart, poured himself a cup, added two lumps of sugar, and stirred. As though they had all the time in the world.

He walked toward the seating area near the cold hearth, peering into the gray ashes. "Fire, please."

The fireplace flared to life upon his command. Then he sat in the oversized wing-backed chair, crossing one leg over the other as though he were prepared for a long chat. Agitated, Leopold moved to sit across from him, clutching the cup in his hands and waited. His valet would tell him what he discovered in his own time. It would do no good to needle him.

"I spent a good portion of the day in port learning what I could about Mr. Enzo Rinaldi."

"Bella's father?"

He nodded. "His boatswain was more than happy to share information with me." There was a twinkle of mirth and confession deep in his eyes.

Leopold sat back in the chair. "You magicked him."

"I felt it was the most expedient course of action, my prince." He paused to take a sip of his tea.

He wasn't too happy that his valet used magic to get information but perhaps he was correct in that it was the quickest way to find out what happened.

"First of all, the merchant's wife passed on several years ago. I understand she was quite ill. Rinaldi took Bella on his sea voyages until she was old enough to remain behind and run the estate in his absence. She is a talented and brilliant woman who has a penchant for libraries and the ability to translate almost any text."

Brilliant and beautiful, he thought. Dickens continued.

"It seems Mr. Rinaldi purchased some odds and ends at a market at a port on the south side of the continent of Cappadocia. He was quite taken with the book and a few other items. The boatswain wasn't sure of the contents of the cargo but he's not one to question his captain."

"The book?" Leopold said. "The book Bella has?"

"It seems so, yes. Once they arrived back in Port Leclare, strange happenings began. Something lurked in the cargo hold. A shadow thing, he called it. No one was quite certain what it was, but it was clear whatever it was frightened the sailors."

"Frightened sailors? That's never a good sign." A fluttering of fear cramped his stomach. He took a sip of tea to quell it. Not that it would do any good.

"There were other signs. A cold wind blowing below deck. Lanterns snuffing. That sort of thing. That night, after docking, the merchant's manor house went up in flames. They were all lucky to escape unscathed."

"That's why they came here to Driftbell?" he asked.

Dickens nodded. "Yes. And then almost the moment they arrived, two of the ships were destroyed in port. One was still at sea, so it was saved. However, the Port Authority opened a formal inquiry into the incident and is investigating to see if there was some sort of prohibited cargo onboard."

"The cargo from Cappadocia?" he asked.

"Likely," his valet said with a nod.

Or perhaps somehow it was the book's doing. He felt it instinctively in his gut the destruction of the manor house and the ships were tied to the book. The *cursed* book. The book that was supposed to save him from living as an immortal beast, forever roaming the wilderness.

But only if Bella was able to translate it.

"There is more, my prince." Dickens placed the teacup to the side and leaned forward as though the next bit of news was the worst yet. "Her father was arrested and placed in a portside jail until the formal inquiry concludes, and he appears in front of the magistrate. His accounts and manifests have been seized, and his license has been suspended."

Leopold stared in cold silence at the man across from him. Dickens' features were pinched with concern and worry. He understood what this meant for Bella. With his license suspended and his account frozen, the family faced financial ruin. Contracts would fall through. Investors would pull out. Debt collectors would close in, demanding payment. Not to mention his reputation as a trader and merchant was shredded.

And the gossip in town. He pressed a hand against his head. He imagined the gossip spreading quickly into town and higher society.

If Rinaldi didn't know what he was bringing on board, the burden of proof would fall on him. If he had no proof, nothing to indicate it wasn't illegal goods, then he'd face accusations of negligence or—worse—smuggling.

Where would that leave Bella?

The thought of her becoming destitute or homeless sent his senses reeling. The arrival of the book was the catalyst, though she may not even realize that. And he only added to her troubles by asking her to translate the book *for him*. He had to find some way to help her. Some way to make sure she remained in Hawthorne Hall. Not only because he needed her, but because he abhorred the thought of her facing such awful trouble alone.

He placed the teacup on the table in front of him. "Dickens, I think it's time I call on Miss Rinaldi at Hawthorne Hall."

"My prince?"

"She didn't return today. Perhaps if I call on her, I could put her mind at ease about coming back here to finish her translation."

A dark brow lifted in apprehension. "Do you think that's wise?"

He cut a glance to the hourglass. By his calculations, if the curse wasn't broken by the next moonrise and the sands ran out...his life as he knew it was forfeit. "I think it's my only choice. We'll go in the morning."

"We, my prince?"

"Yes, *we*. You're coming with me." He got to his feet and held out his wrists. "Best use the iron shackles this time, Dickens."

Dickens got to his feet, his expression one of concern and remorse. "Are you certain?"

"It's the only thing we haven't tried. If it doesn't work, then I don't know what will."

"As you wish, my prince." He bowed low and headed for the door.

Leopold followed, his gut in a tight knot. His transformation followed the phases of the moon, from waxing gibbous, to full, to waning gibbous, giving him ample time to cause mayhem. By the time the quarter moon came around, his transformation went dormant.

But if the curse was getting stronger...well, he didn't want to think about that. They were heading toward a new moon. He hoped Bella found a way to break the curse before the next quarter moon. Otherwise, he'd be lost to this world forever.

CHAPTER 16

Bella stayed in her room the remainder of the night. She didn't go downstairs for dinner, either. And when Emmaline knocked on her door, she feigned sleep so she wouldn't have to talk to her.

She understood the calamity of the situation with her father far too well. For the moment, she wanted to remain in solitude as she tried to collect her spiraling thoughts. It wouldn't be long before the money ran out and the debt collectors came calling.

Her sleep was fitful with haunting dreams of burning ships and cursed books. She awoke several times to the mournful howl of the wolf in the distance. The howl that seemed to grow closer and closer with every passing moment. She was relieved she was in her bed, safe behind her closed bedroom door.

When dawn broke through the lace curtains at her window, she pushed aside the blankets and sat up, staring at the day as though it were offensive. She was still no closer to an answer than when she fled to her room leaving Lord Vincent in the parlor.

A tentative knock on her door sounded. She pushed her hair out of her face, swung her legs off the side of the bed, and took a deep breath.

"I suppose I can't hide forever," she said on a sigh. "Come in."

Emmaline pushed open the door and peered through the crack, looking timid and almost afraid to enter. Bella waved her inside.

The girl entered and shut the door, pausing there with her hands clasped in front of her and worry creasing her face.

"I'm all right, Em," she said at least. "Just...weary. Thank you for seeing to Lord Vincent yesterday. I didn't have the strength."

The girl remained mute and for a moment, it looked as though her face might collapse into tears. Bella stood and reached for her.

"Are you all right? Was he unkind to you?" she demanded.

"N-no, miss. It's just that...well..."

Her shoulders slumped as she dropped her hands to her side. "He told you, didn't he?"

The girl's bottom lip quivered as she nodded.

Fury boiled through her as she turned away from the girl and stepped to the window. How dare he tell her. She stared down at the mess of thorns and vines that had overtaken the garden. The mess she, herself, created. Somehow, she would have to find the strength to clean it up as she fumed about Lord Vincent.

"He didn't tell me to be cruel. He told me because he wants me to look after you, to make sure you have someone to lean on."

Was that true? What she knew of the man was that he had a fabulous library in a lovely manor in port. He was a widower, possibly looking for a new wife. He was never unkind to her. Always pleasant. And there never seemed to be gossip about him. Perhaps he *was* concerned about her and wanted only the best.

"After you left, I walked him to his carriage. That's when he told me. It was nothing more than a mention that your father is in a bit of trouble with the Port Authority."

Perhaps, then, the girl didn't grasp the tragic situation. Best not to tell her yet. She would find a way to continue with the household and make sure everyone was taken care of. Emmaline included.

Finally, she turned from the window and plastered on a smile. "I'm glad you told me of his concern, but there's really nothing to be worried about. All will be well. You'll see. Now, I think I'm ready for some morning tea."

She sounded far more confident than she felt. Emmaline nodded and headed to the wardrobe to select a fresh gown for the day. Bella's discarded gown was in a heap on the nearby chair under the window. Her slippers remained in the middle of the floor. But she ignored all that as they moved about the day as though it were any other ordinary day.

As Emmaline finished helping her dress, she said, "There is one more thing about Lord Vincent, miss."

"Oh?" She slipped on her shoes and turned to face the girl.

She flushed, her cheeks turning pink as she cast her eyes downward. "He asked if he could call again to see me."

Bella was not surprised. A part of her was glad he had taken an interest in her. She was a lovely young girl and would do well in high society with the proper preparation.

"What did you tell him?" she asked.

"I didn't tell him anything," Emmaline replied, lifting her gaze to hers. "I wanted to speak to you first about it."

A smile tugged at the corners of her mouth. She hooked her arm with Emmaline's. "I think it's a fine idea. Write to him and have Gerald post the letter. We can have him for tea one afternoon if that suits."

Her face lit with beaming joy. "That sounds wonderful."

Bella left her to tend to her room as she headed downstairs to the dining room. Her stomach rumbled since she had skipped dinner the night before. After breakfast, she decided, she would return to the garden and clean up the mess she left behind the day before.

As she was finishing breakfast, Gerald appeared at her side.

"Miss, there is a gentleman caller in the parlor. He asked to see you."

Surprise edged through her as she glanced up at the butler. "Lord Vincent?"

"No, miss. He said his name was Thornhurst. He brought this valet."

She froze.

Her heart slammed against her chest in a wild, wicked beat. Her breath caught in her throat. Her breakfast immediately turned sour and threatened to rise but she swallowed hard, keeping it down. What the devil was he doing here?

She hadn't even thought of going into town. Hadn't thought of the carriage, or the return to his shadow-drenched castle. Gods, she hadn't even thought of the book. The cursed thing still sat on the writing desk in the library like it belonged there.

How had she let herself forget?

No—she hadn't forgotten. She'd buried it deep down in the dark recesses of her mind. Ignored it. Pretended for one blissful moment that her life was normal again.

"Shall I bring refreshments?" he asked, blissfully unaware of her inner turmoil.

With precise movements, she folded her napkin in half and then in half again trying to keep her hands from shaking. "Yes, Gerald, and thank you."

She pushed back from the table, rising on shaking legs, and took a deep breath. Gerald went on to the kitchen while she forced her feet to move, one step and then another, from the dining room to the parlor. The parlor where, only a day ago, Lord Vincent gave her the news that made her world come crashing down.

Leopold stood near the parlor hearth, too still for someone merely waiting. One hand rested lightly on the back of a chair, the other tucked behind his back, as if forcing himself into patience. The morning light cast sharp shadows across his coat—a deep charcoal gray, tailored close, with subtle embroidery along the cuffs and lapels. Silver thorns stitched in black thread. His cravat was simple, loosely tied, as if he'd dressed in haste—or with distraction.

He looked entirely out of place in the cozy, well-kept room. Not because he didn't belong, but because he brought the weight of something darker with him. A shadow trailing behind polished boots and noble bearing.

Dickens stood inside the door, hands folded in front of him like a statue carved from stone. His eyes, that unnatural, ancient stillness in them, moved once to track her arrival. Then not at all.

Neither man spoke.

But Leopold's gaze fixed on the doorway as she arrived. Expectant if a bit tense. Like he'd rehearsed what he meant to say and still didn't trust himself to speak it aloud.

When she entered, she put on her best smile. "Your grace, this is a surprise. To what do I owe the pleasure?"

He moved from behind the chair and reached for her hand. She placed it in his gloved one, her heart skipping as he bent over it and pressed a soft, warm kiss there. His lips were featherlight against her skin, sending a tingling sensation through her to the top of her head. When she pulled it back, she clasped her hands in front of her doing her best to pretend he had not affected her.

"Apologies for the early morning calling. I do hope I'm not intruding on your day?"

"Not at all." She moved to the nearby sofa and sat, perching on the edge and crossing her ankles.

Leopold's gaze flickered to Dickens. Silent communication passed between them. His valet gave an almost imperceptible nod before glancing at her.

"Pleasure to see you again, my lady."

And then he slipped out of the room on silent footsteps. The front door opened and closed as he waited outside for Leopold.

"What brings you to Hawthorne Hall?" Bella asked, trying to sound pleasant and cheerful.

She was glad to see him, but she was not glad he had come to the estate to see all the overgrown foliage that seemed to want to take over the manor house. Or the drab exterior that begged for a fresh coat of paint.

"We missed you yesterday." He kept his keen eyes on her.

Bella dropped her gaze to her clasped hands as her palms suddenly turned cold and damp. She had to tell him the truth. She did not want to translate the book, though she needed the money. She did not want to return to his wondrous strange castle, either. She did not want to spend one more moment in his presence, for he affected her in ways she refused to acknowledge.

"Yes, well, I should have sent a note." She lifted her gaze. A shiver of delight shuddered through her at the intensity of his eyes. "I must remain here where I'm needed."

"I see," he said, looking thoughtful.

Before he said anything more, Gerald entered the parlor with his tea cart. He paused in the center. Sensing the tension in the room, he glanced between the two of them, then gave her a brief nod before backing out of the room.

"Would you care for some tea?" she asked, rising.

"No, thank you. Bella, there is no need to fear the library."

She remained where she stood, her hands still clasped in front of her to keep them from shaking. Her nerves were on the edge of snapping. She didn't want to break in front of Leopold. She had to remain strong and sure and confident. She lifted her chin.

"It's not the library I fear."

"Oh, then me?" There was a twinkling of mirth in his pale brown eyes.

She shook her head. "No. It has nothing to do with you or the library. It's—"

Catching herself, she pressed her lips together to keep from saying more. She dare not tell him of her father's troubles. She shouldn't have told him about the ships in the first place.

"Forgive me, your grace—"

"Leopold, please. I insist."

He seemed to bristle at the use of his title. Nodding, she said, "Leopold, then. Unfortunately, I cannot return with the book. It's simply that I'm needed here."

His face remained impassive as he gazed at her. "May I speak freely, Bella?"

It looked as though he had something on his mind. She nodded, a sick feeling creeping through her.

"I was sorry to hear about your father's ships," he began.

She cringed, wishing she'd kept that to herself. Fear sprinkled through her. "Go on."

"You said he was a merchant. I know what happens to a merchant without his ships. I know it could lead to the total collapse of his business."

She clenched her jaw. "Yes." The word came out in a hiss of ice. She said nothing more and allowed him to draw his own conclusions about the situation she was in.

"I can offer you double the amount we agreed upon if you will return tomorrow to translate the rest of the book."

He was serious. She gaped at him, uncertain how to respond. Certainly, she needed the coin to make sure the household didn't fall into ruin while her father was dealing with his troubles. But could she really leave the manor to spend her days in his library with enchanted candlesticks and books that spoke and sang?

But that wasn't the only thing that bothered her. In his offer, she sensed a hint of desperation. He'd told her he was cursed. Perhaps that was why she was desperate to keep her distance from him. He hadn't elaborated about the curse, and she hadn't asked. All she knew was he'd been searching for a book. A book that could break the curse? She assumed that's what he meant. That book was unreadable by anyone—except her.

"Is that not enough?" he asked when she didn't respond. "I can triple it."

"Oh," she gasped. "That's far too much."

"Then double it is." He grinned, his face lighting with joy and perhaps a touch of smugness. He got to his feet. "You'll return tomorrow morning with the book?"

Before she realized what she was doing, she nodded. "Yes."

"Wonderful. I'll tell Dickens to expect your arrival. I'll see myself out." He bowed low. "Until then, my lady."

He left her standing there in the parlor, stunned to the soles of her slippers. When she finally shook out of her numbness, she hurried after him to see him off. But he was already out the door, his ornate carriage rattling down the gravel drive.

She paused there a moment, soaking in the late morning sunlight, when she noticed something odd. The brambles, the overgrown vines, the wild foliage was gone from the front of the manor. The exterior looked as though it was recently painted in a muted green. The abandoned fountain was back in working order, the water bubbling through the decorated stone structure.

Sucking in a sharp breath, she picked up her skirt and hurried around the side of the manor to the back.

She halted at the end of the footpath where, yesterday, she left a mess of thorny cuttings. It was cleared away as though they had never existed. The sweet scent of pink, yellow, and white roses filled the springtime air.

The rose garden, which thrived for years when she was a child, was restored to its former beauty. And so was the manor.

The carriage ride back to the castle was silent. Dickens said nothing but Leopold was acutely aware of what he'd done. He wasn't sure how to chastise him for doing something so kind and thoughtful.

When they arrived, Leopold remarked at the sorry state the manor and grounds were in. But he knew, due to Enzo Rinaldi's current troubles, there was no way for Bella to afford a gardener or anything else. Even when he intended to broach the subject with her and offer help, her reaction was one that said she was too proud to accept it.

Her face had fallen into misery when he mentioned the ships. He hadn't the heart to mention her father, the inquiry, or the fact he remained in a port jailhouse awaiting a trial with the magistrate.

"You wish to scold me, my prince?" he asked, almost as though reading his thoughts.

Leopold was aware his stiff demeanor indicated his internal thoughts. He and Dickens were together for a long time and, by now, he was able to read him without much effort. He expelled a deep sigh.

"How can I, Dickens?"

"My apologies, my prince. I thought it was the right thing to do, given the state of the manor and grounds."

"We could have sent a gardener and a painter," he suggested.

"I have my doubts the lady would have accepted such an offer," Dickens retorted, though it was not meant to be unkind.

He was likely right. She was headstrong and wanted to do things her way. She wanted to find a way to support her household without having to resort to handouts or returning favors. Hence the reason he offered to double her pay for the translation.

"It was kind of you, Dickens."

"Kind?" He sniffed derision. "The gardens were *absolutely* ghastly. How one could let such beautiful roses grow out of control is beyond me. Not to mention the dull, peeling paint on the exterior." He punctuated that with his best *harrumph*.

Though Dickens sounded disgusted by the unruly gardens and the dilapidated exterior, Leopold knew it was merely for show. He concealed the smile that wanted to tug at his lips. Deep down, the crusty valet was a sucker for thriving, fragrant roses in full bloom.

"Will the lady be returning?" Dickens asked then, as though putting the thought of magicking the gardens out of his mind.

"Yes." As he said it, his heart fluttered. A reaction for which he was not prepared.

"Ah, so you were successful then." His valet sounded well pleased. "Will she be staying with us?"

"I don't think so." A pang of disappointment went through him.

"Pity. The hallways seem more cheerful with her in them."

Leopold cut him a curious glance. "My dear friend, it sounds as though you've taking a liking to the lady of Hawthorne Hall."

"And why not? She loves books, doesn't she?"

He grinned, amused at his valet's response. "Indeed, she does."

CHAPTER 17

The following morning, Bella dressed quickly before Emmaline arrived to help her. She chose a light blue gown with pale yellow flowers on it, tied in the back. She was up before dawn, her mind racing with all the thoughts about the book, the man, and his library. She told herself it was not the howl of the wolf that kept her awake most of the night, clutching the blankets to her chin and cowering under them. The howls seemed even closer than the previous night.

She quickly scribbled a note and left it on her pillow, knowing Emmaline would find it. She didn't want the girl to worry, but she didn't want to explain why she was leaving at the crack of dawn either.

In her stocking feet, she hurried down the stairs. At the bottom, she paused to slip on her shoes. And then she hurried to the library where the offending book remained where she left it. The cover was still closed. The parchment with her scrawled notes rested next to it. She folded the paper and tucked it inside the cover and then scooped it up.

Moments later, she was slipping out of the front door and heading down the gravel drive. She only paused once to glance back and see the pristine condition of the manor house. It looked as it did when she was a child, making memories erupt of her mother and father and happier times.

Shoving that aside, she hurried to town to meet Leopold's carriage. He offered to pick her up outside Hawthorne Hall, but she had refused. She preferred instead to meet the carriage in town where she would not have to explain where she was going and why.

The footman and driver and, much to her surprise, Dickens waited for her. He stood tall, stoic, his face devoid of all emotion. Which, she was learning, was normal for Dickens. His dark glittering gaze landed on her as she approached and for a moment, she thought he might smile.

But he didn't.

Instead, he merely gave a half bow. "Good morning, my lady."

"Good morning, Dickens." She said it in her best singsong, cheerful voice despite the fatigue pounding through her. She even plastered on a bright smile.

He opened the door for her. She climbed in and then he followed, closing the door. It surprised her. He perched on the bench across from her and then they were away. An awkward silence stretched between them as they rumbled down the road.

Bella disliked uncomfortable silence. "So," she began, aware she was about to start making small talk. "How long have you known Mr. Thornhurst?"

His gaze flickered from the window to her, a curious glint in his dark eyes. "Many years, my lady."

She toyed with a loose thread on the edge of her sleeve. "How many years is that?"

An inane curiosity fluttered at the back of her mind. Lord Vincent was several years her senior, of that she was sure. But Leopold? She was unable to venture a guess to his age. Why it was so important at the moment, she hadn't a clue, but she was desperate to know.

He lifted one thick dark brow at her, pressing his lips together as thought trying to decide how to answer. "*Many* years."

"Since he was a boy?"

The brow dropped back into place. A strained smile stretched across his lips. "Indeed, my lady."

He didn't seem to want to elaborate, which gave her no more information than when she asked in the first place. Frustration edged through her. She turned away and peered out the window, watching as the countryside rattled by. The closer they got to his castle, the darker and gloomier it got. As if the shadows clung to the estate like a curse etched into every stone.

A curse.

Was the estate cursed as well as the man?

She cut a glance back to Dickens who regarded her with a cool, measured expression.

"You have more questions, my lady?" he asked.

Of course, she did. She had a thousand more questions. But which one or what to ask? It didn't seem proper to ask about the cursed man living in the castle. What was his curse? How did it affect him? And how did he expect to break it? Instead, she shook her head.

"No," she said, though she knew it was a lie.

The carriage slowed as they approached the entrance. She blew out a heated breath, grateful to finally arrive at the castle.

Or was she? It took a lot of courage for her to return to this place, to continue her work with the book, to step foot once again into that library with the hovering candelabras that emitted blue-white light.

"Ah, we have arrived," Dickens said, pointing out the obvious.

Perhaps he was as uncomfortable as she was.

When the carriage halted, he flung open the door and stepped out. Bella clutched the book to her chest as he opened her door and held out his hand. She didn't take it. Instead, stepping down from the carriage of her own accord.

The door opened and Leopold stepped out into the faint morning light. The moment he did, her heart clawed its way to her throat. He wore a long, deep brown coat, the edges embroidered in silver thread, its collar turned up against the morning breeze.

Beneath it, a muted waistcoat of dark wine-red, buttoned with precise care, though one button sat slightly askew as if done in haste. His shirt was crisp but collarless, open enough to suggest he'd dressed quickly or slept very little.

His dark hair was slightly tousled, as if he'd run a hand through it one too many times. And his pale eyes—sharp, searching—were shadowed underneath, the faint bruise of exhaustion etched into the skin below. Even tired, he carried himself with that same quiet gravity, but it was dimmer somehow.

When he saw her, he smiled, and the smile lit up his eyes. He looked genuinely happy to see her. Perhaps he was worried she wouldn't return. Perhaps that's why he sent Dickens to make sure she came.

"Bella, it's good to see you again." His voice was warm, welcoming. He waved toward the open door in invitation. "Dickens, thank you for escorting Miss Rinaldi."

He inclined his head slightly. "The pleasure was mine, my pr—my lord."

Leopold shot him a warning scowl as Dickens slipped past him and into the castle. He turned back to her, extending a hand, the scowl falling away and a more pleasant expression plastered on his face.

"Please, come in. Have you breakfasted? Would you like tea?"

"No, thank you." Despite her response, her stomach growled loudly. She only hoped he didn't hear it as her cheeks flushed hot.

He gave her a knowing grin. "Tea, then. Dickens? Prepare the dining room. The small one."

"Oh, that's not necessary—" she began.

"I must insist. We can't have you working on an empty stomach, now, can we?"

His charming grin obliterated any objection she might have. He extended his arm to her in invitation. How could she resist? She slipped her hand in the crook of his elbow, acutely aware of the fine material of his coat under her fingers.

He led her through a quiet corridor, the floor creaking faintly beneath their steps, to a small dining salon tucked into the eastern wing. The cozy room was paneled in dark walnut, with faded morning light filtering through the tall windows overlooking one of the castle's shadow-draped lawns.

A table was in the center, suited for small informal conversation seating four. The maple surface was polished to a high shine, gleaming softly under the blue-white light of the overhead chandelier. It was set with fine porcelain plates and silver. In the center, a crystal vase with an arrangement of indigo roses, their faint sweet fragrance drifting through the air.

Beyond the windows, the lawn stretched out like a dream half-remembered, framed by mist and distant hedges curving into unnatural shapes. The light didn't quite reach the far edge, where something darker lingered among the trees. Watching, perhaps, or simply waiting.

The fire in the hearth crackled softly, adding warmth to the room, but it didn't quite chase away the chill clinging to the stone walls.

And it was quiet. The room itself appeared to listen.

The highboard to the side of the room had already been laid with delectable smelling food. Steam rose from a silver teapot, the scent of Darjeeling rising through the confines of the room. Fresh from the oven, blueberry scones were wrapped in a linen-lined basket and served with lemon curd and clotted cream. Next to that, a platter of poached eggs.

Elegant, perfect, and far too normal for the eccentric castle, its inhabitants, or the way her heart raced.

He held a chair out for her. She sat, her nerves jangling, and placed the book to the side of her out of the way. He was the epitome of a gentleman as he took the seat opposite her. Moments later, Dickens arrived to serve them. He poured tea, offering her cream and sugar. She waved it away.

Leopold accepted the cream, placing dollops in his cup and stirring with a spoon. All the while, he eyed the book with the parchment sticking out of the edge. Curiosity lined his handsome face. She accepted the poached eggs on buttered toast, sprinkled lightly with parsley. As Dickens served Leopold, she picked up her fork.

"The night I returned to Hawthorne, I translated a few more lines of the book."

Leopold froze, the teacup in his hand halfway to this mouth. His brows rose as he tried to make eye contact with her from across the table. She, however, kept her gaze downcast, focusing on the delicious meal in front of her.

"That will be all, Dickens." His dismissal was curt. Dickens inclined his head and disappeared through a side door, leaving them alone. "Did you?"

She replaced her fork and reached for the paper, slipping it from the cover of the book. Unfolding it, she glanced down at her imperfect penmanship. Placing the parchment on the table, she slid it across to him.

He glanced down at it, his eyes skipping over the words. In a slow, methodical move, he replaced the teacup. But she was certain she saw his hand shake.

"This is incredible, Bella." He breathed the words. He made no other comment about it.

"You told me you were cursed. Do you know what this means?"

He shook his head. "I don't."

His words seemed forced verging on the edge of untruthful. She didn't want to accuse him of lying, but she sensed he might understand what the words meant. Her suspicious senses tingled. She forged on.

"Something strange happened that night," she continued, the memory resurfacing.

He lifted his gaze, his face impassive. "Oh?"

"I was working alone in the library. Everyone else was asleep in the manor. It was late. There was...howling nearby. Something I've never heard before in the country."

She peered at him intently, trying to gauge his reaction. But he gave nothing away. He cut a piece of toast with the edge of his fork as if they were talking of nothing more than daily pleasantries.

"I'm sure it was nothing."

"I heard it the following night. And last night, too," she added.

Again, she kept her gaze fixed on his face. He took a voracious interest in the plate in front of him. When she arrived, she noticed the dark smudges under his eyes, as though he hadn't slept much. She also noticed his somewhat disheveled appearance. Since the moment the word *curse* alighted in her mind, she was unable to shake it.

"Did you hear anything like that?" she asked.

He put down his fork and then picked up his teacup, granting her a knee-melting smile in an attempt to wipe away the worry, the fear, and the thought of curses from her mind.

"I heard nothing like that."

She wasn't entirely convinced he was telling her the truth. She let it go for now and finished her breakfast. When they were both done, he escorted her from the dining salon to the library.

"Will you be staying?" She placed the book on the table. The candelabras emitted their otherworldly glow, leaving a puddle of light in the center of the table.

"I daresay I'd be a distraction for you while you work. But if you need anything, I'll be close by."

He gave her a low bow and then left her alone in the enormous room. Heaving a sigh, she sat and got to work.

Chapter 18

She did not know how much time had passed as she bent over the book writing her translations. She deciphered a name in the margin. *Albert*. Who was Albert? She continued with her writings, her pen scratching along the parchment. Some of her notes were wrong. She struck them out in frustration and tried again. The parchment in front of her had numerous scratched out lines as well as blobs of ink where she'd held the quill tip against it for far too long in her contemplation. She pushed aside the messy parchment and reached for a clean piece and began to rewrite.

Shadows stir. The sands of time slip away. Silence for-
ever in the gloaming.
In the darkest night, no name remembered. No light is
welcome.
The hourglass bleeds its last.

Sitting back in the chair, she examined her perfect penmanship as she read the words aloud.

"In the darkest night, no name remembered. No light is welcome."

She tapped the end of the quill against her chin. What did it mean? Further, what did *the hourglass bleeds its last* mean? Was there an hourglass in this castle? And if so, where would it be?

"Leopold's chamber," she whispered to herself.

The candles above her seemed to flicker in agreement.

She glanced at the door, an idea forming. She needed to see this hourglass. Perhaps it would help her solve the riddle. The only problem was she knew where nothing was in the castle. She'd only seen the library and the small dining room. Did she dare attempt to find his chamber and the hourglass within?

Bella lifted her gaze to the floating candelabra above her. "Do you know where it is?"

It flickered as if in answer.

Her heart thrummed as her breath came quick and hot.

Leopold never mentioned she wasn't allowed in any other part of the castle. Perhaps he wouldn't mind if she took a stroll. Rising from the chair, she bent backward, her hands on her lower back as she stretched her muscles trying to ease away the dull ache. She'd hunched over the parchment and the book for far too long.

As she headed for the library door, the floating candelabra followed her overhead, lighting the way. At first, she had been startled, even frightened, by it. Now, she found it amusing that it seemed to sense where she wanted to go. She pulled open the door and stepped into the drafty hallway, pausing there to scan the area. No one was about. Not even Dickens.

"Which way?" she whispered.

The candelabra flickered and started down the hall. She followed, keeping her gaze lifted slightly to see where it led her. At the foyer, it started up the long staircase. Taking a deep breath, she alighted the stairs, pulling her skirt up to keep from tripping. At the landing, the candles turned left.

They moved down the hall, riddled with opaque shadows that seemed to cling to the corners. She continued on her way until at last the candles halted outside a door that seemed oddly out of place in this long corridor. She glanced left, then right, but no one was about. Taking a deep breath, she wrapped her hand around the knob, turned and pushed it open.

It swung with an eerie creak, the long tendrils of dark beckoning her inside. The candelabra wasted no time as it slipped through the door. The puddle of blue-white light reminding her of moonlight was in the center of the room.

She took a tentative step and paused inside. Faint cerulean light pressed against the panes of glass in the double lancet windows on the far wall. One bookshelf was crammed full. More books were scattered about. Stacked on the floor in neat piles to the side of an oversized velvet garnet chair. A hearth stood cold and dark. Next to it, a stack of firewood.

Her gaze flicked around the room until finally it landed on the writing desk. The chair sat in front of it, askew, as if someone had hastily stood, shoving it backward. The top was littered with scrolls and parchment, a quill, an inkwell.

And an hourglass.

Her breath pooled her throat and for a moment, she told herself she should not be here. In his private chamber, invading his personal space. This was clearly a room meant for a secluded retreat. A place to find solace in an otherwise chaotic world.

But the hourglass.

She had to see it.

Moving closer, the candelabra dutifully following and keeping her in its circle of light, she paused a step away from the edge of the desk. She bent forward for a closer look. It was the most remarkable thing she had ever seen. The iron frame had delicate vines and tiny rosebuds curled around the glass. Inside the glass, shimmering sand in iridescent shades of gold, silver, and a pale crimson. Slowly, the sands dripped through the neck from top to bottom, as if ticking off moments of a lifetime. And, she noticed, it was almost empty. She reached her hand toward it—

"What are you doing in here?" Leopold's voice startled her.

She gasped, pressing a hand against her fluttering heart, and spun to face him. He stood in the half light of the doorway, his hair still tousled. He no longer wore the waistcoat. His collarless shirt was open at the throat, revealing an expanse of golden skin beneath. He didn't sound angry, at least, but he didn't exactly look pleased to see her standing there in front of his desk reaching out to pick up the hourglass.

"I-I'm sorry. I was just...I..." She blew out a breath. "I'm sorry. It was wrong of me to come here. I shouldn't have. I'll leave."

She was aware her words ran together in a quick clipped tone. She dipped a curtsy and headed for the door, but he was blocking it. She decided that wasn't a deterrent, and she'd step around him. The moment she was a breath away from him, he reached for her, placing a gentle hand on her arm and halting her. Her head snapped up, their eyes meeting, and deep within those pale, odd, brown eyes, she saw suspicion and a bit of curiosity.

"What were you doing here, Bella?" he repeated, his voice low, rumbling around deep in his chest.

He stood so close to her. He smelled of cedar and ash, like a fire long since burned out—and something darker beneath, like leather left out in the cold. There was a hint of rose, not sweet, but faded. Dry petals crushed between pages of a book never meant to be opened. And something else. Magic, perhaps. Or sorrow. Whatever it was, it wrapped around her in a tender embrace.

Her mouth went bone dry. Finally, she found her voice. "I-I translated a section of text in the book. It said *the hourglass bleeds its last.*"

With his hand still on her upper arm, he continued to stare at her. His face was expressionless, something he had perfected. But all she noticed was how warm his fingers were on the sleeve of her gown. How his palm pressed against her and his long, slender fingers wrapped around her. And how the curve of his lips seemed to be the perfect shape for kissing.

Whatever was she thinking? She had to get out of here and now, to go back to the library and gather the book and her writings and return to Hawthorne. Her heart fluttered in a mad pulse against her ribcage.

"You know what it means, don't you?" she asked, her voice hoarse and quiet in the deafening silence of the room.

He dropped his hand, his gaze turning to the hourglass on his desk. "Yes."

She searched her mind for something to say, to express a profuse apology. "I should go." With her skirts in her fist, she stepped into the open door, ready to bolt.

"No. Stay. Please."

His voice was low, thin, frayed. As though he could not bear watching her walk away. She stiffened, halting in the doorway with her back to him and the material of her gown still fisted in her hands. She turned her head, looking at him over her shoulder. He looked forlorn, lost, desolate standing there with hope gleaming in his eyes. He didn't want her to go.

But she had questions, and she needed answers.

"You said you were cursed. Is the hourglass part of that?" she asked.

Leopold hid his emotions once again. But now, as he stood there in the pool of blue-white light, something seemed to crack under the surface. As though he had resigned himself to telling her the truth. All of it. His shoulders slumped.

"Yes," he said at last. He held a hand out to her in invitation. "Come. Sit with me. And I will tell you everything I know."

Bella hesitated. Wasn't this what she was seeking? The truth? She'd queried him on it at breakfast, and he had evaded her. Now, he was offering her the truth about him and his curse.

Releasing her skirt, she reached for him, placing her hand in his. His fingers, warm and strong, wrapped around hers, and gave a little tug. Her pulse pounded a wild, hard beat in her throat as she followed him, stepping back into the room. She hadn't noticed before but there was a small seating area across from the hearth on the other side of the room. Two chairs. A low table. He led her there. When they reached it, he released her hand. She was bereft with the loss of his hand on hers.

He turned toward the hearth. "Fire."

The moment he said the word, the hearth ignited into a blazing, warm fire that threw a yellow-orange glow throughout the room and immediately warmed her. When he turned to her, the firelight flickered over his face and in it, she saw sorrow, regret, loneliness, and longing. As though he wanted her to see. As though he was ready to bare all he was to her.

"Please, sit, Bella. And I will tell you the story no one else has heard."

CHAPTER 19

Leopold took the seat opposite her, leaning back into the soft cushions and stretching out his long legs before him, crossing them at the ankles and settling in. He expelled a tight breath ready to dive into a long tale. She waited, her hands folded in her lap while he gathered his thoughts. He pressed a hand against his forehead, rubbing there, trying to find the words and the way to begin.

"For years, I've been searching for a way to break the curse. I never thought I would have to depend upon someone else to help me do it."

His voice was a bit muffled behind his hand. Then he dropped it and looked at her, giving her a faint smile.

"The moment the curse was enacted," he continued, "was the same moment the book disappeared from me. As though it had fallen through a portal, forever out of reach. I have spent my lifetime searching for a way to break this infernal torment. Searching for that book with the thorny language. That day in town, when you tried to sell it, I caught a glimpse of the cover. I could not believe it had finally returned to this world carried by a scribe who was able to read strange languages. I thought my luck had finally turned. I would finally see the end of this vexatious blight. I would finally reclaim my life."

He shoved up the sleeve to his elbow and then extended his arm, tilting it so the light flickered over his forearm. A blood-red brand was there, deeply embedded. It was a crimson rose wrapped in a snarling, twisting vine of brambles and thorns. It was the same image on the cover of her book. The same image in the stained-glass window in the library.

"That's why you stopped me that day," she said, staring at the brand.

She resisted the urge to reach out and run her fingertips over it, to touch it. Was it painful?

"It is." He pushed down his sleeve and placed his arm against his lap, holding it there as if to hide it from her.

But she'd seen it. And it would forever be burned into her mind.

"You know, I was not always a recluse hiding in this enchanted castle, nor was this castle always enchanted." He gave her a faint smile, as he remembered, and then it faded. He cast his eyes downward, as though looking through the material of his shirt to where the brand resided on his forearm. "I was a prince once."

Her lips parted in a gasp, but she remained silent. When he told her he was no lord, he meant it. When she called him *your grace* as she tried to guess his title, he rebuffed her. Now she understood why.

"I was heir to the throne of a powerful kingdom. One that ruled this small province for centuries. It's extinct now. It's nothing more than a myth whispered by those who live in this realm, if they even remember." Finally, his gaze lifted to hers and she saw the depth of his soul in that one glance. So many emotions flickered there—pain, anguish, regret.

"I was determined to be a fair and just ruler, like my father. But then one day war came to our borders. A war I was unable to stop. An ancient enemy returned, one that should have been magically bound for eternity. I sent a small company of warriors and soldiers to the borderlands to fight. They never returned."

He turned his face toward the fire, the light flickered across his hardened features. The story he was telling affected him deeply.

"I assumed they were all dead, and I had sent them to their doom. Days later, a lone survivor returned, bloodied and beaten, his body broken. Nothing more than a ghost of the man he once was. He rambled about monsters made of shadow and smoke. I thought he was mad. No one had seen such things in our world. He was dying, you see. Whatever shadow thing he fought infected him, turning him into one of them."

He paused here, his gaze returning to her. At the mention of the shadow thing, her heart lurched, and a sick feeling crept into the pit of her stomach. She believed without a doubt she had seen this shadow thing along the docks in the port. Her father's crew, too, had seen it. Somehow, it had crept back into their world. She thought of the book and the whispers from the pages. Whispers that had not returned since she started translating it once again.

"He was someone you knew," she guessed.

He nodded. "My brother."

Albert. The name written in the margin of the book leapt to her mind. Though she didn't ask him, she was certain this was the name of his brother.

"I refused to let this dark magical being take him, control him, and turn him against me. He was all the family I had left. My mother died when we were children. My father had recently passed. In desperation, I sought something—anything—to keep him from dying and turning. The old kings forbade dark magic, but I searched for it, anyway. I sent emissaries to seek out libraries and bring back whatever volumes they found, buying them from their owners. Stealing them when they had to."

He paused here, as though remembering that time. His hand brushed across his chin, his palm whispering against his skin.

"At last, I found the spell sealed in an ancient book written in the cursed language. I broke the seal. I said the words in the cryptic, thorny language. It was as though the shadow beast sprang from the pages. I begged it to save his life. To make him whole again. But that came at a steep price. A price I was willing to pay. I offered myself in his place, if only to save my brother."

He pressed his lips together.

"And, so, it cursed you," she finished.

Nodding, he said, "Cursed me to live between worlds. And marked me."

Gooseflesh erupted along her arms and snaked down her spine, leaving a cold tingling sensation. He knew, all this time, the book was the key to breaking his curse. He knew the moment she showed it to him standing on the street outside the bookshop. That was why he insisted he hire her. Why he continued to insist she translate the book despite the strange occurrences in his castle.

He gave a humorless laugh. "When my brother found out what I'd done, he didn't even thank me. He didn't understand the price I paid for his life. Instead, he tried to kill me and steal the crown."

Again, he stopped here and rose to his feet. He moved toward the hearth, leaning on the marble mantle with his back to her, as if he didn't want to tell her the rest of the story. The muscles in his back were pulled taut. Tension filled the space between them.

"What happened then?" she asked, her voice timid and soft in the small room.

His back stiffened, the muscles flexing under the soft material of his shirt. "I killed him."

A sorrow filled her, as she stared at him, and suddenly, unbidden, hot tears pounded against the backs of her eyes. He sounded so desolate, so guilt-ridden, when he said it, it was all she could do to remain seated. She clenched her hands into tight fists, wanting to go to him, to offer him comfort but uncertain what comfort to give him.

Finally, he turned to face her. For the first time, in his face, she saw a hint of something ancient. It struck her then, then. In all her readings, she never recalled an ancient kingdom that once ruled the realm of Cassoné.

She had one more question to ask him. "If I may ask, what was your brother's name?"

"His name was Albert."

CHAPTER 20

In all the long, lonely years of his life, he had never told anyone about his brother or the curse that bound him to immortality. When Albert learned the dark truth about him, he was horrified. He'd started planning the coup almost immediately.

He had not shared with her he was a man by day, a dangerous beast by night. Perhaps it was just as well she returned to her country home every evening and not stay here in this vast castle alone with him. Despite all his and Dickens' precautions, he broke through his bonds every night.

He *was* dangerous. He was evil incarnate. He was death.

At breakfast, she'd questioned him about the howling wolves. She'd heard it near her small estate. It terrified him to know his beastly self was so close to her in the night. Though the full moon was waning and heading toward a new moon, his transformation continued. That, too, terrified him. For he suspected the curse was getting stronger and, eventually, would become permanent.

Leopold finally gathered his wits enough to cast a glance in her direction. She looked bereft, her lovely face creased with sorrow. He didn't want her pity.

He thought he saw tears glistening in her eyes. When she whisked them away, it confirmed his suspicion. She recomposed herself and straightened.

"I'm sorry about your brother."

He wanted to fire off an acid reply telling her to keep her condolences to herself, the anger pumping under the surface. But he remained mute, watching her as she cast her eyes down to her clasped hands in her lap.

"What you did for him...your sacrifice...it should have meant the world to him. His betrayal must have cut you deep."

At that, she lifted her blue-eyed gaze to his. He expected to see horror, fear, or abhorrence there. Instead, he found calm compassion and sincere understanding etched in her lovely face. He was momentarily taken aback by that and struck mute.

"It would have meant a lot to me," she said, her voice quiet in the stillness of the room.

His heart lurched with the sweetness of her words. A sharp pain of longing took up residence in the center of his chest. He was unable to resist pressing a hand there as he got to his feet and turned away, unwilling to let her see the anguish it brought him.

He was certain she was sincere, and it touched him deeply. But in what world could she ever love him—a beast? He was running out of time to find the answer to this curse, and she was all the hope he had left. He needed her but now he was starting to want her.

"How does the hourglass fit into all this?" she asked.

He heard the rustle of her skirts and composed himself, putting on his best emotionless expression. She moved to stand next to him peering at the object on his desk with a curious glint in her eyes.

"Every grain of sand represents a day of my life since the curse took hold."

She sucked in a sharp breath and glanced up at him in question. "But it's almost empty."

He nodded. "Yes."

Bella turned her gaze back to the hourglass. "And what happens when it is?"

It sounded as though she knew the answer but wanted him to confirm her thoughts. The hourglass appeared to him moments after the shadowy monster granted his wish. It came with a warning.

Every grain of sand is one day of your life. When the sand runs out, so does your life. You will be forever bound to the shadow realm.

"Then I am forever cursed."

She took a deep breath, exhaled it. "Well, then. I best get back to the book and finish that translation." She picked up her skirts and started for the open door, determination in her every step. But before she left, she turned once more to him. "Leopold...if I may ask...how old are you?"

He answered quickly, "Five hundred and thirty-seven."

Surprise flickered over her face before she concealed it. Nodding, she turned back to the door and dashed away.

Bella hurried back through the halls of the castle, down the stairs, and returned to the library. She didn't know how much time had passed as she sat with Leopold in his private parlor. Time seemed irrelevant here in this place. There was neither day nor night. Just a constant shadowy existence that seemed to haunt every corridor, every hallway, every corner.

Back in the library, she pressed the door closed and returned to the book. She stared down at the open pages with contempt. Was this the abhorrent thing that caused the curse? Was there somewhere deep in those pages a shadow thing that demanded the price for saving a life of a loved one? She slammed the book closed in agitation. Then she scooped up her pages and neatly folded them. She tucked them on the inside cover and turned from the table.

She intended to return to Hawthorne Hall. Again, that indecision flared bright and hot through her. Every step she took getting closer to the truth—his truth—was another step that terrified her. Another step that took her into a world she had no control over. Another step that pushed her closer to him than she ever imagined.

What did he mean he was cursed to live between worlds? He didn't explain. She didn't ask. She was too terrified to ask.

One thing she was certain of, though. The loss of his brother—by his own hand—haunted him. There was deep sorrow in his eyes and, certainly, in his soul. As though he wanted to absolve himself of the crime but could not.

The strangest thing of all, though, was that he said he was over five hundred years old. *Five hundred.* That didn't sound right.

She tapped the tip of her finger against her chin and turned to face the immense library. Her gaze alighted on shelf after shelf. In truth, she did not know much about the history of the realm. She was never interested in the past. She was only interested in stories about fair maidens and dragon-slaying knights.

While she remained there, pondering all this, her mind returned to the book she was interpreting for Lord Vincent. It was a sad story about a frightening sorceress and the prince who broke her heart. The prince who would forever remain alone in the shadowy recesses of his castle. She never finished that translation and so she didn't know how it ended.

But she couldn't help but see the similarities in that story and the world she was living in now. It would be strange if they were connected.

If Leopold spent his lifetime searching for the book—her book—then what else did he possess in his library? What other strange and exotic volumes perched on the shelf waiting for the day someone would open their pages and let them be free? She'd seen a few of them the first time she was here. But she had never properly explored.

Libraries were meant to be properly explored.

An idea struck her. She darted off toward one of the bookshelves. She started pulling them one by one off the shelf, flipping through them, and then replacing them. She was uncertain as to what she as looking for, but she suspected she would know it when she saw it.

Book after book. Shelf after shelf. Row after row.

When she entered the last row, she pulled a nondescript book off the shelf. It was bound in buttery soft leather with a leather tie wrapped around it. She carried it back to the table, her curiosity getting the best of her.

At the table, she pulled open the tie and placed it on the wood top. Then, with a careful hand, she opened the cover.

The pages were yellowed from age and emitted a musty scent. As though it had not been opened in decades. Perhaps longer.

The only word she recognized in the foreign—not magical—language was one. *Cassoné.*

She turned the page. Someone had spent a great deal of time writing lengthy prose in a careful script. She stared at it hard, willing her mind to translate it. To understand. To *know.*

And then something clicked inside her. That was when she knew the words would flow. She sat in the chair, her heart pumping hard and fast with the first glimmers of excitement and began to read.

CHAPTER 21

Leopold paced the long hallway outside the library. Dickens said she'd returned there, shut the door, and hadn't emerged for the last several hours.

It was nearly dusk.

Part of him was desperate to enter the room, to see her hunched over the book, scratching away with her quill. The other part of him was desperate to hide from her forever. He didn't want to face her. He didn't want to see pity on her face or fear. He didn't want her to turn away from him.

And yet, he was still pacing the length of the hallway when Dickens arrived.

"My prince?" His voice echoed down the long corridor.

Leopold halted and raked a hand through his hair. The brand on his forehead burned and throbbed. The closer full twilight came, the more unnerved he was. He sensed the oncoming shift deep with him. And he feared it.

"She's still in there, Dickens."

Dickens glanced at the door. "Shall I retrieve her? It's nearly dusk."

"I know, I know." He puffed out a breath. "If she's translating, though, I don't want to disturb her."

He lifted a brow in question. "Is she close to a breakthrough?"

The truth was he didn't know. The truth was, deep down, he was afraid. He was afraid his long-sought-after goal was finally going to come to fruition. And if it did, and he was nothing more than a mortal man, then what? Would he still be rattling around this enormous castle with no one but Dickens to keep him company?

A sharp shooting pain sliced through his heart.

He did not want to be alone in this castle anymore with Dickens. Not that Dickens wasn't good company...it was just that after five hundred years one grew tired of each other.

His gaze bored into the library door.

No, he did not want to be alone in this castle any longer. He wanted to share it with someone. He wanted to fill the hollow halls with love and laughter. He wanted... No, he could not think it. He shoved the thought away almost as quickly as it came into being.

But yet, it leapt into his mind, anyway.

He wanted Bella.

"My prince?" Dickens prompted.

"I don't know," he finally said, his voice terse and thin. Agitated. He was agitated.

"If she's to return to town before nightfall—"

"I'll see to her."

Leopold stomped down the corridor, his shoes thumping on the tile. He shoved open the door with a forceful hand and paused inside the threshold, his gaze halting on the table.

She wasn't there. Her chair was empty. The book was closed.

In a panic, he rushed inside, looking through the rows of bookshelves for her. She was nowhere. As he turned toward the small seating area under the rose lancet window, there she was.

She reclined on one of the sofa pillows. Her legs stretched out before her. The edge of her gown floating downward, the hem brushing the floor. A book was upside down on her chest as she slept, her face at peace. Her hand rested on top of the book.

The sight of her sent a pang of longing through him. A desperate need to go to her, to brush the back of his hand across her cheek. To feel the softness of her skin. To watch her eyes flutter open and her blue gaze land on his. Then he would scoop her into his arms and take her away to one of the bed chambers.

But no, that was not going to happen. That was never going to happen.

With his heart clotting his throat, he walked with slow, methodical, quiet steps to her and knelt in front of her. Her rhythmic breathing was slow, deep, constant. Long dark lashes brushed the tops of her cheeks. A loose tendril of hair fell over her forehead. His fingers twitched with the need to brush it away.

"Bella?" he whispered.

She didn't stir.

His gaze landed on the book then. A leather-bound book that was unfamiliar to him. He reached for it, slipping it out from under her hand. The pages fell open, flapping a bit in the hush, as he turned it around to look at it.

The yellow pages were familiar. The drawings iconic. Somehow, she had found the history of his ancient kingdom. There, within the pages of that book, was the rise and fall of his family's empire. How it came to be and how it came to end. His gaze flickered from the pages to her sleeping form.

After their talk, she'd come here to seek knowledge. To find out if he was telling her the truth, perhaps. He couldn't blame her. He'd do the same thing if he was in her place.

It touched him she was interested.

She stirred then, a faint breath escaping her. He flipped the book closed and set it aside.

"Bella?" he said, this time louder.

She snapped awake, her eyes fluttering open as she sat up. "What time is it?"

"It's nearly dusk."

"Oh!" She jumped to her feet then, looking disoriented and confused. "I fell asleep reading. I—" She pressed her lips together, her cheeks turning pink as she realized he must have seen the book she was reading.

"Let's get your things." He motioned to the table where her gloves and bonnet were, pretending as though everything was normal.

She nodded and headed quickly to the table, her skirts swishing with every movement. He watched her fluid movements as she placed the bonnet on her head, tied it, and then reached for the gloves, sliding them over her hands with deft ease. As though she had done it a thousand times and would a thousand more. Scooping up the book, she cradled it against her chest and turned to him.

Their gazes collided and for one breathless moment the world fell away and there was nothing but the two of them in a small sphere. Her eyes were such a startling blue it rivaled that of a perfect summer sky—a summer sky he had not seen in centuries. He longed to see it again with her. Holding her hand, smiling at her, as pride swelled through him to have her by his side.

"I'll take my leave of you now." She dipped a quick curtsy and headed for the door.

Her voice broke through his thoughts, and he realized he was staring. He hadn't meant to stare.

"I'll escort you."

Quickly, he fell in step beside her. The air between them cracked with tension as they walked down the long corridor. What was she feeling right now in light of his earlier confession? Did she despise him? Fear him? He wanted neither of those things.

"Bella—" he began but pressed his lips together again. What could he say?

She glanced up at him. "Yes?"

"Will I see you in the morning?"

"Oh." She looked away, fixing her gaze on the end of the hallway. For a moment, he thought she might change her mind and never return. But instead, she said, "Yes."

Leopold suppressed the smile that wanted to erupt. Relief blossomed through his chest. He would see her one more day. Perhaps one more after that.

Dickens waited at the end of the hallway. As they approached, the brand on his forearm warmed. A familiar feeling. It was a warning. A harbinger of what was to come. He had to get her out of here and in the carriage before night enveloped the estate.

His valet grasped her by the elbow and hustled her to the front door, Leopold on his heels. He wasn't sure if she sensed the urgency that now pounded between them. He followed her out the door, nudging Dickens out of the way as she reached the carriage.

"Goodnight, Bella."

She turned to bid him good night. He reached her, taking her hand in his and bending over it and placing a soft whisper of a kiss on the back of her lace covered hand.

"Until tomorrow, then."

"Yes." The response slipped out on a breath.

Behind him, Dickens stiffened waiting for him to return inside the castle. But Leopold stubbornly remained where he was watching her get into the carriage, the door closing behind her.

"Take her to her manor," he called to the driver.

The man gave a curt nod and then snapped the reins. They clattered down the driveway toward the road.

"My prince, I must insist you come inside at once. The day is late."

Dickens was right. It took everything in his power to turn away from the disappearing sight of the carriage.

CHAPTER 22

That evening, after returning to Hawthorne Hall, Bella stomped up the stairs to her room. Mortification flooded through her as she thought of the way Leopold found her. Sprawled out on the sofa, fast asleep, with the history of the realm on her chest. *His realm.* He must have seen the book and knew she snooped for it. It was no longer on her chest when she came awake and looked up at him as he kneeled beside the sofa.

The way he looked at her so intently made her pulse race. A tingling took residence in the pit of her stomach. His pale brown gaze was as soft as a caress as he peered at her with a spark of something she had never seen before. A spark that seemed to ignite a longing inside her.

Not just a longing to help him, to break his curse. But longing to feel his arms wrapped around her. Thinking that startled her to the core.

"Oh, miss, you've returned." Emmaline's voice broke into her thoughts.

She realized she halted at the top of the stairs, the book still clutched to her chest, as she allowed her thoughts of Leopold to invade her memories.

"Will you help me change, Em?" She headed to her room.

Emmaline fell in step with her. "Were you successful today?"

She knew what Bella was doing—that she was translating the book for Leopold. But she did not know why or what was at stake. Bella nodded.

"Yes, I made progress."

There was so much she wanted to share with the girl, but she felt that Leopold told her the story of his brother and his lost kingdom in confidence. She wouldn't betray that. She couldn't. She wanted him to trust her to keep his secrets, though he had never said they were secrets.

In her bedroom, she placed the book on the table by the bed. Since she had started transcribing it more and more, the strange whispers had stopped. She slid off her gloves and dropped them on the bed, then removed her bonnet. Emmaline scooped them up and carried them to the wardrobe.

"Gerald asked after you this afternoon," she said. "But I told him you were busy in town."

"Thank you," she said, her voice hollow and her thoughts distracted.

"I also got a note from Lord Vincent. He said he'd like to call soon." She turned to face Bella, her cheeks pink and her eyes alight with excitement. "If that's all right with you, of course."

"Lord Vincent? Yes, of course."

Emmaline unbuttoned the back of her dress. As she did, an idea struck Bella.

"Em, I wonder if you could ask him to bring the text I was translating for him? I was never able to finish it before we left for the country."

"I'll ask him."

There was a slim chance finishing the translation of his book would yield any information to help her with the current project. But she wanted to at least try. She had to know how that story ended. If she did, then perhaps she would have an idea as to how Leopold's story would end.

After she was in her nightgown and Emmaline had turned back the bed, the girl gathered up her day clothes and bid her goodnight. She slid under the cool sheets, pulling the blankets to her chin and tucking her arms underneath as she rolled to her side.

Thoughts of Leopold entered her mind once again. Her stomach fluttered as she recalled all he told her that day. There was a profound loneliness that emanated off him. And yet he tried to conceal that from her.

He didn't want her pity. And she didn't pity him. Instead, she had an intense need to help him pounding through her to find the answers in the book. Reading about the long-lost kingdom of Cassoné, though, helped her understand him more. It was once a glorious, thriving kingdom with a long line of kings who protected the realm.

She closed her eyes again, trying to push away the thoughts and quiet her mind. When sleep still eluded her, she huffed and sat up, staring at the book on her night table. It remained silent in the cool darkness.

The chill of the floor bit at her bare feet as she slipped from the bed. Sleep wasn't coming and there was no point pretending anymore. She reached for her dressing gown, shrugging it over her shoulders with a shiver, then slid her feet into her slippers.

Her gaze landed on the book.

It waited on the bedside table where she'd left it, dark and silent, but somehow still watching. She picked it up, the familiar weight settling in her arms. If answers lived anywhere, they were buried in these pages. And if she couldn't rest, then she might as well dig.

Perhaps if she made progress tonight, she'd have something to show Leopold by morning. Something real. Something that mattered. Something that gave him hope.

Her feet were silent as she descended the stairs. The household was quiet, still, sleeping. She moved to the library, her breath pooling in her throat and her heart racing. Determination edged through her as she entered the cold, dark room. The waning moon did little to illuminate the panes of glass of the window. She slipped around the room, lighting the candles.

At the desk, she placed the book down and lit more candles. Then she sat in the creaky old chair that was her father's, pulled out a piece of parchment, and began.

Before long, ink stained her fingers. She ignored it as she continued to stare at the pages hoping something—anything—would become clear. She turned a page, her finger trailing down it. The runes were all the same twisty, thorny vines that had no meaning.

In a huff, she sat back, frustration edging through her. This was a futile attempt. It was as though the translation part of her mind decided to shut off.

She flipped the page once again and then something caught her eye. Leaning forward, the brambles rearranged themselves in an odd shape. Her fingers trembled as she placed them on the paper. She had seen this section dozens of times before. Nothing had ever been there. It was the same knot of impossible symbols and tangled meaning. But tonight, something shifted.

The ink shimmered. Faintly. Like moonlight on black water.

Leaning closer, her breath fogged against the suddenly cold page. The runes rose, bleeding up from the parchment like wounds reopening.

New symbols. New script.

Her heart stuttered. She didn't blink. She held her breath. The translation came slowly, hesitantly, like the book wasn't sure it wanted to give it to her. Her eyes followed the pattern, translating in pieces. Not a passage. Not a spell.

A warning.

A step onto the thorn willingly. Forever altering. A man by day transforms to beast in the moonlight. The sands stilled the moment the vow was spoken. Now they fall again. When the final grain is lost, so, too, is the man. Forever altered.

She stared, mouth dry. The air left her lungs in a cold rush.

She'd seen the hourglass on his desk. The way it gleamed in the candlelight—its sands too bright, too slow, too unnatural. She'd watched it shift, the sands dripping slow. It was as he said.

It wasn't measuring time. It was measuring *him*. Every grain that fell was a breath he'd borrowed. A heartbeat closer to the end. Closer to forever altered.

Her stomach twisted. The book didn't say how many grains remained. Only that when the last one fell, Leopold, the man, would be gone. And she had no idea how to stop it.

A man by day transforms to beast in the moonlight.

What did it mean? He transformed into a beast under the light of the moon? Her heart thundered wildly as she thought of the howls she heard the previous nights. Was it him? Did he follow her in beast form? Would he come after her? Was she in danger?

A cold shiver snaked down her spine. He was far too kind to her. He would never hurt her. He would never hunt her. She rejected the idea of him as a beast. Despite that, she recalled the dark shadows under his eyes. When she queried him at breakfast, he seemed less than willing to give her answers.

A cold breeze shifted through the house, lifting the hair on the back of her neck and snuffing out the candles. She sucked in a breath and stiffened, sitting in the darkness, her hand on the book with oddly glowing crimson ink. Her heart beat hard and painfully fast.

Snatching the nearest candleholder, she shot to her feet. The chair scraped along the floor. Loud in the silence. In the darkness, it was difficult to find the matches. Her hand fumbled on the mantle until finally she found the matchbox. With shaking fingers, she got it open and struck a match, lighting the candle. The tiny glow from the one candle did not do much to push back the shadows and the gloom.

When she turned to face the library doorway, she froze. Standing there was a shape. Nothing more than a silhouette. An outline. With two red glowing eyes. She saw no other features.

The scream froze in her throat. She clutched the candle tight in her hand, her fingers cramping. The shadow thing was here, in her home, its red eyes fixed on her. Was this the shadow thing she saw in the port before their home burned down? Was this *thing* responsible for the fire and the destruction of her father's ships? She dared not scream. She dared not move.

It floated toward her, reaching out with its long billowy arms and slender fingers ending in what looked like shadow claws. Terror gripped her as she watched it approach. It was so close now. It reached for her.

Without thinking, she threw the candle at it. The light flared bright when it touched it. A scream and a hiss and then it was no more than a fine black mist disappearing into the void. Snuffed out.

She was now plunged into darkness once again with a useless candleholder in her hand. She tossed it aside and hurried back to the desk to grab the other one. A quick glance down to see the ink on the page was bleeding, moving, forming a symbol on the page. Swirling now and then lifting, moving, rising. Up and up and up.

Bella stumbled backward, tripping over the hem of her nightgown. As the dark mist rose, it formed another creature. Another shadow thing, for she had no other word to call it. It turned its faceless head toward her and then lunged.

A faint shriek ripped from her throat as ghostly hands wrapped around her neck, pressing into her skin and trying to snuff out her breath, as she snuffed out the candle. She gasped, trying to force air into her lungs, but the sharp fingers were crushing her throat, stealing her life. A burning sensation erupted through her, flaring behind her eyes.

The sound of breaking glass and other noises shattered the moment. The apparition released her and reared back, turned and suddenly the beast was there. It had knocked over the writing desk, the book tumbling to the floor, as it leapt through the broken window.

Bella stumbled backward, her back smacking against the cold marble of the fireplace, her hand on her throat as she gulped in air.

A deep, guttural snarl as it attacked the shadow, swiping massive claws through it. A high-pitched cry and then it was gone. But another quickly replaced it as it surged from the darkness of the hallway through the open library door.

The beast took this one out as well.

Then there was silence. She huddled there, against the hearth, her pulse pounding hard and fast. The beast turned its head and met her gaze. She gasped as she looked into its eyes—its pale brown eyes. Familiar, yet feral. His name whispered through her mind.

But it could not be. Could it?

Shock stabbed her to the core as she got a good look at him.

He was massive. Taller than any man she'd ever seen. He was sinew and shadow. Coarse, thick black fur coated him, the color of charred ash. His limbs were too long, too lean. His hands were still vaguely human, but not, ending in terrifying claws that looked as though they could tear through the hardest stone.

But it was those eyes that stopped her. Not savage. Not mindless. Those pale brown eyes burned beneath a dark brow. Bright and haunted. Terrible and terrifying. Yet unmistakably his. *Leopold.*

His lips peeled back, showing long sharp, teeth. But he didn't howl. He emitted a labored breath as though the fight had taken something out of him. He shifted toward her, and she saw it then—the rose-shaped scar twisted beneath the fur on his forearm. The curse banded into his flesh, even in his beastly form.

Though he stood with the brute power of a predator, he did not move to attack her. He had protected her from the shadows. Deep in his eyes she saw he hadn't lost himself to the beast completely.

Not yet.

And that, at least, gave her hope.

She took a tentative step toward him but suddenly another apparition appeared in the doorway.

"Behind you!" she managed.

He spun as the shadow thing attacked. The dark claw ripped across Leopold's chest, shredding flesh and fur. He cried out in agony, a deep guttural moan that sent shivers skipping through her. The attack angered him, and he surged forward, swiping a paw down the length of the apparition, cutting it in two. That high-pitched whine and then it disappeared in a puff of dark mist.

Footsteps pounded down the stairs and Gerald's voice rang out followed by Emmaline's. She sucked in a breath. The beast's pointed ears perked as he placed himself between the doorway and her.

He emitted a low, guttural growl of warning, ready to fight once again.

"No, Leopold," she said, her voice calm and sure.

He turned his head, his eyes meeting hers once again.

"Go," she breathed. "Before they find you."

"Bella!" Gerald called. He was steps away from the library.

"Please," she begged. Then, she called, "I'm fine!"

She was spurred into action as she hurried toward the door, desperate to put herself between him and the butler. She caught a whiff of his feral scent as she skirted around him, unafraid of him.

"Don't let them see you," she said as she passed by him.

He hurried to the window and leapt through the broken glass, disappearing into the night.

Chapter 23

T he moment he was gone through the window, Gerald was in the doorway. Emmaline held a candle, the flickering glow highlighting the alarm and concern on her face. Edith peered over her shoulder, trying to see what was happening.

"Miss, what happened?" Gerald asked.

"We heard an awful noise," Emmaline added.

When he saw the broken window, he rushed to her. She put her hands up to show she wasn't hurt.

"I think a tree branch, or something must have broken the window. I was working there, and it startled me," she said.

"Are you hurt?"

She shook her head. "I'm fine."

He moved closer to the writing desk to inspect the damage. Broken glass littered the top of it and the floor. A cool breeze ruffled the curtains, letting the evening air pour inside. Emmaline scooted across the expanse of the library to stand next to her, shivering.

"Well, there's not much we can do about it tonight," Edith said from her position in the doorway. Her hands were propped on her hips.

"I'll see if there's some old wood in the gardener's shed to board it up. That will have to do until we can have repairs made." He shuffled out of the room, his shoulders slumped and weary.

Bella, though, knew that such repairs would cost a lot of money. Money they didn't have.

"Gerald will fix it up, miss. You should go back to bed," Edith said before she shuffled off back to her room.

"She's right," Emmaline said. "There's nothing else to be done tonight."

"I'll stay until Gerald is finished," she said. "You go on, Em. I'll be all right."

"If you're certain."

She gave her an encouraging nod and smiled, shooing her from the room. When Emmaline left, Bella returned to the desk. The book lay face down on the floor, pages crumpled underneath itself. Glass glittered across the binding, making it shimmer. She kneeled and picked up the book and gave it a little shake. The glass fell like glitter to the carpet. When she turned it over, she noticed the ink was once more just ink. It was not bleeding like it was before the shadow creature arrived.

Had the strange red ink called to it? She was certain now they were connected. She was also certain these shadow things had something to do with their home in the port burning to the ground and her father's ships destroyed. They were tied to the book, just like Leopold was tied to the book.

Gerald returned with several boards, a hammer and nails. He quickly got to work, closing up the gap in the window.

"That should hold tonight. In the morning, I'll see about trimming the trees in the back."

But she knew no trees needed trimming. She nodded agreement, though. "Thank you, Gerald."

"Get some rest, miss. We can clean up the rest when morning comes."

He yawned and headed off to bed. Reluctantly, she followed.

She had a fitful sleep. At dawn, she was up, shoving away the blankets. Standing before her mirror, she saw the fatigue lining her face. Her hair was a mess of tangles. It would take too much time to try to comb it out, but she didn't have much choice.

Frustration edged through her as she pulled out the tangles. By the time she got her hair combed out in long tendrils, Emmaline arrived at her room.

"Thank goodness you're here. Help me dress, Em. I must go."

"Back to that enchanted castle?"

She nodded as she pulled open the wardrobe door and rummaged through her sparse gowns.

"Miss, what really happened last night?" Suspicion laced the girl's tone.

Bella stopped and peered around the door at her. "Whatever do you mean?"

"I mean...something happened, didn't it? That was no tree branch that crashed through the window."

The girl was smarter than she let on, something Bella did not take into account. They peered at each other for a long, silent moment as she tried to decide how to answer. She did not want to tell her the truth—that it was Leopold in his beastly form that had crashed through the window to save her from the shadow thing. To tell her would mean she'd be giving the girl the whole story about his curse and that she was convinced the shadow things were following them since the moment the book arrived in her possession.

"I can't tell you," Bella finally said, her voice quiet. "But I want to. I want to tell you everything, Em, but I...I cannot. It's not my story to tell."

Emmaline rushed to her then, reaching for her and taking her hands. She squeezed them. "Don't go back, miss. I can see the burden this translation has placed upon you. You haven't slept well in days."

She wanted to tug her hands free but refrained. "How do you know that?"

"Your eyes are tired. And I fear that returning to this castle will cause you more harm. Don't go," she pleaded.

This time, she did pull her hands free as she turned away, focusing on a yellow dress with tiny white daisies. "It's not that simple, Em. I wish it were. I have to go. I have to finish the translation."

As she said it, a low and ragged whisper breathed through the room. Emmaline's head snapped toward the book, her eyes wide and round. She heard it, too. The sound still lingered, coiling in the silence like smoke—not a voice exactly, but intent. Present. Listening.

"That book is cursed," she said, her voice rough. The fear was evident in her features.

Bella remained silent. If she acknowledged that the book was, in fact, cursed...well, she didn't want to take a chance Emmaline would leverage the help of Gerald and Edith to keep her here in this house. She *had* to see about Leopold. She had to know if he was all right. She focused her attention on the yellow dress and then reached for it.

"I have to go," was all she said as she held the gown out to Emmaline.

The girl had no more objections as she helped her dress and pin her hair into a low chignon. Then she pulled on her bonnet and her gloves and picked up the book.

"I'll be back by nightfall."

"Promise?" she asked.

Bella nodded and gave her a reassuring smile. "You have my word."

The carriage ride seemed to take an eternity. Bella peered out the window the entire time, watching the landscape flash by and silently urging the driver to go faster. Worry gnawed at her. Worry for Leopold.

When she arrived, he did not greet her at the door as he usually did. Instead, it was Dickens waiting for her. He waited on the stoop, apprehension creasing his features, indicating the situation must be dire.

As soon as the carriage came to a halt, she was out of it, not waiting for the footman to help her down. She clutched the book to her chest as she came face to face with Dickens. His dark eyes glittering with concern met hers.

"Come with me, my lady," he said, as though expecting her question.

She followed him inside the castle, the door closing with a soft snick behind her. Dickens went to the stairs and headed up and then down the hallway—the same way she had gone when she found Leopold's private sitting room with the hourglass that ticked away every day of his life.

They moved beyond that, down the long corridor that was dimly lit with overhead candelabras. They casted the blue-white light down onto the floor covered by an ostentatious patterned runner.

With every step they went deeper into the castle, her pulse raced harder. Drumming a fast rhythmic beat.

Dickens paused at a closed door with iron hinges. With his hand on the knob, he turned to her.

"He is…not well, my lady," he said, almost sounding as if it were a warning.

"He was injured last night," she said. "I saw it happen."

He nodded, his face solemn. "It will be difficult for you to see him like this. But he asked I bring you to him the moment you arrived."

Her mouth turned to ash. "He did?"

Nodding, Dickens turned the knob and pushed open the door. She got her first glimpse of what mystery lay behind that threshold.

His chamber was large but dim, draped in shadow even in the light of day, though the light of day never really touched this castle. Tall lancet windows stretched along one wall, veiled with heavy midnight blue curtains to block out what light seeped into the room. A small slash escaped between an opening, leaving a puddle of light on the floor covered in a thick garnet rug.

A hearth flickered with warm, yellow light, casting its shadows across the room and splashing toward the bed. The large bed dominated the far wall. It was a massive four-poster of dark oak carved into a motif of vines and thorns that twisted along the footboard, headboard and posts. Amber light illuminated his ashen face where he lay propped up against a mound of pillows, the layered bed linens tucked neatly under his arms. A thick bandage was across his chest and abdomen, the only covering, tinged red from blood.

The brand on his arm was red and angry. She recalled seeing it the night before beneath his fur when he was in the form of the beast.

She halted there a long moment, stiff and panic-stricken as she watched for signs of life. But then she saw the slow rise and fall of his chest as he slept.

The space felt too large for one man. A faint scent of cedar, old magic, and bloodied linen hung in the air. Books lay stacked nearby. Some open, some face-down as if abandoned mid-thought. One chair, pulled close to the bedside, still bore the shape of someone having recently sat there. Dickens, no doubt. The room was quiet, but not peacefully so. It was the silence of waiting, of recovering, of regret.

And even in his weakened state, Leopold fit the space like a shadow fit the night.

Bella hesitated inside the door, still clutching the old, cursed book, desperate to rush to his side yet afraid to do just that.

"Go on, my lady," Dickens said, his voice low and encouraging.

One glance over her shoulder to see the man giving her a nod of reassurance. She forced her feet to move to the side of the bed where she eased into the chair by his bedside and sat in silence, trying to figure out what to say, how to feel.

The bedchamber door closed with a soft click, sealing her inside with the man who had saved her from shadowy apparitions the night before. Apparitions that, no doubt, had a connection to the cursed book in her arms.

As time passed, she waited, finally relaxing enough to drop the book into her lap. She watched him sleep, until his face twitched and he emitted a faint groan. His eyes, those pale brown eyes, blinked open. He focused at first on the ceiling above him then turned his head slightly to meet her gaze.

They stared at each other a long silent moment, her heart pounding so hard she thought it might burst out of her chest. She kept her gloved hands clasped together, resting on top of the book on her lap. A slow smile tugged up one corner of his mouth.

"Bella." His voice was weak, rough, as though rusty from nonuse. "You came."

Surprise flickered through her at his words. Had he not expected her to come? "Of course, I did. Why wouldn't I?"

He turned his head back, as though it were an effort to move, and closed his eyes again. "Now that you know what I am, I thought you would not."

He sounded melancholy when he said it, sending a pang of empathy through her. She wanted to reach for him, to touch him, but she kept her hands firmly in place. He feared she would never return because he had shown her what he really was—that he was a terrifying beast.

She searched her mind for the right words. Words of comfort. Words of encouragement.

"Leopold," she began, her voice soft in the room's quiet. And still her hand twitched, desperate to reach for him and give him a touch of reassurance. "I had to come."

"Because of the book," he said, his eyes still closed.

"Because of you."

She didn't know why she said it, but she felt, deep down, it was true. His eyes blinked open once again. For a breath, she thought he hadn't heard her. But then his sharp, startling gaze found hers. And in that moment, something passed over his face. A flash of emotion so deep, so exposed, it made her breath hitch. Not pain. Not gratitude.

Longing.

Not the kind spoken aloud, but the kind that lived in suffering, lonely silence. Then it was gone. Buried beneath the usual calm. Replaced by that tired, guarded look he wore like a second skin.

But she'd seen it. And now she couldn't forget it. She would never forget it.

She rushed on. "I-I worried about you after last night. That shadow thing, or man, or whatever it was...I saw what it did to you."

Her eyes caught on the bandages first. White and stark against the bruised skin of his ribs and the broad span of his chest. Too much of him was exposed, too vulnerable. She told herself that's all she saw. The injury. The damage.

But the firelight betrayed her.

It traced over him in soft gold, catching the faint sheen of his skin, the rise and fall of each careful breath. And suddenly she was too aware of the strength beneath the wound, the shape of him, the warmth radiating from where he lay.

She looked away. Forced herself to focus on the fire, the chair, anything else. But it was too late. The feeling had already curled low in her belly—quiet, unwanted, and far too dangerous.

Far too undisputable.

"You saved my life. Thank you," she muttered.

Her gaze drifted before she stopped it over the broad line of his shoulders, the quiet strength still visible even in rest. Up to the sharp angle of his jaw, dusted in the beginnings of a beard. He looked rougher like this. Untamed. Real.

And then his eyes. Those eyes that always unraveled her. They caught the firelight just right, deep and fathomless, and for a heartbeat, she couldn't breathe. Couldn't think. She told herself she was checking on him, that she was only worried. But that wasn't the whole truth, was it?

A single lock of dark hair fell over his brow. Her fingers twitched.

She wanted—gods help her, she wanted—to reach out. To brush it back. To press a kiss to his forehead, to tell him without words that she was there. That he wasn't alone. That she wouldn't leave him. Not now. Not ever.

She curled her hands into fists in her lap instead. Because touching him like that? It would change everything. And she wasn't ready for what that might mean.

"I had to," he said finally. He sounded fatigued, as though speaking was an effort. But even so, he added, "I'm glad you came."

And then he fell fast asleep once more.

CHAPTER 24

She sat there in the quiet for the longest moment, watching him sleep. He seemed peaceful and at rest. When she was certain he wouldn't wake again, she rose, placing the book in the seat of the chair. Then she removed her gloves and bonnet, dropping them on top of the book, and then padded to the door.

Once outside the room, with the door closed softly behind her, she paused in the shadowed hallway of blue light, the candelabras dancing overhead.

"My lady?"

Dickens' voice startled her, making her jump. She pressed a hand against her chest. She hadn't seen or heard him approach. He was a man of great stealth.

"Oh, Dickens, you startled me."

He gave her an apologetic look. "Could I offer you some tea and scones?"

At that, her stomach rumbled. Her initial response was to decline, but she skipped breakfast to rush here and see about Leopold. She nodded, viewing this as an opportunity to talk to the valet. He motioned for her to follow him back down the hallway, to the stairs, and finally to the small dining room she had breakfast with Leopold only a day before.

After she was settled, the tea poured and the orange and cranberry scone on her plate, she waited for Dickens to make another appearance. He didn't. So, she ate in the deathly quiet of the room feeling as though the old oil paintings of long-dead ancestors kept their watchful gaze on her. When she finished her tea, it was as though Dickens sensed it and returned to refill her cup.

"Dickens, is it true about Leopold?"

He never reacted to her question as he continued to pour the tea. "Is what true, my lady?"

"That he's a..." *Beast*. She couldn't say the word aloud.

Though she knew the truth of it—she had seen it with her own eyes, after all. She picked up the cup letting the warm steam waft over her face while she peered over the rim at Dickens, her heart in her throat and her gut twisted into a tight knot. He looked as though he would rather be anywhere else than there answering her questions. She replaced the cup in the saucer.

"I must know, Dickens."

Not that she doubted Leopold's words, but she wanted to hear it from another source. And Dickens said he'd known him for many years. She kept her gaze fixed on him as he stood there, stiff as a starched shirt, his dark eyes shrouded in mystery.

"You have seen him at his worst, my lady. There is no one else in this realm who knows his secret." His voice was reedy thin as he stood there, peering at her with a sort of defiance. "I trust you to keep it that way."

She understood then. He wanted to make sure she never spoke of his friend's transformation to anyone. He must worry that if she did, it would bring unwanted attention to him and the castle that was in perpetual darkness.

"I would never violate that trust, Dickens."

It had taken a lot of willpower not to tell Emmaline what was happening here and why she was so desperate to return. She didn't even tell her, Gerald, or Edith what had truly happened the night before. She let them think it was merely a tree branch that shattered the window. It was impossible to explain to them about the shadow monsters that tried to attack her.

"He said the curse is getting stronger. Is it?"

Her determination to get answers pounded through her. She needed to know what she was up against. She needed to know how much time she had left to translate the book.

Dickens seemed to buckle under her persistence and reached for the teapot. He poured a second cup of tea, dropped in a lump of sugar, stirred, and then sat at the table in the chair nearest her.

"It is getting stronger, my lady. I fear what it's doing to him." He took a sip of tea, giving her a look of contemplation over the rim.

"How did he know I was in danger last night?" She ran her finger around the rim of the porcelain cup.

"He sensed it." He took a deep breath, expelled it, and then replaced his own cup. He laced his long, slender ghostly fingers and leaned on the table toward her. "My lady, since the moment you walked into his life, it seems the curse senses when you are near and when you are in danger."

She blinked at that, trying to make sense of what he was telling her. "I heard wolves howling close to our manor house several nights and—"

"He was there. Protecting you in the darkest gloom of the night."

Cold tingles danced up her spine. "You mean, he knew those shadow monsters were out there?"

"The day he saw you in the bookshop was when he sensed them enter the town. It was the night of the full moon. He insisted I bind him to keep him inside the castle, to keep him from breaking free. But nothing I did could keep him from breaking through his bonds," Dickens said.

She thought of that first night as she tried to translate the book and heard the mournful howl of nearby wolves. It was so eerily close, it was enough to rouse Gerald from his bed. They stood there huddled together in the foyer, listening as the night pressed around them. Both shivering with fear of what was out there. And Gerald, being brave or foolhardy, thought to shoo them away with the flick of his wrist.

She thought of the book again. How she saw the shadow apparition skulking around the pier that first night her father was home. The night their house burned to the ground. And then when they learned of the destroyed ships.

These shadow things must be tied to the book. For she had it with her in Hawthorne Hall when she heard the howling wolves.

"These...monsters...they're tied to the book, aren't they?"

"They are the *veil-shade*. Neither living nor dead. Demons of the night. Creatures tied to the book that hide themselves in shadow and illusion. But they are dangerous. With lethal claws. Mindless enemies that have one thing only in mind—reclaim the book." He sat back in the chair and reached for the teacup, taking another sip.

"Where did they come from?" she asked.

Dickens looked at her over the rim as he considered his answer. "My prince told you of the curse, did he? How and why he used the darkest magic imaginable?"

She nodded.

"They were unleashed with the curse. When the book disappeared that night, they were meant to hunt it down and find it again. Only when it resurfaced in your possession were they able to do just that."

That night...he referred to the night Leopold used the old spellbook to try to save his brother.

"And it's true about his brother, Albert?"

His face was solemn. "It is."

With a shaking hand, she reached for her cup and sipped, trying to hide the fear that pulsed through her.

"Were you there that night, Dickens?"

He didn't answer. When she glanced at him, she saw the unease shifting through his aged face. He didn't want to remember. Or if he did, it disturbed him greatly.

"Yes, I was there," Dickens said, quietly. His eyes were distant, his voice flat in a way that said he did not want to remember.

"It was far past midnight. The castle was silent. Everyone else had given up hope the young man would live. But not Leopold. He was desperate to save the only blood he had left in the world. He sent away the guards. He barred the door behind me and told me not to speak, not to stop him. He needed me there. He wanted me there. To bear witness. I know that now.

"He'd found the book, you see. Somewhere deep in the archives of an old monastery that had long since been deserted. When he opened it, it was as though the book had been waiting for him. He didn't need to read the spell aloud. It already knew what he desperately wanted. What he was willing to give—himself."

He paused there to take a sip of tea. His eyes didn't meet hers.

"The air shifted from hot to cold to hot again. Then crackling with the fiery, metallic tang of magic. Dark magic. Acrid and foul. The *veil-shade* came first. Long, thin things, clawing toward him like smoke. They did not speak. But I felt them. So did he.

"He accepted his fate with a deep, unrelenting courage. He placed his hand on the page and waited. That's when it took him. Light shattered. Every candle in the room snuffed out. A scream ripped from deep within his lungs. Just once. But I will never forget that sound. The sheer terror. The pain. The anguish of it all. Then a sound. Like bones breaking. Like skin ripping.

"When it was over, he still stood. But the mark was there. Burned into his forearm. The rose and thorns. And his eyes..." He paused again, swallowed hard. "His eyes changed to that pale brown. And deep within them the hint of something feral and savage."

He fell silent then, his gaze fixed on the tawny liquid of his tea.

"He was no longer the man who walked into that room."

Her cold fingers pressed against her trembling lips as he told the story. She didn't know what words to say once he had finished. What *could* she say?

Leopold did all that for his brother. His brother who feared and loathed him and tried to kill him for his crown. Hot tears pressed against the backs of her eyes as she tried to imagine the horrible scene.

Dickens lifted his gaze to hers then. And in them she saw the desolation, the despair, the fear, the burden he had carried all these long years.

"The brand on his forearm...it steals a little more of him each time he turns. It's taking a little more of his soul, of his very life essence. And he is running out of time."

The conviction in his voice hit her like a spark to dry kindling. Sudden, searing, and impossible to ignore.

It lit something deep inside her. Not just hope but need. A pounding ache that pushed against her ribs, rising into her throat. The helplessness, the fear, the wanting to do something all crashed into her at once, fierce and unrelenting.

She had to find the answer. She didn't know how. Didn't care how. Only that it was there. Buried somewhere in that infernal whispering book, tangled in the thorns and the ink and the truth it never wanted her to see.

And she would find it. Even if it destroyed her. *She would find it.*

"How much time does he have?" she asked.

He shook his head. "Only the hourglass knows."

The hourglass that was nearly empty. The hourglass that ticked away more of his life with every drop of sand.

He leaned forward, and for the first time since she'd known him, Dickens reached for her.

It startled her—not the touch, but the choice to touch her at all. His hand settled on her forearm, cold and light, like he wasn't quite sure he was allowed to make contact. His fingers were long, too long, and there was something off about them. About *him.*

The chill of his skin bled through her sleeve.

Not cold from the draft. *Lifeless.*

Her breath hitched.

It felt like he was fading before her eyes. Like he'd been carrying this story for too long, and it had finally begun to hollow him out from the inside. His hand trembled faintly, and still he didn't let go.

For one awful heartbeat, she wondered if death had already begun to take him, and he was simply trying to leave something behind before it finished the job.

"You must help him, my lady. You *must* break the curse. If you do not, he will roam this world forever in his beast form. And this…" He swallowed hard, shook his head, and leaned back in the chair releasing her. "This place will be no more."

"This place?"

"This castle will disappear. And so will I."

CHAPTER 25

*D*isappear.

The word haunted her.

The thought of Leopold remaining a beast forever sliced pain deep within her. The thought of Dickens disappearing from this world forever distressed her. And she was the only one to save them from this abhorrent fate. The weight of that knowledge pressed down on her as she carried their desperate hope on her shoulders alone. Her hands broke into a cold sweat. Her mouth turned bone dry.

She never wanted this responsibility. She never asked for it. She did not know what she was agreeing to that day on the street outside the bookshop when Leopold—a prince—hired her to translate the book with no name. But she accepted it now and she would do her best to finish translating the book. She rose from the table, smoothing her damp palms down the length of her skirt.

"I *will* find the answer, Dickens." She sounded far more confident than she felt.

A rush of relief flickered over his face as he gave her a rare, weak smile. Then it was gone in an instant, his expression returning to the passive one to which she was so accustomed.

Her attempts to read the thorny language were, at best, difficult. The runes were not willing to give up their secrets so easily. And though she had not figured out the remaining words in the book, her resolve remained strong. She experienced moments of breakthrough. And other moments when she simply stared at the page, the thorny lines swimming before her tired eyes.

The idea of going to that cavernous library alone, divided from Leopold, sent a cold pang of longing through her. She couldn't bear it. She didn't need the library's endless shelves or ancient tomes to find the answers. She only needed her magical mind to work. And she needed to be close to him while she worked. Not only to be near him with nothing more than the small space separating them, but to ground her. To help her focus. To help remind her what was at stake and what she was fighting for.

Him. She fought for *him.* For his very existence as a man.

It would give her courage and motivation to untangle the thorns.

"I wonder if, perhaps, I would be able to remain with Leopold while I work?" she asked.

It was a long shot. Dickens may want her to stay far away from him while he was in his current state. But the old valet didn't seem bothered by her request.

"There is a writing desk in his bedchamber you can make use of. You should be able to find parchment and a quill and inkwell there as well."

She hadn't seen it when she entered the room, but then, her sole focus was on Leopold lying ashen-faced in the bed.

"Thank you, Dickens."

As she turned to go, his voice stopped her. "I do hope you find the answer, my lady."

"So do I, Dickens. So do I."

He didn't offer to escort her back to his room. She was able to find her way alone. She headed back up the stairs, the blue-white candelabra following her the whole way. She paused at the door, taking a deep breath to calm her nerves, and then she pushed open his door and entered once again.

He continued to sleep. She watched the slow rise and fall of his chest as he breathed in deep.

On silent feet, she walked into the room, closing the door and heading through the chamber. The heavy curtains on the window blocked out all the light, not that there was any to block. She headed for the writing desk Dickens mentioned. A pile of books were haphazardly stacked on the floor to the side of the desk. The top was cluttered with papers, scrolls, more books, unopened letters, invitations to long-ago balls that had gone unanswered. A navy coat hung over the back of the chair as if he had put it there only moments ago.

The unlit hearth was cold and dark. She peered at it a long moment as she recalled when he told her the tale of his cursing in his private sitting room. How he said one word, and it sprang to life. She clutched her elbows, warding off a shiver. The room was chilled. So, she approached the hearth, peering down at the gray and black ash that was under the grate.

"Fire, please," she whispered.

And moments later, the hearth lit with a crackling, vibrant fire that immediately warmed the room.

She smiled, pleased. "Good. Now, keep it going."

Turning back to the room, her gaze swept over it. The ornate wardrobe carved in a flowing elegance was to one side. The door was left ajar, as though someone reached for something in haste and forgot to close it. A pair of boots sat nearby, polished and perfect yet with a scuffed bottom, worn from pacing or walking halls he rarely let himself leave. Shoes and clothes of a man who kept himself together on the inside, even as he frayed on the outside.

There were no portraits here. No tapestries or family heirlooms here. No crown on display. No reminders of his distant past. Nothing to show he was once a prince.

But that wasn't right, was it? Dickens called him prince, but Leopold was truly a king. When his father was killed, he had taken the crown of the kingdom—a kingdom that now only existed in books of myth and legend. The remnants of it swept away into the shards of the past.

This place, this room with its solemn quiet and palpable loneliness, was his throne room. Even the light moved differently here as it dragged across the rug-covered floor in long, sweeping lines. The way the shadows stalked him. He called himself a recluse. But she had met him in daylight. In a bookshop. Surrounded by stories. Was it coincidence? Or something more?

Fate, perhaps.

She wasn't here by accident. She felt that now, deep in her essence. She was meant to be here, just as she was meant to find the rose among the thorns.

Bella shook herself out of her thoughts and tidied up the desk to give her enough space to work. When she had all the loose papers neatly stacked and put aside, she returned to the chair beside the bed to pick up the cursed book. As she approached, he emitted a faint moan, as though he were in pain.

She halted there, frozen mid-reach as her gaze landed on him, watching the slow rise and fall of his chest. He still breathed but his face was contorted in pain. Despite her better judgement, she moved to the side of the bed. A desperate need to touch him skipped through her.

Leaning down, she intended to whisper to him, to let him know she was there, to give him that comfort. As she did, he lifted his hand and touched her cheek, as though he sensed her nearness. His skin was cold, clammy and yet the moment he touched her, every part of her sang in elation.

His eyes fluttered open, meeting hers. Her breath halted, pooling deep in her chest as they locked eyes. Her pounding heart throbbed, and she was certain he heard it, too. As he looked at her, she saw there such deep, raw emotion it nearly ripped her in half. His features softened. His hand brushed over her cheek again, sliding to the back of her neck and resting there, tugging her closer with a gentle nudge.

She did not resist him.

Oh, he was going to kiss her. She sensed this deep within her and suddenly it was her dearest wish. To feel his lips brush against hers when she had only felt them on her hand. The breath she held shuddered out of her.

"Bella." Her whispered name was on his lips as though it were a longing.

But he made no move to pull her closer.

"Yes?" she finally said, her voice trembling.

He didn't answer. His eyes fluttered closed, and his hand dropped as though all strength left him in a rush. In moments, he was asleep once more. The absence of his hand on her cheek left her mourning the loss of his touch.

She straightened, trying to calm her ragged breathing and the wild beat of her heart. She pressed her hand there, closing her eyes and taking deep breaths. It was silly to think he was going to kiss her. She shoved away the thought, then snatched the book. She hurried to the desk and got to work.

Bella did not know how long she hunched over the desk, writing and scribbling and scratching out words. She was no closer to solving the strange language than she was that morning. Frustration edged through her. She tossed the quill on the desk in annoyance.

The longer she stared at the runes, the more discouraged she got. The letters simply were not forming for her. Why? What had changed? Was it because she was no longer in the library? Was it because she was so close to Leopold? Or perhaps it was because she was close to solving the riddle.

She didn't know.

Her back ached. She had ink stains on her fingers. Her head throbbed and, she realized, her stomach rumbled from desperate hunger. She had not left the desk or the room since returning. The only thing she had earlier that day was a bit of tea. She didn't recall if she actually ate the offered scones.

When she tired of sitting at the desk, she stood up, arched her back to stretch it, and then walked around the desk. Keeping distance between her and the bedridden Leopold, she made sure he was still breathing and all was well. The *veil-shade* that had attacked him must have taken much from him, for he hadn't moved again. He hadn't made a sound.

A light knock on the door sounded before it pushed open and there was Dickens on the other side.

"My lady, it's nearing dusk."

"Oh," she said breathing the word in surprise. Had she really been here since nearly sunrise?

"The carriage is waiting for you." He pushed the door wider and stepped aside in anticipation of her leaving.

Her gaze slipped from Dickens in the doorway to Leopold still sleeping in the bed to her discarded bonnet and gloves still in the chair.

"Do you think... what will happen to him tonight?" she asked. She cast her glance back to Dickens.

Worry lines creased his forehead. "He will likely shift again. It's best you are not here when that happens."

She wanted to question him why, but she remained mute. It occurred to her the beast inside Leopold *knew* who she was the night before when his pale brown gaze landed on her. He made no move to hurt her. Her gaze swiveled back to Leopold.

"Because he's dangerous?" she asked.

"Because he does not want you to see him like that. Come, my lady. The day wanes."

She understood then. Leopold was proud and there must be something deep inside him that despised knowing she saw him in his beast form.

"I'll gather my things."

She returned to the desk and gathered the book and the notes she made. Then, at the chair by the bed, she snatched up her gloves and bonnet but didn't put them on. She cast one more longing look at Leopold, but he remained sleeping.

At the door, she looked up at Dickens. "Look after him for me."

"As I always do, my lady." He gave a low bow and a faint smile as he said it. Then he ushered her out the door.

CHAPTER 26

She was gone again.

The moment she stepped out his bedchamber door was the moment the loneliness returned.

Leopold prided himself on his restraint when it came to Bella, but in his weakened state, his guard was down, and he was quite overcome with emotion. He sensed her stepping closer to the bed when he emitted a faint moan. He hadn't intended to let that slip, but the pain was intolerable. And then there she was, bending over him. The faint aroma of her perfume—something soft and delicate, like her—wafted to him. He inhaled it with a silent breath, relishing it, savoring it, basking in it.

His first mistake was lifting his hand to touch her face. When he did, everything changed forever. Her skin was velvety, her cheek warm. He heard the almost imperceptible intake of breath. He was quite overcome as his hand slid around to the nape of her neck where tendrils of wispy hair rested.

Then he made his second mistake. Opening his eyes to gaze up at her. He had no words for her beauty. No words to describe how she made him feel. Her brilliant blue eyes were wide and round and gleamed with wonder. The dark pupils expanded with yearning. Her face was flushed. Her pulse pounded like a hummingbird's delicate wings. Her delicate lips parted in anticipation, and he realized with a wild, unfettered emotion, he was going to kiss her.

Her name escaping through his own lips was a prayer, a plea, a desperate need. She had no idea she looked at him with yearning. He pulled her closer with a gentle nudge. When she did not resist him, the surprise and delight edged through him. Oh, how he wanted to kiss her. To taste those delicate, pink lips. To pull her into his arms and ravish her.

Deep down, the warning clanged through him, pounding his mind. If he kissed her, if he touched her lips with his, he would never be able to stop. He would pull her into his arms, into his bed, and he would love her forever.

So, he released her, closed his eyes and feigned sleep once again. A fervent prayer flickered through his mind for her to step away, to move out of arm's reach, to expand the distance between them.

She did just that, but to his horror, she remained in the room with him. He heard the shuffle of papers, the sigh as she sat in his chair at his writing desk. He imagined her nimble fingers picking up his favorite quill and dipping it into the inkwell. Then the scratch of the tip on parchment, her faint muttering as she continued to try to translate the book.

Why had Dickens allowed her to stay here with him? Why did he not send her back to the library? That cold, cavernous library where she would remain alone. Thinking of her alone in that room sent a pang of despair through him. He did not want her to be alone. Not there. Not ever.

He chanced a peek at her. Across the room, shrouded in shadows, she was absorbed in her work, her head bent over the book. One hand rested on the aged page before her while she scribbled madly, then scratched out in frustration. He watched her from the haven of his bed, knowing all the while he was falling madly in love with her. Knowing all the while he would never have her.

Now, in the deafening silence, he stared at the ornate ceiling. Dickens had arrived to usher her home. Dickens knew, like he did, what was to come when the sun dipped below the horizon. The brand on his arm already started to burn, to sear, to throb. Though the full moon waned and was nothing more than a crescent, he continued to change into that horrendous beast. His alteration had not stopped as the full moon diminished.

Returning footsteps signaled Dickens came back. The door pushed open. His valet remained in the entrance, not moving.

"Come in, Dickens." His voice was raw, thick, and heavy with emotion. He had wallowed in his self-pity long enough.

Dickens appeared at his side, moving the vacant chair out of the way. Concern etched his pale features.

"Is she safely away?" he asked.

Dickens nodded. "In the carriage returning to Hawthorne. It's time, my prince."

He waved him away. "No, Dickens. The bonds do not help. I will only break through them again."

He shoved off the blankets and swung his legs to the side of the bed, the hot pain from the slashes in his chest lancing through him. He winced and uttered a low groan.

"Are you certain, my prince?"

"Help me up. Take me to the gardens, Dickens," he said, ignoring his question.

"But—"

"The time is near. I cannot stop it, even if I wanted to. Take me to the gardens where I will do the least amount of damage," he insisted.

Dickens nodded, though it was clear he wanted to protest. He remained mute as he placed a hand under his arm and hoisted him to his feet. He wore nothing but the torn trousers and the bandage around his mid-section. When his bare feet hit the floor, he shuddered. He stayed upright, though, despite the agony spreading through him.

His valet wrapped an arm around his waist and helped him across the room, to the door. Leopold focused on every step as he made his way out. One more step and then another step and on and on until he reached the landing at the top of the stairs.

He paused there, to take deep breaths and stave off the shear pain. Dickens did not speak. He waited patiently for him to begin again.

Down the stairs. One slow step at a time. He needed something to distract him, so he turned his thoughts back to Bella.

"Why did you allow her to remain in my room?"

"She did not want to spend the day, alone, in the library, my prince. I thought it would do no harm for her to watch over you." He said this as though he were speaking of nothing more than the weather on a fine day.

He wanted to retort that it was quite harmful—to him. To his psyche. To his very existence. Could his valet not see how much she affected him? How much he wanted her?

"She's quite taken with you," he added, his voice soft as though whispering a secret.

Oh, gods, he didn't need to know that about her. He wanted to forget her. He wanted to push her out of his mind forever. But he knew that was folly.

He would never be able to forget her. He would never be able to push her from his mind forever. He loved her.

It was impossible to think she loved him back, though. He was cursed to live as man and beast. And, if she didn't find the way to break the curse, he would roam the world forever as that immortal beast. Never to feel her touch again. Never to see her beauty again. Never to hear her voice again.

He couldn't bear the thought. The anguish was too raw, too real.

They were at the bottom of the stairs. He paused to take another deep breath, to take a rest while he regained his strength once again for the remaining journey to the dark gardens.

"Is there any reason to hope?"

"She's quite determined to succeed," he said. "Do not give up yet, my prince."

He glanced at his old companion to see the optimism and the hope glinting in his dark eyes. If Dickens continued to have faith, then he would, too.

Nodding, he said, "Let's continue."

After a laborious long walk to the castle gardens, where night flooded the area, he was relieved to perch on the edge of a bench. Dickens released him and stepped back, waiting no doubt for the inevitable.

A glance overhead to see the sky dotted with twinkling stars and the quarter moon glaring down at him. He closed his eyes as the shift took hold of him. The burning sensation from the brand on his arm was the first sign. Then, the pain ripped through him. He staggered to his feet, the guttural feral scream ripping from his throat as the shift started in his legs, then moved upward to his torso, down his arms, and finally his head and shoulders.

He tilted his head back and snarled, then howled at the quarter moon, his transformation complete. With his feral instincts taking over, he bounded from the castle gardens and into the night.

The familiar carriage was parked outside Hawthorne Hall when she arrived. *Lord Vincent*. A wave of apprehension shifted through her as she froze there, staring at the house with the yellow candlelight dancing behind the lace curtains. Warm. Cheerful. Welcoming.

A contrast to the enchanted castle she left behind with a secluded man who needed her.

Lord Vincent had come to call, and she was not at home. Dread pounded through her. She did not want to see him, but she suspected he was there to see Emmaline. At least, she hoped he came to see the girl and not her.

The distant howl sounded through the night. She halted on the stoop and turned to stare into the inky darkness. Squinting, she tried to make out any movement that was there, but she saw nothing and no one.

An eerie sensation swept up her spine, the hairs on the back of her neck stood on end. There was something out there. Something that skulked through the shadows, searching. Though she didn't see the *veil-shade*, she suspected they were still out there.

The howl sounded again. Sucking in a breath, she reached for the doorknob and pushed open the door, stepping inside quickly and closing it with a snap behind her. She pressed her back against the door, her heart beating wildly.

Movement in the parlor caught her attention. She straightened and did her best to put on a bright smile, as if nothing was amiss. Emmaline appeared in the doorway. Lord Vincent stood behind her. They both gave her a curious look.

"Oh, Bella, you've returned," Emmaline said. "Lord Vincent is here." She motioned to the man standing behind her, her cheeks turning a pale pink.

"I see that." Bella moved toward the foyer table and placed the book there, hoping neither of them saw it. She pulled off her gloves in haste, dropping them on top of the book. Then she removed her bonnet and turned to the two of them and continued to force a pleasant smile. "You've come to call on my Emmaline, have you?"

Lord Vincent moved around the girl to greet Bella. He reached for her hand, taking it in his, and kissed the top of it with his cool lips. She slipped her hand away.

"I do hope this is not an imposition," he said.

"Not at all. Is there tea?" She peered into the parlor hoping there was something to eat. Her stomach emitted a fierce rumble.

"Yes," Emmaline said and moved back into the room.

She immediately started to work and poured a cup as Bella entered, Lord Vincent on her heels. Bella gratefully accepted the warm brew, relishing the bergamot scent wafting up to her. It was a long, tiring day, and the last thing she wanted to do was entertain a guest.

"Miss Emmaline said you were interested in the unfinished manuscript you were translating," Lord Vinent said. He motioned to the book and a stack of papers on the low table between the chairs. "I brought it."

"Oh, thank you for bringing it. Now, I can finish my work." She sat near Emmaline, holding the cup and eyeing the small finger sandwiches on the tray. It was long past dinner time.

"I can pay you the remaining fee in advance, if you like," he said.

Her gaze lifted to him, peering at him over the top of her cup. It occurred to her he suspected she wanted to finish the translation because she needed money. Because her father was still in the port. Because her father's business was in ruination. Because she was facing the downfall of the estate.

"That's not necessary," she said with a pleasant smile. She wanted to make it clear she was not desperate. "You can pay me upon delivery of the final translation. I should have that ready for you in the next day or so."

An awkward silence descended between the three of them. She was desperately tired, yet she was unable to think of nothing else but the cursed book on the foyer table.

"I should be going." He rose to his full height, his gaze flickering between the two of them before landing on Emmaline. "Miss Emmaline, thank you for your hospitality." Then he turned to Bella. "I shall take my leave."

He headed for the door where he paused to collect his hat and overcoat. Guilt slashed through her, though she was unsure why. It was as though her arrival had interrupted their intimate meeting. She was at a loss for words, though. She glanced at Emmaline who looked disappointed by his leaving.

Bella placed her cup on the table and followed him to the door. Emmaline remained in the parlor.

"Thank you for bringing the book, Lord Vincent."

He had paused in the foyer, his keen gaze on the cursed book underneath her bonnet and gloves. Her nerves rattled, and she resisted the urge to dash to the book and scoop it up. He turned to her, then, his gaze meeting hers.

"I do hope all is well with you, my lady." He said no more, but the hint was there. He hoped she was all right while her father was absent and faced who-knows-what terrible things in the port.

"I am well, thank you."

She reached for the door and pulled it open. The balmy night air spilled inside along with a scent of something wild and untamed. Her breath caught as she snapped her head toward the darkness. She thought she saw the flash of pale brown eyes in the night. Her heart clawed its way to her throat. Her first impulse was to put her hand on Lord Vincent's arm to stop him from stepping outside.

"Are you sure you can't stay for another cup of tea?" she asked.

"The hour is late, my lady," he replied as he placed his hat on his head. He gave her a brief nod and stepped out the door.

The moment he did, a low, savage growl sounded through the night. Close. It was so close. He halted one step outside the door and stiffened, his gaze flickering through the shadows. A shudder of fear ran through her as she remained rooted to her spot within the threshold. If she darted into the night, Lord Vincent would try to stop her. She feared what would happen if she did that and if Leopold, the beast, saw him do it.

She stepped through the threshold and planted herself between Lord Vincent and where she suspected the beast was.

"You're quite right, Lord Vincent. The hour *is* late. I do thank you for calling on us to see how we're faring while my father is otherwise indisposed. It was quite gallant of you." Her incessant chattering was far too brash.

He cut her a curious glance. "Yes, well, please let me know if you need anything. I'm happy to help."

"I will," she said with a nod and a smile that was painful.

Another low growl nearby. Her heart rammed hard and fast, and she silently begged Lord Vincent to get in the carriage and ride away before Leopold decide he was a threat.

"Good night, my lady," he said finally.

And then he was stepping toward the carriage, the footman was opening the door, and he was climbing inside. The door closed, the footman returned to his place, and they were off. The carriage rattled down the gravel drive, the wheels clattering in the night. She waited, watching it disappear, swallowed by the night shadows, before she turned back to the open door. She paused in the slash of light from the house, her head turned to one side. Though she couldn't see him, she knew he was there.

"He means us no harm," she whispered, hoping he heard her. "He is a friend. Nothing more."

A muffled rumble, as though he understood but detested the thought there was another man in her life.

"Go home, Leopold," she pleaded on a whisper.

Then she stepped inside and closed the door.

CHAPTER 27

As soon as the door snapped shut behind her, she exhaled the breath she held while Lord Vincent departed. She couldn't risk him knowing about Leopold, in beast or human form. But especially in beast form. If he found out about him—if anyone found out about him—she feared the consequences.

She appreciated the man's offer to help her and her household by offering to pay her before she finished her work. Refusing his offer was likely an insult, something she would have to deal with later.

Her duty of taking care of the household had been sorely neglected. It was something she had taken pride in before, when they lived in port and she had a full staff to help her. Now, she was down to Gerald, Edith, and Emmaline, and she hadn't even looked at the ledgers since they arrived. Helping Leopold, though, seemed far more important and urgent.

She waited there until her heart returned to normal. Emmaline exited the parlor with an unreadable expression on her face, her hands clasped in front of her. Perhaps she was disappointed at

Lord Vincent's hasty retreat. Or that she had barged in on their private meeting.

"Shall I help you retire for the evening, miss?" the girl asked.

Bella glanced at the cursed book still resting on the foyer table. She shook her head. "No, thank you. Not yet. I need some time."

Some time to continue to look at that book, to try to read the thorny language and find the answer to Leopold's wicked curse. The girl gave her a nod and headed up the stairs. Bella stepped to the foyer table and scooped up her belongings.

"Welcome home, miss. This arrived for you this afternoon." Gerald appeared from the other side of the manor, an unopened letter in his hand. He extended it to her. "It's from your father."

Her heart returned to its throbbing as she reached for the letter. "Thank you, Gerald. I'll read it in the library." Before she hurried away, she turned back to him. "I apologize for not being here, Gerald, but—"

"There is no explanation necessary, miss. I know you are doing what must be done to make sure we and the household is cared for."

She blinked surprise, unsure what he meant. Did he know she spent her days in the gloom of Thornhurst Castle?

"You do?" she asked.

"Yes, miss. Miss Emmaline said you've been in town. I assumed that meant you had taken a position at the bookshop to keep the larder well stocked, and the other bills paid until this nonsense with Mr. Rinaldi is settled."

She gaped at him. Emmaline covered for her? She owed that girl a debt of gratitude. Something else he said stood out. Apparently, there was a mysterious benefactor keeping them afloat. Words fled her mind, and she searched for some reply that sounded appropriate. Gerald stepped closer to her, then, his expression one of caring and concern.

"The three of us, that is Edith, Miss Emmaline, and I, appreciate all you're doing to make sure we're taken care of. I wanted you to know."

She was stunned. "Thank you, Gerald."

"Do get some rest, my lady. You look exhausted."

With that, he left her standing in the foyer shocked to the soles of her slippers. It took several moments for her to regain her senses. He didn't understand she had no time for sleep, though he was correct in that she was exhausted. Fatigue pounded through her, making her weary. Somehow, she found the energy to push onward through it all.

She glanced down at the letter in her hand desperate to read what her father had to say and hurried to the library where she shut the door, enclosing herself in deafening silence.

The window was still boarded, but the glass was cleaned up. She placed her things on the writing desk and quickly lit the candles to give the room a warm glow. Then she sat and stared down at the letter with the Port Leclare seal. Taking a deep breath, she broke the seal.

The penmanship was not his normal, careful script. It looked as though he hastily scribed or was under duress. Ink blotches appeared along the page and a few scratch-outs existed here and there.

When her father arrived back in Port Leclare, he was immediately taken into custody. He was in a portside jail awaiting the formal inquiry to conclude. Then he would appear in front of the local magistrate to attempt to clear his name. They suspected he was a smuggler of some type of contraband. His crew was dispersed. The manifest confiscated. His accounts seized. His merchant license suspended.

It was worse than she thought. Her hands shook as she read the last few lines.

I begged to write this letter to you so you would hear from me the situation. By now, I'm sure the gossip-mongers are doing their swift work. I did not do these terrible things, Bella. I am not a smuggler and would never put our livelihood at risk, nor would I put our reputation in jeopardy. But I fear this terrible misunderstanding will have cataclysmic consequences for both of us. I hope you can forgive me.

Stay in Hawthorne Hall for as long as you can. Do not come to the port to see me. I will not have you be a part of this abhorrent situation, too.

Numb. She was numb. There was no other word for how she felt at the moment as she read her father's letter. Lord Vincent didn't tell her he had been apprehended. Perhaps to save her feelings.

What was she to do now? He didn't want her in port. She understood that, and she agreed with his assessment. If she showed her face in the port, then she would face ridicule and haughty derision from the locals. Her father had carefully built his merchant reputation over the years and now it was in tatters.

She stared down at the cursed book, certain it was to blame for all the ill will that came to her and her father. With a careful hand, she refolded the letter and placed it aside, then reached for the book.

Her hands still shook as she cracked it open to the last page she was studying before she left Leopold's. Now, she was determined more than ever to find the answer and be rid of the book forever.

Silence encircled her. The only sounds were that of her shallow breathing and the scratching of her quill against the parchment, pausing only to dip it into the inkwell. The clink of the tip against the glass seemed deafening in the quiet.

Her hand wrote furiously, scratched out, wrote furiously again. As she peered at the runes, they seemed to move and transform before her eyes. As though rearranging when she was close to a breakthrough. If she didn't know any better, she suspected the book did not want her to find the answers buried there amongst the thorns.

Dropping the quill, she sat back in the chair, immense frustration edging through her. She covered her face with her hands, the hot tears pounding her eyes and threatening to fall. It took all her self-control not to swipe the book and the parchment with her notes to the floor.

She shoved up from the chair and paced the small confines of the room. Her back and neck muscles were stiff. Her hands ached from the tight grip she had on the quill. Her fingers were stained with ink.

The hope she would find something useful in the final translation of Lord Vincent's book diminished when she completed it. The story was nothing more than a child's bedtime fairytale. It did not aid in her translation of the cursed book at all. Another irritation.

What was she missing? What was she not seeing? There had to be *something* that eluded her. She halted there in the middle of the room, clutching her elbows and glaring at the book still open on the desk, the parchment next to it.

As she stared at it from across the room, she thought she heard a puff of breath. Then the parchment next to the book stirred. She remained where she was, frozen in place, as her eyes went wide and round.

There appeared to be faint movement on the page. As if the thorny vines and brambles shifted.

It had to be her imagination. She rubbed her tired eyes. She should retire and try again tomorrow. Forget about this cursed book for the rest of the night.

Outside, the mournful wail of the wolf's howl.

She glanced at the boarded window, expecting something to barrel through it. The beast. Or perhaps another *veil-shade*. But nothing happened. Nothing else stirred.

The candlelight flickered over the page, the shadows dancing across the aged paper. Again, she thought she saw the twisting vines moving across the page. And then it formed a word followed by an eerie whisper. As though it rearranged itself for her while she stared.

Tentatively, she moved closer, still clutching her elbows. When she was close, she peered down at the page. The word appeared before her tired eyes.

When

That was all. Nothing more.

Excitement pumped through her. She reached for the quill slowly hoping the book did not see her do it. Holding her breath, she picked up the pen and then inched closer to the desk. Standing behind the chair, she waited.

Two more words appeared.

the sky

Her gaze landed on the parchment next to the open book. She was desperate to sit and record the words. She pulled out the chair slowly, stepped around it, and perched on the edge. She wrote the three words *when the sky* and then sat back and waited.

The moment she jotted the words, they disappeared. The vines and thorns and brambles rearranged themselves and covered the letters. In place of the letters, a rose bloomed, the petals unfurling as though seeing the sunlight.

"Oh."

The word slipped out between her lips on a murmur.

She sat back in the chair and waited, gripping the quill so tight her fingers cramped.

Movement again on the page and this time, the vines revealed more words.

is blind and the stars

She sucked in a sharp breath and wrote the next line. As she finished, the pages changed. The roses bloomed.

Never in all her years of translating strange texts had she seen anything like this before. It was astounding.

Quickly, she dipped the tip of the quill in the ink and waited again.

Again, the same thing happened. The thorny vines wound around the odd shaped runes and then more words appeared. She wrote them in a hurry.

dare not shine

A breath hiccupped out of her as triumph flooded her. She made progress. Sitting back in the chair, she read the line altogether in a low voice.

"When the sky is blind and the stars dare not shine."

What did it mean?

Outside her boarded window, the wolf howled.

"When the sky is blind..." she repeated, her mind racing.

She shot from the chair and prowled the small library, her heart drumming against her chest as excitement pounded through her. She thought she knew what it meant as she searched the shelves for a book that might tell her. Her father was always bringing home new and wonderful books about anything and everything. He loved all subjects and read voraciously.

When she found the one she wanted, she pulled it off the shelf and flipped it open, the musty scent of the ancient pages fluttering up to her nose. Then she saw it and halted, staring down at the page that was a drawing of the phases of the moon.

A blind sky. The new moon?

Stars dare not shine might indicate the total darkness of night that seemed to swallow the stars.

Was the new moon the key to breaking the curse? Or did it mean if the curse was not broken by the new moon, he would forever remain a beast?

She glanced at the cursed book. The book that played tricks and liked to hide the meaning behind cryptic messages that she was forced to unravel. She understood, now, how it worked. She understood how to reveal the hidden messages behind the brambles and thorns and vines.

Patience was key. Let the message reveal itself.

Now more determined than ever, she tossed aside the celestial book and went back to the desk. She had more work to do.

CHAPTER 28

Morning came.

When she awoke, her neck hurt. At some point in the night, she moved to the small two-seat sofa unable to sit upright anymore. The decorative pillow under her face was scratchy and uncomfortable. Her back ached. Her head throbbed. Her stomach growled. She was still in her dress from the day before. Her fingers were still stained with ink.

Sunlight seeped around the edges of the boarded window. She sat upright, the book that was on her chest falling to the floor with a thump. The candles she had burned were down to nothing but nubs and snuffed out of their own accord.

But she had made progress. The book revealed one more line to her.

The final form shall take root.

The final form must refer to the beast form. Leopold would forever be a beast when the sky was blind, and the stars did not shine.

A swift knock on the library door sounded. She stiffened and waited as the door opened a moment later and Gerald stood there gaping at her.

"Miss?"

"Oh, is it morning already?"

She gave a yawn and a stretch, pretending as though she merely fell asleep reading. She reached down and picked up the fallen book, closing it with a snap. It was the book about celestial events. She tucked it in her arm, holding it.

"Did you sleep here?"

"Yes, I suppose I did. I was exhausted when I returned yesterday. I must have fallen asleep reading."

It was, after all, the truth.

She forced a smile and cut a glance to the cursed book, now closed, still on the writing desk. Rising, she stepped casually toward the desk and picked it up along with the parchment with her notes. She held it in her arms along with the book on celestial events.

"What time is it?" she asked.

"Half-past eight, miss."

Oh, gods. She missed the carriage. "I'm late."

She hurried past Gerald. He said something about breakfast, but she wasn't interested. She needed to change her dress and get to town, hoping Leopold's carriage was still there waiting for her. If he wasn't...she didn't know how she would find her way to the shadowy castle.

Emmaline was coming out of Bella's room when she bounded up the stairs.

"There you are, miss. I was looking for you." Her gaze flickered up and down her. "You're still wearing yesterday's gown?"

"Yes, and I need you to help me change. Quickly."

Emmaline followed her into her room. Bella tossed both books on her still made bed. She kicked off her shoes. She caught a glimpse of herself in the mirror on her dressing table and halted. She hardly recognized herself. Deep shadows lay under her eyes. Her face was lined with fatigue. Sprigs of hair sprung from the side of her head. Her perfect chignon was untidy. In a frenzy, she tugged the hairpins from her hair, dropping them on the table.

Emmaline was at her wardrobe pulling out a pale blue dress.

"You're leaving again today?" the girl asked.

"I have to. I must." She pulled her fingers through her tangled hair.

When she looked at Emmaline, she saw the worry on the girl's face. Then her gaze flickered to the book resting on the bed.

"It's that book, isn't it?"

"What about the book?" Bella tried to make it sound as though it was nothing special, nothing important.

"You've never let it out of your sight since the night of the fire."

Bella gaped at her. What could she say to that? She was right, of course. She had carried it with her almost everywhere. Emmaline's gaze met hers.

"What is it?"

"A translation. Nothing more." The words rushed out of her. She tried her best to make it sound as though it was nothing more than an ordinary book. "Help me with the dress, Em."

She turned, pulling her hair to the side and waited for the girl to unbutton the back of her gown. There was a long silence, then she put aside the dress she held and went to work. Bella blew out a breath between her lips, grateful for Emmaline's help.

Minutes later, she was dressed in the pale blue day dress. Her hair was tidied once again. Rather than her normal chignon, she pulled it back at the nape and tied it with a matching blue ribbon. She didn't want to take the time to fuss with the elaborate hair style. She grabbed her bonnet, her gloves, and then slipped her feet into her shoes.

"Thank you, Em. I hope you know how much I appreciate you."

"I do." The girl chewed on her lower lip. "But are you certain you have to leave again?"

"Yes," she said with conviction. "Send a note to Lord Vincent. Tell him I finished his translation. You can find it and his book in the library. I left it there on the desk."

"Yes, miss."

"I'll be home by nightfall."

And then Bella picked up the books and left, her heart pounding a wicked beat as she hurried down the stairs and out the front door without stopping for breakfast. She hoped the carriage was still there, waiting for her to arrive. If it wasn't, she decided, she'd start walking. Determination pounded through her. She had to get there. She had to see Leopold.

She hoped she didn't have to start walking.

At the edge of town, with her legs burning from her hurried exertion, she thought she spied the carriage with the familiar Thornhurst emblem of knotted thorns, vines, and blooms. Pushing herself to go faster, a jolt of relief spiked through her. It was truly there. Standing beside it was Dickens with a pinched look on his face as his dark eyes scanned the crowd.

She started to lift her hand in a wave when a sudden movement to her left caught her attention. A familiar voice called her name. She halted where she was, startled to see Lord Vincent headed right for her.

Oh, gods, what was he doing here in Driftbell? She was dismayed to see him and that he had not returned to his palatial home in Port Leclare.

"Good morning," he called, a smile plastered on his face as he greeted her.

She did not want to see him. She did not want to delay getting to Leopold. She cast a glance toward Dickens who had stiffened next to the carriage. His dark, baleful eyes under bushy brows observed her with keen interest as Lord Vincent halted next to her.

"I'm delighted to see you here this morning," he said, reaching for her gloved hand.

She didn't want to be rude, so she allowed him to take it. A breath of a kiss passed over the back of it. Then she tugged it away and clutched the books to her chest.

"Lord Vincent, what a surprise. You stayed in town?" Her voice was breathless from her near sprint to get to town.

"I thought it most prudent since it was late when I left last night. Are you well? You look a bit flushed."

"I'm fine, thanks, but I'm running late for an appointment. I must go."

His gaze landed on the book in her arms. He nodded toward it. "At the bookshop?"

He mistakenly assumed her appointment was there. How was she going to get away from him? She kept her focus on him, watching as the morning sun played upon his features. She didn't want to glance at Dickens and give away her next move.

Before she answered, he extended his arm to her. "I'll escort you."

He was determined to keep her close. A sense of urgency to get to Leopold pounded through her. She opened her mouth to reply, when Dickens was abruptly at her side.

"My lady, your carriage awaits." When he spoke, he gave a low bow.

"Who's this?" There was no mistaking the suspicion lacing Lord Vincent's words.

"This is…" But her words trailed off, an explanation escaping her.

"Her servant, sir," Dickens replied and gave Lord Vincent a bow. Then he turned to her and extended his hand to the carriage. "Shall we, my lady?"

Confusion etched on Lord Vincent's face. She didn't want to explain her situation. It was too much. She dipped a curtsy.

"Good day, Lord Vincent."

Then she hurried toward the carriage waiting for her. Dickens fell in step behind her. As they approached, he moved around her to open the door. She climbed inside quickly, sitting back into the cushioned seat and expelling a breath, placing the books in her lap. Dickens followed, closing the door behind him and moments later they were off.

"Thank you, Dickens."

As the carriage turned toward the road, she glanced out the window and saw, with much dismay, Lord Vincent watching them hurry away. A sense of foreboding flooded her. She hoped he would not follow, that he would forget he saw her. It was almost too much to hope.

Dickens settled into the seat across from her. "It appeared you needed assistance, my lady. I was glad to oblige."

"I appreciate it. Apologies for being late. I overslept." A feeble excuse, but it was the truth.

"Who was that man?" he asked, sounding more curious than accusatory.

"A business associate. I translated some text for him. Nothing more. Yesterday, he called on my maid."

A bushy brow lifted. "Your maid?"

"He has an interest in her." She waved it away as though it were nothing.

"I daresay that interest is not in her but you."

Her eyes snapped up to him. "Why do you say that?"

"My lady, I do still have keen senses despite my advanced age. It's not so difficult to see how he looked at you."

Oh, blast it all. She didn't need that kind of attention. But it was hard to ignore the way he gazed after the carriage as they rode by.

"I hope he doesn't follow us," she said with fervent conviction.

"Fear not, my lady. There are few who have the courage to approach Thornhurst Castle."

He sounded so sure of himself, it was hard not to believe him. "I do hope you're right, Dickens."

As soon as they arrived at the castle, she leapt out of the carriage the moment it halted. There, standing in front of the open door waiting for her, was Leopold. Pale shadowy light framed him, as if he'd been waiting there for hours. Perhaps he had. Her arrival was normally after sunrise. He was dressed, composed, not entirely whole, surely, but unyielding the same.

A dark high-collared coat hung open down the front, tailored but looser than usual which, she assumed, was meant to conceal the bandages wrapped around his torso. Beneath it, a soft black shirt, unbuttoned at the collar to hint at the expanse of smooth skin below, and untucked at the waist. Black trousers and his polished boots completed the look.

His dark hair was tousled as it usually was with one lock falling over his forehead, fluttering in the faint breeze.

There was no cravat. No waistcoat. Merely the quiet strength of the man who showed up to greet her.

The moment she was out of the carriage and their gazes met, the question glinting in his eyes faded away to be replaced by the light of elation. He didn't bother to hide his delight. A sweeping sensation coiled low and hot in her gut at his unabashed adoration. She was completely caught off guard with the sudden surge of feelings. Heat flamed in her cheeks. And though she met him on many occasions, today was different. Today, she sensed a deeper emotion emanating from him.

Saints preserve her. Her breath caught in her throat as he reached a hand to her in invitation. Gods, he was handsome in every way.

"You came," he said, his voice low and soft in the quiet morning. As though he worried she may not arrive at all.

"I overslept," she said.

He reached out for her hand as Lord Vincent did. But for Leopold, she jostled the books in her arms to willingly place her hand in his. He covered it with his free one. He held it there, the warmth of his skin pressing through the cotton gloves. A fervent wish to touch his hand without the barrier of the glove clanged through her.

He studied her for a long moment, the only sound the breeze swishing through the trees of the nearby forest. That and the wicked pounding of her heart against her chest. He tilted his head to one aside.

"Your hair is different."

She flushed again. "Yes, I didn't have time to—"

"I like it. It suits you," he said. "Much better than the other way."

Behind her, Dickens cleared his throat. "Shall we go inside, then?"

"Ah, yes." Leopold released her hand and stepped aside, motioning for her to enter first. "Would you like tea?"

She stepped into the grand foyer and spun to face him. "No. Leopold, I have news."

He blinked surprise at her sudden announcement. For a moment, they stood staring at each other and the words she practiced fled her mind. Did he remember last night? Did he recall, as the beast, that she sensed him outside the manor while Lord Vincent made his departure? Did she tell him she worked in the library into the wee hours of the night while listening to his distant howls?

"What news?" Hope tinged his words.

"I had a breakthrough." She reached inside the cover of the cursed book and slipped out the parchment with her messy script. She hated her handwriting was almost indecipherable, but she wanted to get down the words before they disappeared. "I was able to translate this line. *When the sky is blind and the stars dare not shine.*"

He leaned closer to her to get a better look at the paper, the scent of him washing over her. That familiar smell of winter and wildfire she came to associate uniquely him. That and the heat radiating off him that warmed her.

"What does it mean?" he asked.

"I think it has something to do with the new moon." She lifted her gaze from the parchment. Close. He was standing so close. "The new moon is coming."

Elation ignited deep in his eyes with a hint of relief. "Dickens, bring tea and breakfast to my sitting room. We will work in there today."

"As you wish, my prince."

CHAPTER 29

Leopold pressed a hand to the small of her back. With his other hand he motioned toward the grand staircase. She didn't hesitate as she turned toward them.

It was difficult not to touch her. With her standing so close, he scented her sweet, intoxicating fragrance. He was unable to resist touching her. She didn't recoil from him, much to his delight.

Together, they ascended the stairs and walked in silence down the hall to his private sitting room. The room with the offensive hourglass that ticked away the days of his life. With every shift of the sand, his end grew closer. But now, there was hope. Hope that she was closing in on the answer, the way to break the curse.

When they entered the room, he immediately hurried to the desk and began tidying it to give her space. She stood inside the door, clutching the book, and watching him with those ocean-colored eyes. Eyes he felt it was impossible not to get lost in.

He stacked papers, neat and orderly. Closed books and removed them, placing them on the floor. Found fresh parchment for her writings, his favorite quill, and an inkwell. But the hourglass remained.

He hadn't been able to move it. Not even touch it. It sat on the desk like a silent sentinel, its sand glowing faintly, unnatural, like starlight bleeding through a wound. Grain by grain, it marked the end, steady and unforgiving.

His end. Every time he looked at it, the urge to smash it warred with the knowledge that he couldn't. That it would outlast him. That it was already winning.

Finally, he stood back and waved her toward the desk.

With tentative steps, she headed toward him, still wearing her bonnet and gloves. With careful motions, she placed the book on top of the desk. That's when he noticed she carried another book as well. Something with a blue hardback cover and silver writing. When she tilted the book just so, he caught a glimpse of the title in silver. *Celestial Events.*

He stepped back to give her space. She removed her gloves and bonnet and dropped them on the desk next to the books. In one fluid motion, he scooped them up and removed them, placing them on one of the nearby side tables so they would be out of her way. Her lashes fluttered as she watched him do it, then granted him a smile.

"It's all right if I sit here?" She pointed to the chair behind the desk.

"Yes, of course."

Determined not to stare her down or fidget, he snatched up one of the books off the floor and flipped it open, pretending to be suddenly engrossed in the pages. Truthfully, the words were nothing more than dots on the page.

"Dickens will arrive soon with tea," he said, as though he needed to explain about the delay.

"Last night, I was able to decipher a second line," she said.

That caught his attention. "You did?"

"Yes. *The final form shall take root.*"

Her gaze was fixed on the paper in front of her, as though she were afraid to look at him. A strange sensation shifted through him as the words played over and over in his mind.

"The final form..." he said slowly, carefully. Though he was afraid to ask, he said it anyway. "What final form?"

"I take it to mean your beast form," she said, her voice barely above a whisper.

She looked up.

Whatever words he'd been holding onto scattered like leaves in the breeze.

Her eyes—gods, those eyes—held a depth that hit him like a blow. Raw dread. Grief. Something else he didn't dare name. All of it crashing into him in a single, unguarded look.

It gutted him.

The force of it struck deep, sharp and unrelenting, like she'd reached inside and found the last fragile piece of him still left untouched.

He couldn't look away. Wouldn't. Because at that moment, she saw him. All of him. The beast, the curse, the man.

And she didn't run.

"Well, then, we best unravel the rest of the riddle, eh?" He said it with bravado he didn't quite feel.

Before she replied, Dickens charged in with the cart. The teacups rattled with every roll of the wheels as he pushed it into the room. The decadent smell of delicious food wafted from the tray. Warm, golden freshly baked scones rested in a linen-lined basket. Clotted cream and strawberry preserves were served in delicate porcelain dishes. Soft-boiled eggs, crusty toast, and fruit completed the ensemble.

The faint aroma of Darjeeling tea wafted from the teapot. Comfort disguised as civility. Next to it, cubes of sugar and creamer.

"Shall I serve, my prince?" he asked.

"No, that will be all for now, Dickens."

He gave a nod of his head and departed.

Bella rose from the desk. "Oh, that smells wonderful."

"I take it you missed breakfast." He grinned at her as he poured her a cup of tea, then one for himself.

"Yes, I was in a bit of a rush to get out of the house." She gratefully took the tea, sipped it, and closed her eyes to enjoy the fruity, muscatel notes.

He picked up a small plate and handed it to her. "Help yourself."

Taking the plate from him, she filled it with reckless abandon. As though she hadn't had a proper meal in ages. When he had his plate, they sat together in the small seating area with the low table in the center enjoying the light breakfast in silence.

He was so overcome with emotion at having her there with him in this quaint almost perfect moment, his stomach cramped. He placed the plate on the table and sat back in the cushions of the sofa. He didn't want her to notice, but she noticed.

"Everything all right?" she asked. She stabbed half a soft-boiled egg with her fork and popped it into her mouth.

"Bella…" He pressed his lips together, unsure what he wanted to say.

No, that wasn't right. He knew exactly what he wanted to say. The words pressed at the back of his throat. So many things and all of them wrong. Too much. Too personal. Too dangerous.

What were they to each other, really? Associates?

It began that way. Simple. Transactional. He told himself it would stay that way, that he needed it to. But somewhere between the silence and the shared glances, the hours spent unraveling curses and shadows, the lines blurred.

And now? He couldn't name what they were anymore.

But he knew what he felt.

Undeniable. Irreversible. *Hers.*

And yet, how could she possibly feel the same?

Not when he was like this—broken, cursed, marked for ruin. He couldn't even offer her a future, only the weight of a name stained by magic and loss.

So, he said nothing.

Because the truth of what he wanted wasn't safe. And worse—it wasn't fair.

"Yes?" she asked, her tone light as she spread a touch of clotted cream over the end of her scone.

He watched her hands instead of her eyes. It was easier to look there. Easier to pretend this was a morning like any other. Tea and scones and not the moment everything might change.

He swallowed. The words he almost said twisted inside his chest like a knife in the gut.

Don't say it.

But she looked up then. A flick of her gaze. Not teasing. Not expectant. Just open. As if she already knew what he wanted to say and wasn't going to stop him.

"Nothing," he said finally, voice rough. He swallowed hard, forced a smile. "It's nothing."

She raised a brow, but didn't push as she took a bite of the scone. Somehow that felt like mercy. She set her plate aside with careful precision and rose to her feet.

"I should get back to work," she said, her voice soft. Neutral. Too neutral.

He didn't move. He watched her, every part of him wanting to reach out—to say something, anything—but the words remained locked tight in his thoughts.

She headed back to the desk. Though she remained in the same room with him, there was distance. As though there was a vast ocean between them. The tension pressed against his chest like a weight. Still, he said nothing.

He was a coward.

He picked up his book and pretended to read. Looking but not really seeing the words. Because if he spoke, it would come out wrong and ruin what little time he had left with her.

For now, he was going to relish the time he had left with her.

Bella opened the book to the page she studied the night before. She sat back in the chair, acutely aware of his presence in the room. His back was to her as he remained on the sofa, stiff and on edge. The tension stretched between them, taut and thin.

Something shifted between them. He emitted a silent form of communication she did not know or understand.

She told herself she didn't want to know. She didn't want to understand. She told herself there was no use in hoping for something more intimate between them. If she did not find the way to break the curse, he was doomed, and she would blame herself for that until she took her last breath.

The hourglass within arm's reach ticked away the hours and minutes with every shift of sand. The top had nearly emptied into the bottom. Time—his time—was running out.

Her gaze drifted back to the book. In the flicker of light from the overhead candles, the thorny vines shifted. With a careful hand, she reached for the nearby quill. As though a quick movement would startle the book into stilled silence.

A rune appeared with the letter N. Nothing more. She held her breath and waited. This was how it began the night before. How the letters and words formed. With stealthy movements, she slid a piece of parchment toward her, watching and waiting.

The letters formed words. The words a phrase.

Not beast. Not man.

She hastily wrote down the words. The vines rearranged, and the words disappeared as it had the night before. Now, she waited again. The letter S appeared. She gripped the quill tight in her hand until her fingers cramped. Her eyes were dry and gritty as she stared hard at the page watching the transformation. The phrase appeared moments later.

Something in between.

Dipping the tip in ink, she wrote this down under the previous line. Shifting vines. Disappearing words. Roses blooming in their place. Again, she waited.

How much time passed? Leopold shifted on the sofa, his book snapping closed. The only movement. The only sound. She wanted to tell him what she discovered and opened her mouth to do so when the thorns and vines revealed more words. She waited, holding her breath, watching every letter appear and writing down each one. The moment she did, blooming roses replaced each letter, covering the words. When she finished, she sat back again and stared at the words she had written.

Bound by thorn. Named by none.

Then she put the phrases she had discovered all together, writing them down on a clean parchment in careful script. She started from the beginning.

Shadows stir. The sands of time slip away.
Silence forever in the gloaming.
In the darkest night, no name remembered. No light is
welcome.
The hourglass bleeds its last.
When the sky is blind and the stars dare not shine.
The final form shall take root.

Not beast. Not man. Something in between.
Bound by thorn. Named by none.

"I have something." Her voice sounded loud in the quiet.

Leopold shot to his feet, moving around the edge of the sofa and coming to stand beside her at the desk. She looked up and watched as he stared down at her writing. His eyes flicked over every word, every line.

"When the sky is blind...you said that had something to do with the new moon?" he asked.

"Yes." She reached for the celestial events book, flipping it open to the page she marked. She lifted it up to show him. "We have very little time before the new moon."

He studied the phases of the moon as depicted in the drawing on the page. His brows pinched together.

"Tell me what you think it means?" he asked.

"I think *no light is welcome* means the darkest part of night, when there is a new moon and nothing to light the way. *The hourglass bleeds its last* must signify when the sands run out coinciding with this phase of the moon."

His gaze cut to the hourglass. He gave it a good stare before his eyes flicked back to the phases of the moon.

She continued, "*The final form shall take root.* That means you will become the beast and remain that way forever. I'm not sure what the last two lines mean."

"I do." His voice was rough, raw. *"Bound by thorn. Named by none.* It means the brand will never go away and my name, my castle, my very essence will be forgotten forever."

He straightened and stepped away from her. She sensed his unease, his distress, and shoved back from the desk. She got to her feet, the inkwell shivering on top of the desk by her sudden movement. Following her impulse, she stepped in front of him and took his hands in hers.

"This is not the last of the book. There are more pages yet. More runes to uncover."

Leopold stilled, not moving. Perhaps not even breathing as he looked down at their entwined hands. He was warm to the touch. His hands smooth, yet not soft. His grip strong, yet not cruel. Her heart thudded once, hard. She started to pull away, but he tightened his hold in a way that said *do not release me.*

Her mouth turned to ash. Her stomach threatened to heave her breakfast. As their eyes met, she saw the shimmering tenderness deep in his gaze. She recalled the day she stood beside his bed, the way he touched her face, the way he looked at her. It was much the same now. Then she thought—hoped—he might kiss her. Then she was afraid of how that made her feel. Now, she was no longer afraid of those feelings.

She tilted her head back, her lips parted as she loosed a breath. He dipped his head closer to her. The surroundings disappeared. Fading to the background. There was no sound other than her heart pounding like a war drum, the whoosh of her pulse in her ears, and the warmth of his hands on hers.

"Shall I remove the breakfast dishes, my prince?"

Dickens' voice made them jump apart, shattering the moment. She stumbled back toward the desk, her hands shaking as she reached for the chair to sit. Disappointment flooded her at the interruption. Leopold straightened and turned to his valet, as though nothing was amiss. As though they were not standing intimately close.

"Yes, thank you, Dickens." He sounded normal, strong and sure.

Bella busied herself at the desk, fiddling with the quill and keeping her gaze downcast. Her cheeks were warm, her nerves ragged. She allowed herself to be caught in the moment, to hope there was something between them.

Dickens picked up the discarded dishes and loaded them on top of the tray. He wheeled it out of the room, disappearing through the door without even so much as casting a backward glance at the two of them.

"I'm afraid I'm a distraction. I'll leave you to your work," Leopold announced.

Before she was able to protest, he was gone.

Chapter 30

Leopold did not return, much to Bella's dismay. She remained in his private sitting room at his desk, staring through bleary eyes at the book. The vines and brambles and thorns decided not to give up any more secrets. Yet she remained there. Waiting. Hoping.

Nightfall approached and that meant her time was up at Thornhurst Castle. She would have to leave and return to the village, then walk home alone in the gloaming. She dreaded it yet staying was not an option. Emmaline already had suspicions about her disappearances. It was only a matter of time before she started asking more prying questions. There was no explanation Bella wanted to share with her.

Coming here to Thornhurst, being with Leopold, was a secret she held dear to her. She didn't want to share him or his library with the rest of the world. Eventually, if—when—she broke the curse that would no doubt change. Something for which she was not prepared.

Dickens rapped softly on the door frame to get her attention. When she looked at him, she saw the disappointment, the desperation, the almost loss of hope deep within his gaze.

"It is time, miss."

She closed the book with a snap, then folded the papers with her writing in half and tucked them into the Celestial Events book. She scooped up both, retrieved her bonnet and gloves but didn't bother putting them on.

It was hard not to think about the way she touched Leopold's hands, the way she grasped him, the way he did not pull away. It was hard not to think about the way he looked at her, the way his gaze scanned her face, the way desire shadowed his eyes.

Her heart thumped.

She mustn't think of him this way. She must stop. She saw no future with him even when the curse was broken. She saw no way to explain him to her father. She saw no way to be with him in society.

"Miss? Are you well?" Dickens remained at his place in the doorway, his face shielded by the shadows, concealing his expression.

"Apologies, Dickens. I was lost in thought." She did not tell him she was lost in thoughts about Leopold.

She said nothing more as she walked out of his private sitting room and followed Dickens down the hall, the stairs, and to the front door. She half expected Leopold waiting there to bid her farewell, but he wasn't. Disappointment flooded her.

The carriage waited in its usual spot outside the door. Dickens escorted her out and pulled open the door like he did every night.

Hesitation swept through her as she paused there, then cast a glance at the valet.

"Leopold...is he...?"

"Still recovering from his injuries, my lady."

She nodded understanding. Then she stepped into the carriage. He closed the door behind her, sealing her inside deafening silence. Moments later, the carriage was away, bouncing over the gravel road in its haste to return her to the village.

A sigh escaped her as she peered out the window into the gloom. As the distance expanded between her and the castle, so did the loneliness.

Dickens returned inside the castle and immediately went up the grand staircase to Leopold's bedchamber. He hid out there all afternoon, almost as though he was avoiding the young lady.

And he suspected he was.

He would have to be blind not to see the way they looked at each other. They way his prince gazed with longing need at the beautiful young scribe. How could he not? She was alluring and kind-hearted. When he entered the private sitting area to remove the breakfast dishes, he walked in on a moment between the two of them. She held his hands clutched in her delicate ones. Her head was tilted back, her lips slightly parted in anticipation.

Interrupting them was the right thing to do. The only thing to do. Not that he wanted to keep them apart, but he feared Leopold faced emotions he had not had for anyone in a very long time.

Certainly, the usual dalliances with ladies existed in the past. They had come and gone like the wind. But he had never looked at those women with such utter overt longing. And when the curse took hold of him, everything changed. He changed.

But as he escorted the lady to the carriage that evening, he understood a deep yearning existed.

She loved him, even if she refused to acknowledge it. Likewise, Leopold loved her, though he refused to acknowledge it.

This was Dickens' chance to push them together. To make them see they were meant for each other. They belonged together.

At Leopold's bedchamber door, he knocked as a courtesy before entering. When he pushed open the door, Leopold stood at the windows, his hands behind his back, as he peered through the opaque curtains into the night.

"She left, I take it," the prince said without turning.

"She did."

"Another day gone." He inhaled a deep sigh, expelled it. "The sands of time are running out, Dickens."

"Yes, I know, my prince."

"She was able to translate more of the book, but the answer still eludes her."

Leopold remained with his back to him as he spoke, his voice stripped bare—bereft, almost hollow. Dickens said nothing. Better that way. Better to let him hold on to the last shreds of his pride.

He imagined it was difficult watching the sands slip away. Slow, relentless, cruel. The enchanted hourglass never hurried, never faltered. It simply drained him, grain by grain, and made him watch. To know one's fate was tied to that. To understand that when the last grain of iridescent sand fell to the bottom, life as he knew it was over.

Dickens tightened his jaw.

It would be the end of Leopold's cursed life. It would also be the end of the man he had once been.

The end of this castle. The end of *himself.*

Even so, he held onto hope the girl would find a way.

"I have faith she will find the answer," Dickens said.

At last, Leopold turned to face him. For the first time, he saw fear in the prince's eyes. It didn't sit well with him, for the prince always faced his fate with bravery and courage. He had never let the burden of the curse wear him down. Now, it appeared it was doing just that. Eroding away what was left of him.

"I hope you're right, Dickens," he said.

He swiftly moved into the room. "I am right."

Leopold's brows drew together in question. "You sound certain about that."

"I am and you should be, too. After all, it's clear the girl has feelings for you."

He gaped at him for a long moment, his jaw clenched. The muscles ticking along the edge. Then, he scoffed, "That's preposterous."

"Think what you will. But I saw the look she gave you earlier and the way she held your hands. She looked for you when she left. Hoping to see you before she got into the carriage and it took her back to the village."

He didn't know why he said it. It wasn't like him to push himself into Leopold's business. But for this—for her—he had to make him see she wasn't giving up. He shouldn't either.

If he didn't know any better, he'd swear the man blushed. When he got that under control, Leopold's face registered regret for not seeing her off. Though he didn't lie to the girl, the prince was still recovering from his injuries, it seemed kinder to tell her that than to tell her he was hiding in his room like a coward.

"The sun has almost set," Leopold said, ignoring his last words. "We best get to the garden."

CHAPTER 31

The clatter of the carriage was in the distance as Bella hurried down the footpath from the village. A longing burned through her with every step as she headed back to Hawthorne Hall. She wanted nothing more than to shut herself in the library and stare at the book, trying to see the shifting vines and thorns and brambles.

She saw the hourglass that day on the desk. There wasn't much time left.

Insurmountable pressure pounded through her. The deadline for his final transformation loomed like the last heartbeat of a life she hadn't realized she was fighting for or one that she so desperately wanted.

As she approached the manor, she saw the outline of the familiar carriage sitting out front. She halted there a moment, cradling the books in the crook of her arm and her gloves crushed in the fist of her hand.

What was *he* doing here again? This was the second night Lord Vincent visited while she was out.

She dropped the books at her feet and hastily pulled on her gloves, then dropped the bonnet on her head, foregoing tying it. Scooping up the books, she headed for the door, trying to squelch the sudden panic that rose to her throat.

Once she was inside, soft laughter emitted from the parlor. Candlelight danced in the foyer and the strong aroma of roasted meat filled the air. She'd missed dinner again. Her stomach let her know its displeasure at skipping yet another meal.

When the door closed with a snap, the voices stopped. Footsteps, then Emmaline popped out of the parlor with an expectant look on her face.

"Oh, Bella, Lord Vincent is here."

"Again. Yes, I see."

She moved to the doorway of the parlor, stepping around the girl. Lord Vincent stood by the fireplace. His pristine white gloves were on the low table as well as his top hat.

"I came for the final translation of the book you provided," he said, without greeting. "I'm impressed you finished it so quickly." His gaze raked over her, studying her, as though looking for something out of place on her person.

She clutched the books tighter. "I'm glad I was able to finish it for you."

"Miss Emmaline was gracious enough to allow me to stay for dinner," he said, a smile playing upon his lips.

Bella cut her a glance as annoyance lanced through her. The girl, at least, at the decency to flush, her cheeks turning pink.

"Is that so? I don't recall her being the lady of the house."

"I-I'm sorry, Bella. I—"

"Miss Rinaldi, may I have a word with you?" Lord Vincent interrupted, effectively hushing Emmaline. "Alone."

Her gaze swiveled back to him as curiosity—and a tiny bit of distress—flicked through her. "Em, will you take these books to the library and leave them on the desk for me, please?"

"Yes, miss." She nodded and gave a little curtsy as she took the books from her and slipped down the hall.

Bella stepped into the parlor, closing the door behind her and remaining where she was. Thick tension filled the air. There was something disturbing about the way he looked at her from across the room. As though he had a sordid secret he was prepared to share with her. As though he knew something that would ruin her reputation forever.

She didn't like it.

And she thought of their morning encounter and worried that somehow he followed her to Thornhurst Castle. Perhaps he thought he knew something. Perhaps he was wrong.

She tried to steer the conversation the way she wanted it to go. "If this is about my father—"

"No," he said. "It is not."

She stiffened. She refused to sit and invite him to do the same. Because that would mean she accepted him into her home, and she was perfectly fine with him here. She wasn't. She wanted him to leave. She wanted him gone.

She lifted a brow, trying to remain calm. "And what is it then?"

"Where did you go this morning when you climbed into that carriage?" he asked, point blank.

She was momentarily caught off guard by the question. For a moment, she could only blink at him, the words lodging somewhere useless in her throat. She hadn't expected the edge in his voice. A flicker of something ugly—hostility, maybe even suspicion—broke through his otherwise polished demeanor, and she felt it like a slap she hadn't seen coming.

It rattled her. More than she wanted to admit.

She straightened instinctively, gathering the shreds of her pride around her like armor, even as something small and raw twisted inside her chest.

"I don't think that's any of your concern, Lord Vincent."

He paced the confines of the small room, prowling up and down as though he were a predator about to pounce. The tight clasp of his hands behind his back did little to disguise his stiff energy.

"Perhaps not." His voice too smooth, too sharp around the edges. He turned, fixing her with a look that made her spine stiffen. "I asked around about that carriage," he went on, each word deliberate. "The one with the carvings of thorns and roses in bloom."

She forced herself to hold his gaze, even as her pulse stumbled in her throat.

"No one knows it." His tone dropped lower. "No one seems to have seen it. No one...except for me." A beat of silence "And you."

The room seemed to shrink around her, the air growing heavier with each syllable he spoke. The unspoken accusation in his voice wrapped around her like thorns. Tight, cutting deeper with every breath.

"Where did you go?" His gaze narrowed as he asked it. "Or perhaps I should ask, who were you with?"

She backed up to the door, reaching behind her for the knob. With a twist, she shoved it open. She didn't want to answer. Didn't *need* to answer. Where she was every day was none of his concern.

"I think you've worn out your welcome, Lord Vincent. You have your translation. You should go now."

A faint, oily smile flickered over his lips. "As you wish then."

He reached into his pocket and dropped a small coin purse onto the table. It jingled with the volume of coins inside. Payment for her translation, no doubt. Then he picked up his gloves, his hat, and the book she translated for him the night before. As he approached, she stepped aside to let him exit the room. She stiffened as he passed by her and headed for the front door. She hurried to get to it before he did.

She followed him out the door, pausing on the stoop as he stepped toward his carriage. A stiff breeze blew, and she scented it then—a feral smell that was all wolf. *Saints help her.*

He was nearby.

Her back straightened as she scanned the evening shadows looking for his beastly shape but saw nothing. It was a moment of distraction. She hadn't realized Lord Vincent turned back to her and stopped inches from her.

"Are you in danger?" he asked, his voice low and quiet.

Her gaze flickered to him as she made a valiant effort to ignore the low muffled growl to her left.

"I can assure you, I am in no danger," she said. "There is nothing for you to worry about."

"If you were, would you tell me?" He clenched his jaw so hard, she saw the muscles flexing along the edge. Then he stepped closer and reached for her, placing a hand on her elbow.

The growl erupted next to her and, before she realized what was happening, the beast leapt from the shadows. Lord Vincent stumbled backward a step, his eyes wide with panic, as he released her instantly. The snarling beast placed himself between her and the nobleman.

"No, don't!" Bella shouted. "He means no harm."

The snarling beast turned his head and peered at her with those pale brown eyes she had come to love. But of the man, not the beast. She stepped closer, putting out her hand.

"Don't hurt him, please," she whispered.

"Bella—" Lord Vincent began.

The beast turned his head and snapped and snarled at the man. He shrank back against the carriage.

"No," Bella said, her voice firm. "He is not a threat."

She was close enough to touch him now. Her hand landed on his neck, her fingers sinking into the thick, coarse fur. His head swiveled to look at her, those wild eyes instantly taming to something softer, something warming. As though he recognized her.

"No threat," she said again, her voice soft and soothing. She leaned her head toward him and dropped her voice to a whisper. "Go back to the shadows. Where it's safe."

They stared at each other for a long moment, her heart beating a wicked beat. She silently begged him to leave, to return, to be gone.

He reared back then, gave one last growl at Lord Vincent, and then melted into the shadows once more. The darkness concealed his form, but she knew he was still there, lurking. Protecting.

Finally, she turned back to Lord Vincent who cowered against the carriage.

"That beast is a menace," he said, his voice as hard and cold as the steel in his eyes. "And I will see its end."

The words hit her like a slap. For a heartbeat, she couldn't breathe past the rush of fury and fear that crashed through her. Before she summoned a reply—before she could even find her voice—he turned, climbed into the carriage, and barked an order to the driver to make haste.

The wheels rattled against the gravel drive, carrying him away into the shrouded darkness, leaving her standing there with a storm gathering in her chest.

Chapter 32

Bella rushed inside the manor, closing the door with a snap behind her. She headed straight for the library with only one thing in mind—find the answer and break the curse. She *had* to because now time was of the essence.

Dread pounded through her. Dread at knowing Lord Vincent saw the beast. He must have followed her from the village to...where? Dickens seemed sure that no one would be able to penetrate the shroud around the castle unless they were wanted, welcomed.

If Lord Vincent followed her that morning, what would be to stop him from following her again tomorrow?

She closed the door to the library and hurried around the room lighting the candles. She paused a moment to light a fire in the hearth to ward off the chill of the room. Then she hurried to the desk and stopped short. She stared at the window. It was no longer boarded. In its place, a new pane of glass was there, letting the pale light of the evening slash through the casement. Her heart thumped as she gaped at it, uncertain when it was repaired.

Surely, Gerald would have mentioned it had someone come to replace the window.

She shoved away thoughts of the new window, trying to push it out of her mind and focus on the task at hand. Emmaline had left the books where she told her. She sat down hard in the chair and stared at the cursed book with its shimmering embossed rose on the cover. The book that was the bane of her existence. The pages were not so willing to give up their secrets, but she was determined.

She reached for a clean piece of parchment, pulling it to her, then snatched her quill. Taking a deep breath, she slammed open the book and flipped to the page where she had left off earlier that day, trying to make the runes appear and the roses bloom.

Sitting back in the chair, she gripped the quill, waiting, holding her breath. But the pages did not yield any movement.

Frustration edged through her as she leaned forward and peered once again at the page.

"Please," she whispered. "Show me the way to break the curse."

Still nothing.

The vines remained in place. The runes did not appear. No letters faded into existence.

She dropped the quill and clenched her fists, pounding them once against the desk on either side of the book with aggravation.

"I know you can hear me," she said to the book.

The pages didn't move. The ink didn't shimmer. The book sat still. Silent as a tomb when she needed it the most. Not even a ghostly whisper in response.

She pressed her palms against the frigid pages, fingers trembling.

"I've done all I can. I've translated the riddles," she said, barely holding back the sob. "But I'm running out of time. *He's* running out of time."

Still nothing. Only the faint rustle of the fire, the distant howl of wind outside the window. The howl of wind and the howl of the beast out there, somewhere, lurking in the shadows. Ever watchful.

Her throat tightened. A nagging pain seized her chest. The threat of tears burned the backs of her eyes.

"I love him."

The whispered words came out on a quiver. She pressed her cold, shaking fingers against her lips, squeezing her eyes shut.

"Saints preserve me, I love him. Do you hear me?" She cut a glance down at the infernal book. "I don't know when or how it happened. But it's real. If there's anything left of him to save, please. *Please,* I beg you. Show me how to save him."

The silence stretched so long it hurt. She dropped her head, her forehead resting against the page.

Then a pulse. Faint, but there. Under her fingertips. Like a heartbeat.

She looked up.

The ink on the page began to shift, vines and thorns and brambles rearranging themselves in slow, deliberate strokes, as if something inside the book stirred. As if her words had reached it. Pierced whatever enchantment kept it sealed and silent.

A single line of new script appeared at the center of the page.

Love is the name the curse could never bind.

Her breath caught.

Below it, more runes took shape. The final key, the last piece of the riddle she hadn't been able to solve. But now...the book was showing her.

Because now, it believed her.

She snatched up her quill and wrote, fast and furious, before the letters disappeared and were replaced by rose blooms. Her handwriting was awful, but she didn't care as she scribbled the words. Her hand cramped as she scribed the last few lines.

Then she sat back in the chair, staring down at her messy handwriting and reading over it.

> *One shall bleed, though no*
> *wound is seen.*
> *One shall choose, though no*
> *path is clear.*
> *To break what binds, name*
> *what was given freely.*
> *Not taken, not stolen, not owed.*

*A crown cast down. A heart left
open. A vow made in silence.
Speak the truth that lives between the thorn and the bloom.
Name it, and he shall be unmade and made whole again.*

"Speak the truth that lives between the thorn and the bloom," she whispered.

The thorn...did that mean Leopold?

The bloom...was that her?

Her mind raced as she worked out how to break the curse. She shoved aside the parchment and searched through her other writings. Desperation pulled at her. She had to put it all together. She found her previous scribbles and writings and organized the pages. Then she took out a fresh sheet of parchment, dipped her quill in ink, and rewrote the phrases.

*Shadows stir. The sands of time
slip away.
Silence forever in the gloaming.
In the darkest night, no name
remembered. No light is welcome.
The hourglass bleeds its last.*

MICHELLE MILES

When the sky is blind and the
stars dare not shine,
The final form shall take root.
Not beast. Not man. Some-
thing in between.
Bound by thorn. Named by
none.

One shall bleed, though no
wound is seen.
One shall choose, though no
path is clear.

To break what binds, name
what was given freely.
Not taken, not stolen, not owed.
A crown cast down. A heart left
open. A vow made in silence.
Speak the truth that lives be-
tween the thorn and the bloom.
Name it, and he shall be un-
made and made whole again.

As she rewrote the last line, she read it again. And then sucked in a sharp breath.

"Merciful skies! I know how to break the curse."

She shoved aside the parchment pages that didn't matter. Then took the one with the fresh ink and the completed curse—spell?—and folded it in half with a gentle hand. She slipped it between the pages of the book, then slammed the cover closed.

She scooped it up and hurried across the room to the library door with one destination in mind—to get to Leopold.

But then she halted in the open doorway, her heart racing. Leopold's carriage would not be waiting for her at this time of night in the village. She would have to walk alone in the dark. The only thing that gave her comfort was knowing the beast was out there to protect her.

No, it was too great a risk. Other perils existed on the dark road at night. Vagrants. Highwaymen. She did not want to risk her safety—or that of the beast's—trying to get to Thornhurst Castle in the middle of the night.

She turned back to the room, headed inside, and snuffed out the candles. Still clutching the book, she toed off her slippers and settled down on the small sofa in front of the fire. This would have to do for tonight. Still holding the book, she watched the flickering flames until, finally, she was fast asleep.

An ethereal mist crept through the trees, thick and unnatural, as the beast sat on the edge of the forest, his keen eyes focused on the small manor house she called Hawthorne Hall.

Something had changed. A subtle tremor in the world his wolf senses picked up. He could not name it, or explain it, but it was there. Stirring. Shifting. Coming.

It was not the wind he sensed. It was something else. More determined. More desperate. More dangerous. His senses pricked against the air. His instincts were on edge. The brand on his foreleg burned with a wicked intensity.

A ripple in the curse.

The *veil-shade* were coming. The curse was no longer dormant.

It was awoken by something or someone.

He glanced at the girl's library window. For a brief time, yellow light flickered there. He saw movement through the opaque lace curtains. And then the light snuffed out abruptly. No more movement there, either.

Perhaps the girl left the room.

She was not safe. He knew this. He sensed this with a deep thrumming through him. His paws padded through the garden to the front of the manor house where the strange man who threatened her parked his carriage. Marks from the wheels still showed in the dirt.

Overhead, only the quiet stars twinkling in the night. The moon barely a crescent. His time was near. The time when he would transform for the last time. He swung his head toward the door, thinking of the girl there. The one who told him to go back into the shadows.

She protected him. As he protected her. She sensed he wanted to pounce on the pompous man who threatened her, who threatened him.

A clatter of distant wheels out on the road caught his attention. His head snapped in that direction, his sharp eyes piercing the darkness. There was nothing and no one.

But then he caught sight of it. The shadows moving against the wind when there was nothing. Forming shapes in the unnatural mist.

He knew who and what they were. He knew they were coming for her, for the book.

He dropped his head and growled low and deep in his throat. His front paws were spread, ready to pounce.

This was his last stand against the *veil-shade*. And he was not going to let them get to the girl behind that closed door.

He would stop them or die trying.

CHAPTER 33

Faint sunlight slashed across her closed eyes. The moment she came awake, she sat up, panic lancing through her. It was past dawn.

The book was no longer in her arms. Frantically, she searched the area. It had slid to the floor and was upside down, the pages curled there. Her parchment was scattered across the rug. She hastily picked up the papers, gathering them together. She put them inside the pages of the book.

Before she flipped it closed, she noticed something different. Every single page had a blooming rose. Even the pages she had not yet read.

What did it mean? That the book held no more secrets? The curse was broken? Or—worse—the curse was forever?

She had to get to Leopold. She dashed from the room, flinging open the door and rushing into the hallway.

And halted in the foyer.

She gaped at the open casement.

There was no longer a door. And what remained was nothing more than shredded, splintered wood. As if something had tried to claw its way into the manor. Her heart thumped a wild beat.

What happened? She didn't recall hearing anything the night before, but she had been so tired she must have slept through whatever it was that tried to get inside.

Stepping closer, she saw droplets of blood on the floor inside the doorway.

"Oh, gods," she whispered.

Leopold.

Urgency pounded through her. She had to get to him.

She started for the open door, when suddenly Gerald stepped in front of her.

"It's not safe, miss."

She blinked surprise as her heart jolted. He startled her. She hadn't seen him. She wasn't even sure where he'd come from. She stared up at him, then looked back at the door. The claw marks were evident.

"What happened here?"

"All I can say, miss, is that a beast tried to get inside last night."

"Last night."

Her mind pounded with unanswered questions. Why would Leopold try to get inside the manor? He wasn't a threat to her. In the instances she saw him in beast form, he protected her.

Unless...unless there was another threat. She clutched the book tighter in her arms, suddenly worried about Leopold. She knew he was there last night when Lord Vincent left.

His haughty words rang back to her.

That beast is a menace, and I will see its end.

A shadow fell across the open casement, catching her eye. She glanced up to see Lord Vincent stepping through the destruction, a look of smug satisfaction on his face. Instantly, she knew he was responsible for something. Dread washed through her, making her stomach cramp.

"What did you do?" It took everything in her not to shout at the man.

His surprised gaze flickered to her. "What do you mean?"

"I see it in your eyes, Lord Vincent. The triumph. You came back last night, didn't you?" Accusing him was farfetched. It was nothing more than a guess, but she saw the gratification in his eyes.

"And a good thing I did, too." He ignored her as he glanced at the butler there. "The threat has been eradicated."

"What does that mean?" Her heart thudded like a war drum, sending terror pumping through her. Bile rose to the back of her throat. All she thought about was Leopold.

Lord Vincent's cold eyes turned back to her. "It means the beast will no longer threaten you or this manor."

Her knees nearly buckled. "He was no threat to me or us."

Emotion clotted her throat. Hot tears burned the backs of her eyes. She *had* to get out of this house. She had to find Leopold. She had to know if he was all right.

But judging by the delight oozing from the nobleman, she wasn't sure.

"That's not what I saw last night. And so, I returned and took care of the beast."

Unable to stop herself, she emitted a strangled gasp. Gerald placed a concerned hand on her elbow as he moved to stand next to her. She was grateful for his strength. But Lord Vincent's eyes narrowed to suspicious slits.

"Do you care for this beast, Miss Bella? Is that it?" He moved closer, closing the distance between them. Stifling her. Making her shrink back with his disdainful expression.

"I-I—"

But she didn't finish her answer as Emmaline bounded down the steps. She halted at the foot of the stairs, her eyes wide as she took in the situation. The destroyed front door. Lord Vincent standing over her, threatening her. And Gerald holding her elbow as though to keep her upright.

"Ah, Miss Emmaline. Please escort the lady to her chambers and see that she remains there until this situation," he waved to the door, "can be properly handled."

Emmaline nodded as she stepped toward Bella, reaching for her. Fury ignited through her as she shrugged off the girl and the butler. She rounded her ire on Lord Vincent.

"Who are you to give my maid orders? And my butler? Who are you to walk into this house as if you are the lord of the manor? Who are *you* to seek justice for some infraction that has never even occurred?"

He was startled by her heated words and took a step back. "Bella, I—"

"Do not use my given name," she spat. "You are not worthy of that. Or of Emmaline. I tire of your meddling, my lord. I tire of you coming here demanding answers from me—me!—when I owe you nothing. *Nothing.* I finished your translation. I gave you back the book. You paid me handsomely for it. That was nothing more than a business transaction. *We* are nothing more than a business transaction. Coming here pretending to be interested in Emmaline is disgraceful."

She regretted the words the instant she heard Emmaline choke out a sob. Lord Vincent's face drained of color. Gerald stepped toward her, placing a hand on her elbow again.

"Miss Bella—" the butler started.

"Enough." She jerked away and rounded on him. "Find someone in town who can repair the door, Gerald. If no one will come, find someone in Port Leclare. Perhaps one of my father's old contacts. I don't care who. Just get someone here today to fix the door. As for you." She turned back to Lord Vincent, who had stumbled back toward the open door. "Leave this place and never return. If you do, I shall call the constable and have you arrested for trespassing. Is that clear?"

He stiffened then, unaccustomed to being accused of any sort of crime, and straightened his cravat even though it wasn't askew.

"You have made your wishes *perfectly* clear, my lady." He started to go, then turned back, a spiteful look on his face. "I do hope your father is released from the port jail soon, though I daresay the magistrate won't take kindly to him being a smuggler."

It was a parting shot as he stepped through the open casement. Bella clenched her jaw tight as she stared daggers at his retreating back. The only sound was the man's retreating footsteps on the gravel drive, then the rattling of the carriage as he rode away.

Silence descended between the three of them. She took a deep, cleansing breath to get her emotions under control.

"Miss Bella…is Mr. Rinaldi a smuggler?" Gerald asked, his voice low. Confusion and concern etched his brow.

"No," she snapped. "He is no smuggler. Lord Vincent knows that. He just wanted to insult me. You've known my father longer than me. You know he is no criminal."

He seemed to take her words as truth and nodded. "I will find someone to repair the door."

"Thank you, Gerald."

She turned to Emmaline, then, who still stood at the foot of the stairs. Her eyes were wide and watery with tears, her fingers pressed to her lips. Guilt immediately swamped Bella. Her words were cruel, she knew, but she was certain they were truth. After all, the nobleman did not deny them.

"I'm sorry, Emmaline."

She shook her head, spun, and hurried up the stairs. Moments later, a door slammed.

Bella sighed. The damage was done. She would find a way to make peace with the girl later. Now, though, she had to find Leopold.

The moment she stepped out the door and into the morning, she smelled the blood and death that seemed to permeate the air. Her stomach twisted into a knot as a sick feeling crept over her. She glanced around the area and saw more drops of blood dotting the front of the manor. A trail led away toward the gardens to the side of the house.

She followed it down the footpath. But it disappeared under one of the rosebushes. Crouching low, she saw the ground stained with a wide pool of blood. There was nothing more. No indication he had dragged himself out of the bushes. Thankfully, his body—in beast or human form—was not there either.

"I hope you're all right."

There was only one way to find out.

CHAPTER 34

B ella's legs burned with exertion, a jolt of fire through her calves, as she hurried to get to the village. As it crested into view, familiar roofs rose against the gleaming morning sun. Her gaze snapped to the usual spot where the carriage waited. No thorn and vine and rose encrusted carriage. No lacquered door. No Dickens waiting for her arrival.

Her heart sank. Her breath caught in her throat as she gulped in air. Despite the warmth of the morning, a chill swept through her, sending a shiver to the depths of her soul.

Leopold.

Lord Vincent alluded to "taking care of" the beast, which terrified her. What had he done to Leopold? If Dickens wasn't there to pick her up, then something dreadful happened to him. The man she loved.

Panic rose through her breast as she glanced around the bustling village. No one took notice of her. They were all far too busy with their own lives, their own drama. The rattle of carriages heading down the main thoroughfare blended in with the cacophony of the everyday noises. The hum of voices. Laughter. Merchants hawking their wares. In the distance, the jingle of the bookshop bell as a patron entered or exited.

A painful throb took up residence in the center of her chest as she clutched the books in her arms, trying to decide what to do next. Although she had traveled to the mysterious castle every day, she wasn't sure of the direction. But she had to try. She turned toward the road that disappeared through the thick trees that loomed like phantom sentries guarding a secret. Sucking in a breath, she started down the side of the road. Alone. With nothing but hope to guide her.

It was late in the day when she arrived at the gate of Thornhurst Castle. The imposing fortress never failed to exude its eerie appearance. Though the afternoon light was behind her, splashing across the road not far away, the dark-blue façade still appeared as though it belonged to shadows, its outer walls glistening with starlight. Tilting her head back, she looked up at the spires and towers that reached for the indigo sky that was in perpetual gloom.

The curse made it imposing and threatening. She knew that now. But she had never been afraid of the castle.

Hurrying toward the door, she paused there, unsure if she should knock or simply barge in. She decided to follow decorum and fisted her hand to pound on the thick oak door with all her might. Then stood back and waited.

No one came.

There was no bell, either.

She tried again, pounding once more. "Dickens! It's me! Please let me in. *Please.*"

Still nothing. Every moment that passed was a moment wasted.

Finally, in desperation, she tried the knob. It turned, and the door swung open with ease. She burst through it, kicking it closed with her heel. Then she made a mad dash for the grand staircase. Up and up, her muscles objecting to the hurried pace with every step. She ignored it as she sprinted down the hallway and paused at his bedchamber door. It was closed.

Gulping air into her burning lungs, she decided propriety be hanged. She hadn't come all this way alone to lose her courage now. She opened the door and stepped inside.

The first thing she noticed was the horrible smell. The metallic odor of blood hung thick and redolent in the air barely masked by a sickly-sweet medicinal scent. She covered her mouth and nose with her free hand as she forced away the bile that wanted to rise to her throat.

Dickens was sitting by his bedside. The moment he saw her, he jumped to his feet and hurried around the bed. He blocked her view, but she caught a glimpse of a prone Leopold in the bed. The valet's face was pinched with concern and now a hint of annoyance as if she were nothing more than an unwelcome intruder.

"My lady, you should not be here." As he approached, he reached for her as if to take her by the arm and turn her away.

"Dickens, I know how to break the curse." The words spilled from her before she stopped them.

He dropped his arm to his side, listless. Limp. "It's too late."

A sharp breath sucked in through her teeth with a hiss. "What do you mean?"

His face turned solemn, serious. A look she had never seen before from Dickens. That terrified her.

"He's dying," he said, his voice nothing but a weak whisper.

She shook her head, refusing to believe. "No."

"I'm afraid there is nothing I can do for him."

She stepped around him and headed for the bed. Dickens was on her heels.

"You do not want to see him like this, my lady. Please." He had never begged her for anything, but his sharp tone caught her off guard.

Pausing, she looked at him over her shoulder and saw the anguish, the distress, the concern creasing his aged face.

"What happened to him last night, Dickens?"

He swallowed hard, cutting a glance at the man in the bed, then looked back at her. "Don't you know?"

"I know he was there last night, at the manor. Lurking in the shadows. I know he was trying to protect me."

But it didn't make sense to her he was trying to protect her from only Lord Vincent. She swallowed hard, her mouth turned to ash as she recalled the previous evening. She told Dickens about Lord Vincent and his threat to end the beast once and for all.

"I never thought he would actually make good on that threat," she said. "But then this morning, the door to the manor was torn to shreds. There were claw marks and..." Her heart thudded. "...blood."

Dickens stretched a frail hand to her. It struck her then. He was fading away. His life-force was tied to Leopold's.

"Come away, my lady."

She shook her head. "I don't want to leave him."

"He doesn't even know you're here. Come away." He beckoned with his hand.

Reluctance shifted through her as she cast another glance at the bed. Leopold was covered completely with the white sheet. His face was ashen. Drops of sweat beaded his forehead. Death stalked him, now.

Dickens stepped closer to her, taking her free hand in his, and tugging her away. Out of the room. She said nothing as she allowed him to do this, all the while knowing the answer to all their hopes and wishes resided within the pages of the book she held.

He took her to Leopold's private sitting room, leading her to the desk where the enchanted hourglass sat. The sands inside were glowing and shifting at what appeared to be a much quicker pace than she remembered. The top was nearly empty.

"What...what does this mean?"

"It means he does not have much longer to live. The hourglass *knows*."

Hot tears sprang to her eyes. "No."

"He was mortally wounded last night," he continued as if she hadn't spoken. "The *veil-shade* came. They attacked. He was all that stood between you and them. He fought them off. They wounded him. He was already wounded when the other man returned. This Lord Vincent."

She pressed cold, shaking fingers to her lips as she stared, wide-eyed, at the hourglass.

"He shot him."

A gurgled gasp escaped her as her knees gave out. She sank to the floor, dropping the book on the rug. Her papers scattered like leaves in an autumn wind.

"The prince tried to claw his way inside to get to you, to get help. Lord Vincent wrongly assumed he was trying to hurt you. He shot him again. In the back."

Bella shook her head. The tears slipped down her cheeks as she watched the iridescent glow of the shifting sands.

"He dragged himself to the rose garden where he hid under the bushes until the attacker left."

"How...how do you know all this?" she asked, her voice quivering.

"That's where I found him early this morning before dawn. As a man. I pulled him out and got him back here before sunrise."

She lifted her gaze. "But how did you *know* to find him there?"

Dickens sucked in a deep breath through his nose, expelled it. "We have been cursed together in this castle for hundreds of years. I am his caretaker when he shifts. From the first moment you arrived, he insisted on protecting you. As a man and a beast. He knew the *veil-shade* would come. And so did I."

He was there that first night, when she heard the howls from the library. And again, the next night when she cowered under her bedcovers listening. He was there. He was the one protecting her from the demons of the dark.

"You shouldn't be here, my lady. It's too late for him."

She shook her head, coming back to her senses. She reached for the scattered pages, shuffling them back into order. For good measure, she snatched up the cursed book and cradled it all in her arms. She pushed to her feet and turned to Dickens.

"I *should* be here, Dickens. I can help him."

"My lady, he's far too gone. His wounds are fatal. Twilight is upon us now. You need to go."

Twilight. That meant a night with no moon—the new moon.

She refused to believe Leopold was too far gone. There was hope yet. "Take me to him."

"Bella—"

"*Please.*"

He clenched his jaw tight, his lips forming a thin line. The reluctance was written all over his face. Finally, he nodded and turned back to the open door. His footsteps were unhurried which drove her mad. It was nearly nightfall. And when night came, the new moon would come. The sands would drain from the hourglass and Leopold's fate would forever be sealed.

She hoped she could get there before that happened. Before he was turned into a beast and lost to her forever.

At his bedroom door, Dicken pushed it open and stood aside. She entered, holding her breath and clutching the papers so tight in her hands, the parchment wrinkled. Apprehension swamped her as she approached the bed.

She did not like what she saw.

Leopold's face was bathed in sweat. His skin was pale. His eyes were closed. His face turned to one side to reveal horrible scratches along the jaw and neck. His forehead was bandaged. Blood stained through the linen cloth. The bedsheets were tucked around his hips, his chest bare. One shoulder was wrapped tightly and another bandage around his upper torso.

How she loathed Lord Vincent at the moment for what he did to Leopold. There was no revenge in the world to exact on the man. Only one thing.

Save Leopold.

Juggling the pages and the book, she pulled the chair closer to the bed and reached for his hand. His skin was cold and clammy, but she did not recoil.

"Leopold, can you hear me?" Her voice was tentative, quiet in the silence of the room.

He stirred, his face twitching as he turned his head toward her. He groaned as though in terrible pain. She clutched his fingers, squeezed his hand to let him know she was there.

"I'm here."

"Bella?" He croaked her name. His voice sounded scratchy.

She squeezed his hand in answer.

His eyes blinked open. Those beautiful eyes that were so pale brown they were terrifying to everyone else but her. He focused on her a long moment.

"You came back."

"I had to." Emotion clotted her throat as she made a valiant attempt to hold off the tears. "I know what happened."

He grunted, closed his eyes again. "I should have killed him."

"But you didn't," she said.

She noticed then the brand on his forearm. It was red and angry and pulsing, ready to consume him to turn him forever into the beast. The ink was darker than ever, which terrified her.

"Leave me," he said. "There is no help for me."

"There is hope," she insisted as she eyed the brand. "I have found the answer."

"It's too late."

"No."

She released his hand, placing the book in her lap, and shuffled the papers, looking down at her handwriting that seemed so foreign and strange. She didn't know how the curse worked, but she suspected she had to start at the beginning and speak the words. With her hand shaking, she reached out and placed it on top of his as she read.

"Shadows stir. The sands of time slip away. Silence forever in the gloaming. In the darkest night, no name remembered. No light is welcome. The hourglass bleeds its last."

He groaned. She held his hand tighter and forged on.

"When the sky is blind and the stars dare not shine, the final form shall take root. Not beast. Not man. Something in between. Bound by thorn. Named by none."

Underneath her hand, his muscles twitched. It was impossible to know if it was full on night or not. The castle was constantly shrouded in darkness and shadow, never letting in a drop of sun. Still, she hoped.

"One shall bleed, though no wound is seen. One shall choose, though no path is clear."

He sucked in a sharp breath. His eyes remained closed. Still, she hoped. Still, she read.

"To break what binds, name what was given freely. Not taken, not stolen, not owed. A crown cast down. A heart left open. A vow made in silence. Speak the truth that lives between the thorn and the bloom. Name it, and he shall be unmade and made whole again."

Leopold inhaled one last breath. His eyes fluttered open. He looked at her one last time.

Her name was nothing more than a whisper on his dry, cracked lips. He closed his eyes once again. And then he was gone.

CHAPTER 35

N^{o.} The word didn't escape her.

Shock pounded through her. A cold force slammed into her, gripping her chest and holding her there, frozen.

It should have worked.

It was supposed to work.

She said the words. She felt the truth of them burning through her. Binding her. She poured her heart and soul into the translation. Into *him*. But the curse had not broken and Leopold...

Leopold lay still and quiet wrapped in bandages and bed linens that had suddenly become his tomb.

His chest did not rise and fall. His face was devoid of emotion. There was no pulse beating in his throat.

He was gone.

Something deep inside her fractured, breaking. It was her heart. She knew it. She wasn't in time. And she wasn't strong enough to weather the storm that was to come without him in the world. Her world.

Suddenly, Dickens was at her side. "Come away, love."

He reached for her arm, giving her a gentle tug upward to propel her out of the chair. She shrugged him off, standing at the side of the bed. The parchment fluttered to the floor at her feet. She dropped the book in the vacated chair. Her mind refused to believe what her eyes saw and yet, how could she not believe?

She leaned over him, the tears burning her eyes. Her voice was low, quiet, nothing but a murmur.

"I love you."

As she said it, one tear slipped from her eye and landed on his forehead.

Then she turned away, toward Dickens. She allowed him to take her by the hand and pull her along, numb, from the bed. Away from Leopold. Away from the man who was everything to her. Her unhurried steps headed for the open bedchamber door. She was almost to it, when suddenly the air shifted.

A cold breeze swept through the room. A ghostly whisper sounded. She jerked free from Dickens and spun around. She watched, her eyes wide and her heart ramming against her ribcage, as the book slammed open on the chair. The pages flapped in the peculiar breeze. A white mist lifted from the pages, soaring higher and higher and higher. Forming an image. A cluster of thorny vines. And then brambles. And then it transformed into a rose-bud that bloomed full, the petals unfurling at an unnatural rate. Expanding into a rose that was nothing more than misty vapor.

That misty vapor surged toward Leopold. She took a step, to intervene, but Dickens caught her by the arm and stopped her. Glancing up, she met his dark gaze. He shook his head to indicate not to interfere. Looking back, she watched as the brand—the intertwined rose and thorn—lifted from his skin. It joined with the mist and then, together, the mysterious fog shot downward and into Leopold.

There was a beat of silence. Then, something that sounded like glass shattering outside the windows. The odd blue-white candlelight flickered as if it was hit with the breeze and then snuffed out. She sucked in a breath as the floor rumbled. The castle shook. The walls vibrated. Dickens' hand tightened on her arm, pulling her closer as if to protect her from whatever threat might happen next.

As quickly as the candles flickered out, the flames returned. Not the blue-white to which she had become accustomed. But a warm yellow-orange light that lit up the chamber casting away the shadows and the dark and the gloom.

Then, from the bed, Leopold sucked in a deep breath, a gasp of renewed life. He sat bolt upright in the bed, his gaze searching, seeking until he found hers. Those pale brown eyes she came to love that once were full of sorrow and despair were now full of life and wonder.

Bella jerked her arm away from Dickens and charged toward the bed. He was breathing. His face had returned to a normal pallor. He was awake. *He was alive.*

She launched herself at him, not thinking about anything other than falling into his arms, touching him, making sure he was real. As though anticipating her, he held his arms out to catch her. He wrapped her into his embrace, clutching her to him, holding her close, their foreheads pressed together.

"You did it." His soft voice floated over her, warming her.

Words died in her throat as she searched his gaze, diving deep into the recesses there. Floating on a cloud. Her mind devoid of all thoughts.

He lifted a hand, the back of his fingers grazing her cheek. A tentative touch, as though he were afraid to touch her. For a moment, she stopped breathing, stopped thinking. His palm settled at the side of her neck. No longer cold and clammy. Now it was warm and steady as he gently guided her toward him.

Yearning shuddered through her. She waited her entire life for this moment.

And then his lips met hers.

Tentative at first. Nothing more than a brush. As if he feared she might pull away.

She didn't.

She leaned into him, her arms slipping around him, wanting him closer, and deepened the kiss before second-guessing the way her soul unraveled under his touch. The touch she had craved longer than she was able to name.

He kissed her back with reverence. With hunger. With something that felt like home. And a deep, unabating devotion that made her knees weak.

It was everything she hoped for and more. So much more.

When his mouth claimed hers fully, she gave her heart to him without hesitation. She was his, and he was hers.

There was no more curse.

Only him.

Only them.

Breaking apart, the realization she was trembling shattered her. He pressed his hand against the small of her back, holding her steady, keeping her close. Holding the pieces of her together with the very essence that was him.

He pressed his forehead against hers, their breath mingling in the small space between them as they shared this intimate moment. He didn't speak. Neither did she, for words seemed inconsequential. She was incapable of conveying her feelings to him. Her heart fluttered hard and fast. Like a hummingbird had taken residence there.

She met his eyes. Her breath stopped. His, searching and seeking and wanting and needing with a hint of wonder.

"You did it," he said again, nothing more than a whisper.

"I thought I lost you," she replied, her voice weak.

"You nearly did." He pressed his brow against hers.

She drew in the scent of him. Different from before. No longer like frost and sorrow. No longer like wood smoke and wildfire. No. Now, she caught the faintest scent of roses. Not cloying or sweet or perfumed. Different. Alive. Like petals brushed with morning dew. Like a bloom after being too long in the dark.

In a rush of emotion, she buried her face against his neck, inhaling that freshly bloomed scent and loving it. Loving *him*.

He was no longer fading into that dark world where he was a feral beast. He was a man. He was becoming.

And so was she.

His arms tightened around her as he held her close. So close. As though they would never be parted. A hand brushed down her messy hair. It was only then she realized her hair was still tied with the ribbon from the day before. Only then when she realized she wore the same gown.

"You brought me back from the dark, Bella," he said, his voice soft in the glow of the room. He pulled back then to look at her, his eyes searching her face. "I am yours."

A breath shuddered out between her lips. "And you are mine."

"Always?" A smile tipped the corner of his mouth.

"And forever," she confirmed.

In the dusky gloom of Leopold's private sitting room, the final grain of sand slipped through the hourglass. It landed with a soundless thud. The glow vanished. Snuffed out like a candle in a storm, leaving only cold glass. No shimmer. And at last, Leopold's life was his own.

Chapter 36

Bella remained in the castle until morning. With Leopold still recovering, she took a bedchamber down the hall, thanks to Dickens. She slept that night for the first time in days. A deep sleep that was not interrupted by howls or curses or shadow things.

Before she left, Bella peeked into Leopold's chambers to see he still slept. Likely he would need rest after the ordeal of the curse for the last several centuries. Plus, he had wounds that needed healing.

The old valet walked with her down the stairs to the front door in amicable silence. As if perhaps, he was trying to decide what to say and how to say it. After she left Leopold to rest, Dickens took her to a room without a word. It was an unspoken acknowledgement between the two of them that she had broken the curse and he was grateful.

Dickens was much changed. No longer did he have baleful eyes or frightful pale skin. He had color in his face once again. His eyes had changed from dark and piercing to a sparkling blue. His hair, once slicked back, now fell across his high forehead. The shaggy ends dusted his thick eyebrows. He looked different. Alive. Healthy.

He turned to her, grasped her hand, and held it a long moment. His fingers were warm around hers. There was relief deep in his eyes as he looked at her. Relief and admiration.

"My lady, what you did—"

"No need to thank me, Dickens," she interrupted.

She didn't need accolades for doing the right thing. She'd grown fond of the old valet and didn't want him to shower her with his praises. She cast a glance back to the stairs.

"I hate to leave him."

"When he's strong enough, he will call on you at Hawthorne Hall." For the first time, Dickens smiled. A genuine smile that lit up his face and warmed her from the inside out. Then he kissed her hand.

"I look forward to that, Dickens."

When she stepped outside the door of the castle, she inhaled a sharp breath. Morning sunlight filtered through the tall trees. Gone were the shadows and shade. In front of her, the carriage waited on the curved gravel drive. Beyond, a lush verdant lawn immaculately trimmed. On the breeze, the sweet scent of roses which caught her attention. Along the stone wall, where once the night rose bloomed, now there was nothing but color. Pink, yellow, orange. The petals vibrant, their soft faces turned upward reaching for the sun.

She stumbled outside and turned to look up at the castle. Even the dark-blue façade was changed. No longer did it resemble twilight. Now, the stone walls gleamed in the light. The spires and towers rose toward the brilliant blue sky. Even the gargoyles who once peered down with soulless, stone eyes were now nothing more than statues carved from alabaster.

Dickens joined her and followed her gaze. He stared at the much-changed exterior of the castle for a long moment, his face impassive as though processing what was before his eyes. A complete transformation from dark and bleak to light and welcoming.

"It has been restored to its former glory," he said at last.

The curse had truly affected everything.

"The prince will be overjoyed to know," he added. Then he turned to her and for a moment, she thought she saw the mist of tears in his eyes before he blinked them away. "Safe travels, my lady. I will send word when his highness is better."

She nodded. "I look forward to it."

Then she climbed into the carriage and headed back to Hawthorne Hall for a good long rest.

When she arrived back at Hawthorne, she sensed a shift in the air. Gerald paced the length of the small foyer with a pinched expression on his aged face, a paper clutched in his hands. The moment she saw him her senses went on high alert.

"What is it, Gerald?"

"Oh, miss, there you are."

He came to a stuttering halt, looking her up and down. She realized then she wore the same dress as yesterday. Glancing down, she saw it was full of wrinkles. Her hair was a mess about her face. She'd long since lost the ribbon that tied it. She didn't know where it was. She flushed as she realized she must look a mess, and she didn't have a ready explanation to share with the old butler.

Then she decided she didn't need to explain to him where she was. She was the lady of the house, after all. She eyed the paper clutched in his fist.

"You have news?" she asked.

"Yes." He handed her the letter. "This arrived earlier this morning."

She took it, her heart climbing its way to her throat as she glanced down at the handwriting. It was unfamiliar, but the seal was all too familiar—the Port Leclare Magistrate. By the way Gerald was acting, he likely already knew what was written there.

"I'd like some tea and whatever breakfast you have, Gerald. I'll take it in the parlor."

She didn't wait for a reply as she stepped into the parlor and sealed herself inside. Her hands shook as she opened the seal and walked toward the nearest chair. As she flipped open the paper, she sank into the worn cushions.

In two days, her father faced the inquiry to respond to the charges of smuggling, violating port regulations, and colluding to traffic contraband. The magistrate was ordering her to testify on her father's behalf.

You are hereby summoned to appear before the Magistrate's Court two days henceforth at the hour of eleven bells in the forenoon, at Port Leclare Hall of Justice, to offer testimony in the matter of Rinaldi v. Port Leclare Port Authority.

It was signed Magistrate Eldred Halverson of Port Leclare.

Her first instinct was to crumple the letter in her fist. But she didn't do that. Instead, she laid it on the table before her and stared at it. She drew a deep breath and clasped her hands in her lap to stop them from quivering.

Moments later, Gerald arrived with the tea cart and leftover scones from the day's breakfast. But she found she'd suddenly lost her appetite.

"Everything all right, miss?"

"Yes," she said, the word nothing more than an icy hiss. "It appears I will be returning to Port Leclare."

"Mr. Rinaldi?" he asked.

"Yes," she said again, keeping her eyes forward. "I'll need to pack a bag. Emmaline can travel with me, but you and Edith should remain here."

"Ah..." He cleared his throat as tension filled the air between them.

She glanced up at him. "What is it?"

"Miss Emmaline left this morning to return to her family home, miss."

"Oh." The word came out on a rough whisper. "I see, then."

With stiff movements, she rose and poured herself a cup of tea. It was the only normal thing that felt right about the moment. Pouring tea. Eating scones.

Gerald remained where he was, clearly unsure what he should do.

"You may go, Gerald. Thank you for telling me about Emmaline."

He gave a quick bow and left her alone in the parlor.

CHAPTER 37

Two days later, Bella took the first train out of Driftbell back to the port. She traveled alone. There was no one to accompany her and so she felt adrift in the sea of the crowd, her mind numb. She thought of sending a message to Dickens, but what good would that do? Leopold was likely still convalescing. And since she hadn't told him anything about her father or the situation, it didn't seem proper to include him.

She arrived mid-morning and disembarked the train. She dressed in a pale-yellow gown. But she didn't want to fuss with her hair, so she left it down, tied at the nape with a matching yellow ribbon. Her bonnet shaded the morning sun from her eyes as she headed to the Hall of Justice which was near the docks. She did not relish the thought of testifying, but a little part of her looked forward to seeing her father once again. The last she heard from him was his letter. That seemed like an eternity ago.

A crowd loitered outside the stone building, likely waiting to get inside and hear the proceedings. The hum of voices melded with the sounds of the port—the calls of the seagulls, the clang of rigging on the ships in port, the boisterous laughter of sailors.

The small building had high arched windows to let in the light. The main double doors were carved from heavy oak with thick iron hinges that creaked when opened to let in the crowd. They surged forward, as though excited to see the proceedings. But all Bella felt was sick to her stomach as it twisted into a tight knot.

She went up the stone steps and entered, pausing inside the doorway to take in the old building. The high ceiling had wooden beams that stretched across in an arc. It smelled faintly of old wood, dust, and wax. Wooden benches lined the viewing gallery along the bottom floor. The men and women jockeyed for the best viewing position. Lifting her gaze, she saw more seating in the balcony area filling in with curious onlookers. The floor was polished granite, shining in the slashes of sunlight from the arched windows.

At the front of the room, a table and one empty chair—likely for her father—faced the magistrate's dais, which was lifted high enough for him to cast his beady gaze at the defendant and into the gathering. Two constables on either side flanked the dais.

She swallowed hard and approached one of the constables. He gave her a disdainful yet questioning glance. She practically shoved the summons at him.

"I am Isabella Rinaldi and I've been summoned here today."

He took the summons, read it over with a bored and annoyed look, then handed it back. He pointed to a seat behind the empty chair. "Sit over there."

He was less than cordial, but Bella tried not to take it personally. She headed to the chair and paused there, her hands shaking. It felt as if every gaze was on her. She scanned the spectators and saw a familiar, youthful face peering back at her with wide, apologetic eyes. Emmaline. An older woman was with her and a girl that looked much like her. Her mother and sister. Bella granted her a smile, glad to see the girl, and nodded to acknowledge her presence.

As she was about to sit, another constable brought in her father, clutching him by the elbow and leading him to the empty chair in front of the dais.

Her heart banged hard as she watched him led to the chair. He looked old, haggard, with dark lines of fatigue under his eyes. For a moment, their gazes met. She saw the joy light in his eyes followed quickly by regret and misery. He didn't want her there anymore than she wanted to be there. But she *was* there, and she was going to do everything within her power to free him from this sham.

The magistrate, dressed in black robes, banged his wooden gavel on the desk, the sound cracking through the small building.

"All be seated."

His deep voice boomed across the crowd. As she sat, a familiar figure caught her eye. She glanced up and saw, much to her horror and dismay, Lord Vincent taking a seat across the aisle from her. He flashed her a smug grin as he settled on the edge of the chair, then pulled off his top hat and placed it in his lap.

She didn't like this at all.

Not at all.

"I call this court to order," the magistrate boomed. His eyes were focused on a stack of papers before him. "Proceedings herewith begin in the matter of Mr. Enzo Rinaldi, owner and merchant of the Rinaldi Trading Company. Allegations of illegal shipments, defying port authority, and a plot to traffic contraband are now under review and the purview of this court." He lifted his gaze, pinpointing her father. "How do you plead, sir?"

Her father straightened up to his full height. His face was pale but composed. "Not guilty, your honor."

A murmur rippled through the crowd.

The magistrate glanced back down at his papers. "We begin with testimony from the petitioner, Lord Vincent Blackwell, who filed the complaint."

Bella's heart thudded painfully in her chest as her head snapped in his direction. How *dare* he. Disbelief followed by shock pounded through her as she stiffened in her chair, her gloved hands clenched so tight they ached.

Lord Vincent stood, not giving her a second glance. "The facts are simple, your honor. Two of Mr. Rinaldi's ships were destroyed by a mysterious fire while the third was still out to sea carrying unlisted cargo of questionable origin. One in particular known to be cursed."

She clenched her jaw. How did he know about that? The only viable explanation was Emmaline suspected and must have told him. He looked directly at Bella, then.

"His daughter, your honor, has possession of that cursed item."

Saints preserve her. The loathing for the man shot through her in a hot, wild beat. More whispers swelled throughout the room. She shot to her feet, her mind working to come up with an explanation—any explanation—that was less condemning.

"My father had nothing to do with the book. He didn't even know it was on board."

Her father sucked in a sharp breath. "Bella, no."

"Is that so?" Lord Vincent smirked, knowing the truth all too well.

"What was this object, Lord Vincent?" the magistrate asked.

"A book, your honor. A book of dark enchantment that was likely cursed. Why, every nobleman in port knows the girl can translate arcane languages. That she skulks around dusty libraries. She wanted the book for herself. She wanted to use it to cast dark spells."

Fury boiled through her. "I did no such thing."

But he was not to be dissuaded in his impassioned argument. "I saw the book myself. She conjured a beast with it. She is a witch, your honor."

Gasps rippled through the gathering, followed by a rumbling of voices as the onlookers formed their own opinions of her.

"What?" The word burst through her before she realized what she was saying.

Her father leapt to his feet. "My daughter is no witch!"

"Silence." The magistrate banged his gavel to calm the crowd.

"How *dare* you," she muttered, her hands still clenched into tight fists.

But Lord Vincent continued. "What made you think you had the authority to remove and conceal an object of such power, Miss Rinaldi?"

"She acted on *my* authority."

The familiar voice sent a tremor through her as her heart stopped. She turned, as did the entire court. Even Lord Vincent.

The man rose from the last row and stepped into the aisle. Straight-backed. Sure-footed. Pale brown eyes gleamed with control.

Leopold.

He walked toward the bench with quiet authority, his gaze never leaving that of the magistrate. He wore a dark high-collared coat, finely tailored. A thorn pattern trimmed the cuffs and collar in a muted silver thread catching the light. His waistcoat was equally tailored in dark charcoal with silver buttons lying flat against his frame. Perfectly pressed trousers, tall boots polished to a high shine. Not ostentatious. Not flashy.

High born. Royalty. An undeniable force.

And everyone in that room knew it. Especially Lord Vincent who glowered at him as he passed by to pause at the front of the room. He was so close to her, she caught the faint scent of roses lingering on his coat.

"And who are you, sir?" the magistrate asked.

"Leopold Thornhurst, your honor. Prince of the Southern Mountains. I can assure you Miss Rinaldi is no witch. Nor is Mr. Rinaldi a criminal. I claim full responsibility for the cursed item in question. If it can be called cursed."

The magistrate lifted a brow. "Do you?"

The room fell into a deathly silence. Bella found it difficult to breathe. Here he was, the man she loved, standing here defending her honor and her father's reputation. How did he know to be here? She hadn't told him. She hadn't told anyone. Not even Gerald.

"The book came into port at my behest. Miss Rinaldi removed it—quite reluctantly—at my persistent request. Her father had no knowledge of the item, either. If charges are to be brought, they should be brought against me."

"You can't be serious," Lord Vincent scoffed. "The man's a liar, your honor. He comes here touting a phony title. You cannot take his word over mine. Or *hers*. She's clearly been swayed by some dark magic."

Oh, how she despised that man. Leopold remained still and calm, unaffected by Lord Vincent's outrageous accusation.

"I've seen the beast he becomes at night!" Lord Vincent snapped. "He's dangerous. He's a *creature* that should be locked away or put down. Not standing here pretending to be a highborn princeling."

Leopold lifted a brow as he regarded the man with a cool expression. "You seem quite interested in my downfall, Lord Vincent. I wonder why that is? Perhaps my existence threatens you in some manner?"

Bella suppressed a smile that wanted to erupt. Her aching hands unclenched.

Vincent sneered. "You think she loves *you*? She'll come to her senses soon enough. And I'll be the one here for her."

"I already came to my senses, Lord Vincent," she said, her voice shaking with emotion. "The moment I saw who you truly were."

"Enough of this," the magistrate snapped. "Sit down, Lord Vincent, or I shall call you in contempt."

He banged his gavel to punctuate his point. Lord Vincent sat, fury smoldering in his eyes.

"Now, then." He turned his gaze back to Leopold. "Is this book you have cursed?"

"Gods, no," Leopold said with a chuckle. "Merely an old family heirloom an ancestor of mine created. He considered himself a bit of a linguist. He thought creating a language related to our lineage would be his legacy." He laughed as though it were a family joke.

"And how did it end up on Mr. Rinaldi's ship, your highness?"

Upon hearing *your highness*, Lord Vincent snorted derision.

But Leopold was not to be derailed. "It disappeared some centuries ago. Sold off by one of the servants for ten gold pieces. I've been searching for it my entire life. A book seller across the sea found it and sold it back to me. For a thousand gold pieces. Can you believe that?" He clucked his tongue at the exorbitant price.

Bella hid a smile behind her hand. She was impressed with how he wove the truth with the lie.

Leopold continued. "Your honor, I have nothing to gain by coming here. No title to restore. No favor to win. I came to speak the truth. Miss Rinaldi acted with courage and kindness. Not malice and certainly not with witchcraft. Her father is innocent of all charges."

The magistrate sat back in his oversized chair, the wood creaking with his weight, silent. A thoughtful expression crossed his face as he glanced down at the papers, shuffled them, straightened them. No doubt stalling as he came to a decision. Deathly silence pierced the room.

Finally, he said, "Lord Vincent, I find your testimony to be lacking substance. You have presented no evidence to prove to me or this court that Mr. Rinaldi is guilty of these heinous charges. Your personal grievances have no place here in my court."

Lord Vincent's mouth dropped open, as though he were prepared to object when the magistrate continued.

"The court, however, does recognize Prince Leopold's testimony as valid. I hereby dismiss all charges." His gaze swung back to the man sitting stiffly across from her. "As for you, Lord Vincent, any further public accusations will find you sitting on the other side of the law. I hope I make myself clear. Mr. Rinaldi, you are free to go."

With that, he stood and stepped down off the dais and headed toward a door on the side of the court. The two constables followed. With the proceedings done, the disappointed spectators began to leave.

Bella's breath exhaled in a rush. Her father was next to her an instant later, hugging her so hard it nearly crushed her. But she was happy for it. Because it meant he was a free man.

Lord Vincent rose stiffly from his chair and exited the building without giving her a sideways glance, every line of his body taut with fury.

Leopold watched him go, his keen eyes keeping him in sight until he was out of the building. When he was gone, Emmaline made her way toward Bella, shame burning in her face. Bella gave her a bright smile as she intercepted her, engaging her in a quick hug.

"Thank you for coming, Em," she said.

"I'm ever so sorry, miss."

"Whatever for?" she asked.

"I trusted him." The girl jerked her head behind her, indicating the departing Lord Vincent. "I shouldn't have. I shouldn't have let him coerce me into telling him things."

Bella took the girl's hands in hers and squeezed. "It's all right. Don't you fret. It's over now and all turned out well."

Emmaline cut a glance to Leopold, who remained standing behind her. "Yes, it did. I'm glad."

"Me, too. And I'll be glad to have you back at Hawthorne Hall. After you have a proper visit with your mum and sister, that is. Come whenever you're ready."

Her face lit with a mixture of relief and joy. "You mean that?"

"Indeed, I do." Another squeeze of her hands and then she released her.

Emmaline bid her farewell and hurried back to join her family. Bella watched as they departed, glad to have reconciled with the girl. Then she straightened and turned to Leopold. Her heart swelled at the sight of him standing there, a half-smile on his handsome face. He looked well pleased.

"How did you like my performance, my lady?"

A laugh bubbled through her. She sailed into his arms, hugging him. The moment her arms were around him, he grunted, as though in pain. She stepped back.

"I-I'm sorry."

"No need," he said. "I'm a bit sore still, that's all."

She had a thousand questions to ask him but didn't dare in the presence of her father. She needed Leopold all to herself for that.

"Bella, my dear, I don't know who this man is, but I'm certainly grateful for the help," her father said.

She flushed hot, her cheeks burning. She didn't know how to introduce the two of them. Thankfully, Leopold stepped in.

"Leopold Thornhurst, my lord. Your daughter and I met in Driftbell." He gave her a sideways glance, that playful smile still lifting the corner of his mouth. "In the bookshop."

"Indeed? I should like to hear all about that," her father said. "Do you enjoy books, too?"

She recognized the hopeful look on her father's face and laughed. Not only at the way her father hoped she had found someone like her, but the fact that Leopold more than liked books.

"I enjoy books quite a lot. Especially ones written in strange languages," Leopold replied. He held his arm out for her. She took it, sliding her hand in the crook of his elbow. "My carriage is waiting outside. Shall I give you a ride?"

"Hawthorne Hall is quite a ways," her father said. "Are you certain?"

Still grinning, he said, "Oh, I'm counting on it." He slid her a roguish glance.

They filed out of the Hall of Justice, the last of the dispersing crowd.

Her father said, "Did you know my Bella has a talent for translating strange languages?"

"Does she, then?" Leopold gave her a surreptitious wink. She stifled a giggle. "I should like to hear all about that on the ride back to Hawthorne Hall."

Her cheeks ached from smiling as they stepped out into the golden wash of midday sunlight. His fingers brushed hers, then laced through them with quiet certainty. He gazed down at her with love and adoration gleaming in his pale brown eyes. And for a moment, everything was perfect. Whole.

The curse was broken. Her father was safe. And Leopold had chosen her. The weight of courtrooms, shadows, and whispered fears lifted, burned away in the light.

Everything was right. And with him beside her, it finally felt like her life had begun.

EPILOGUE

Marigold emitted a wistful sigh as she leaned back into the cushions of the sofa holding the now-cold mug of tea. Fatigue lined her eyes as she fought back a yawn.

"I loved that story," she said. "That was the best one yet."

"I'm glad you enjoyed it." Hilde smiled, happy to have put her in a better mood.

But it was late. And Linnea would have her head for keeping her up far past her bedtime. There was a doctor's appointment in the morning. Though her sister hadn't returned from work yet—she called and said she had to stay another shift—Hilde was certain she'd want her daughter in bed at a decent hour. Now, it was approaching midnight.

"We best get you up to bed now." She rose and motioned for Marigold to do the same.

She frowned. "Do I have to? How about another story?"

Hilde chuckled. "It's far too late for that. We'll have to save it for another time. Come on."

Reluctantly, Marigold peeled herself off the sofa, placing the half-drunk tea on the coffee table, then trudging toward the stairs. Suddenly, she halted and turned back.

"But, auntie, you didn't tell me the whole story."

"I didn't?" Confusion edged through her. There wasn't much she left out.

"No. What about Leopold? How did he know to find Bella and her father in the Hall of Justice?" Her brows drew together with sincere concern.

"Oh, well, that's an easy one. Dickens, you see, was magical and had watched over Bella, her father, and her household from the moment Leopold sent him to find out more about them."

"He was the mysterious benefactor, wasn't he?" she asked.

Hilde nodded. "He was."

She wrapped her arm around her niece's shoulders and started for the stairs once more. As they headed up, Marigold yawned.

"But...what happened after they got in the carriage? Did her father get his merchant business back?"

"Of course, he did. Enzo Rinaldi was a resourceful and smart man. After he was exonerated, he rebuilt his ships. He started sailing the seas once again, looking for rare treasures for Bella."

Enzo Rinaldi became the most successful merchant in Port Leclare. His business boomed. He had a whole fleet of ships with a thriving business there in port while Bella remained at Hawthorne

Hall running the estate. They never rebuilt the home in the port, though, as Bella preferred to remain close to Leopold.

Another yawn. "Did they live happily ever after? Did they get married?"

"They did marry. Afterward, Bella sold Hawthorne Hall and moved into the castle with Leopold and Dickens."

The wedding was small, intimate, lovely. They married under a bower of roses in the gardens at Thornhurst Castle in the late Spring.

They had four children, filling the once lonely and silent halls with music and laugher and a lot of love between them all. Leopold never reclaimed his title as king, preferring to remain nothing more than a nobleman who spent hours in his extravagant library. Bella taught her children how to read and write, and one precocious young lady inherited her magical gift—the gift of reading strange languages.

Dickens remained stoic and, eventually, the children referred to him as Uncle Dickens. Something he, at first, resisted but quickly accepted when he realized he was as smitten with them as he was with Bella.

A lovely family.

At the top of the stairs, they turned into Marigold's room. She dressed for bed as Hilde pulled back the covers. Then she helped her brush out her long golden hair.

"Someday my prince will come," Marigold said, sounding wistful.

"Perhaps he will."

"And he'll be just as handsome as Leopold."

"I'm sure he will," Hilde agreed. She tucked her into the bed and kissed her forehead. "Good night, sweet girl."

It was hard to turn and walk away when all she wanted to do was watch over her for the rest of the night. But her energy was fading, and she knew she had to return to her own home soon.

"Aunt Hilde?"

At the door, she paused, her hand hovering over the light switch. "Yes?"

"Do you think I'll ever fit in with those other girls?"

Her initial response was *no*. She didn't belong with those mean, envious girls. One day, Marigold would understand that.

But she didn't want to tell her that. Instead, she smiled and nodded. "I think some day you might. Good night."

She flipped off the light and closed the door behind her. Her heart ached for the girl. She *had* to tell her the truth. Marigold needed to know. Because in the morning, when she awoke, her arm would no longer be broken. The bones would knit themselves back together into one piece. As if it had never happened.

Linnea thought keeping the truth from her was protecting her. Hilde knew differently and someday, when the time was right, she'd tell her. The time was almost right.

Afterword

Dear Reader,

Welcome to the *Enchanted Realms*, where magic shimmers between the lines and fairy tales are retold with fresh twists, heartfelt romance, and a touch of the unexpected.

You'll notice that each full-length book in this series begins and ends with a special pair of characters—Aunt Hilde and her curious niece, Marigold. These brief scenes serve as a *framing device*, inviting you into the tale and gently guiding you back out again, as if you've just spent an evening curled up beside a fire listening to a beloved story passed down through generations.

Hilde and Marigold are more than just storytellers. Their journey unfolds across the series, each book revealing a little more about who they are, where they come from, and the magic that ties them to the Realms. If you read in order, you'll catch glimpses of their evolving relationship, hidden lore, and maybe even a few secrets that connect everything together.

So settle in, open your heart, and let yourself be swept away. The Realms are waiting.

With love and a pinch of stardust,
Michelle

Next in the Series: Once Upon a Midnight Dreary

A Poe's The Raven Retelling

Once Upon a Time... in the shadowy halls of Ravenwood Manor

A beautiful heiress seeking solace. A brooding mysterious caretaker burdened by dark secrets. And a forbidden love threatened by malevolent forces determined to tear them apart.

When tragedy shatters her family, Victoria Ravenwood inherits the crumbling estate of Ravenfell Manor, a place she once called home but no longer recognizes. Hoping to escape her grief, she returns to its ivy-choked walls and forgotten rooms, determined to start anew. But Ravenfell is no sanctuary—it is a house of sorrow, steeped in secrets, and alive with something that should be dead.

Gabriel Allward, the manor's reclusive caretaker, has remained at Ravenfell for years, his presence as rooted as the ancient stones.

Cold and mysterious, he keeps to the shadows, guarding a truth he dares not reveal. Yet Victoria is drawn to him and to the darkness that clings to him like a second skin.

As their fragile bond deepens, something awakens in the manor. A raven watches from the eaves. Whispers echo through the halls. And a long-buried secret claws its way to the surface. One that binds Gabriel's soul to the estate...and could drag Victoria into the same eternal night.

Can they uncover the truth behind Ravenfell's curse before it claims them both? Or will their love become just another tragic tale whispered within its walls?

YOUR FREE BOOK IS WAITING!

Step into the Enchanted Realms—Magic and Adventure Await!

A fierce huntress sworn to protect her village. A cursed dire wolf bound by a dark past. And an ancient curse that ties their fates together.

In the heart of the Enchanted Woodlands, where shadows prowl and magic reigns, Poppy is no ordinary girl. Trained by her warrior grandmother, she is the protector of her village, armed with a bow, a sharp mind, and a cloak as red as blood—an heirloom granting her untold power. But when a new terror rises, a fearsome dire wolf known as the Wolf King, Poppy must confront a danger greater than she ever imagined.

Tasked with hunting the beast threatening her home, Poppy soon discovers a dark secret—the Wolf King was once a guardian like her, bound by an ancient curse tied to her own bloodline. Now, Poppy faces an impossible choice—kill the beast and save her people, or break the curse and risk the wrath of the village she has sworn to protect.

With the fate of both worlds hanging in the balance, Poppy must decide what kind of huntress she truly is.

Part of the Enchanted Realms world. Perfect for fans of fierce heroines, cursed beasts, and slow-burn fantasy romance set in lush, magical forests.

Get a free copy of Once Upon an Ancient Curse, An Enchanted Realms Novella

Available to newsletter subscribers only
https://viplist.michellemiles.net/enchanted

ABOUT THE AUTHOR

MICHELLE MILES believes in fairy tales, true love, and a little bit of magic in every story. She writes fantasy, paranormal, and young adult books packed with adventure, action, and swoon-worthy romance—because what's a story without a bit of danger and a whole lot of heart? From angels and demons to dragons, elves, and time travelers, her books are filled with epic quests, fierce heroines, and the kind of heroes worth falling for.

When she's not crafting new adventures, she brings stories to life as a narrator and hosts *Miles Beyond the Page*, a podcast where she chats with authors about their writing journeys. A Texas girl through and through, she loves getting lost in a good book, binge-watching movies, hiking the trails, and sipping a glass of wine. Come hang out with her on Facebook, Instagram, Pinterest, and more!

Magical Worlds, Daring Adventures, Unforgettable Romance!

Read more at MichelleMiles.net

www.ingramcontent.com/pod-product-compliance
Lightning Source LLC
Chambersburg PA
CBHW051307300726
48976CB00002B/297